SURPRISES AT THE OLD TICKET OFFICE DARLING ISLAND

POLLY BABBINGTON

POLLY BABBINGTON

PollyBabbington.com

Want more from Polly's world?

For sneak peeks into new settings, early chapters, downloadable Pretty Beach and Darling Island freebies and bits and bobs from Polly's writing days sign up for Babbington Letters.

The curtains were open in the top room of The Old Ticket Office, the sash window at the front was slightly ajar, and a breeze coming in from the sea nudged the curtains back and forth. Emmy loved her bedroom; it was one of the best things that had come about since moving to Darling. Her own lovely, quiet little sanctuary. Divine. Sometimes, when she was tucked up in her room, it felt as if she was just that bit removed from the ins and outs of the world as she pottered around at the top of the building, rugged up for an early night, or sat in bed reading, getting lost deep down in the depths of a good book.

Today, she was doing just that – sitting up in bed with her iPad alongside her, a notebook open by her side, her phone in her hand, and a steaming cup of hot chocolate beside her on her bedside table. There may have been a large, round, turquoise fancy box of salted caramel truffles nestled next to her. It might have been delved into quite a few times.

On her tallboy dresser opposite the bed, two oversized linen-scented candles flickered, and a fabric-covered lamp glowed. Emmy's glasses were on her head, and she had various things open on various contraptions – a spreadsheet open on her laptop, the traffic analytics of her shop on her phone, a profit-and-loss equation in her notebook, a half-read fiction book, and a list of tips for digital store success on a printed out sheet.

From the window, she could hear the sounds of Darling drifting across the air, the foghorn in the distance, the far-off sound of the ferry, and the trams trundling past on Darling Street below. Emmy thought about her day as she peered into the box of chocolates and dipped in, trying to kid herself that she hadn't already nearly stuffed half the box. Tom had brought home the box of chocolates for her from a business trip, and she'd loved them from the first bite.

As she sat surrounded by her things, her mind swirled with the trappings of her new life – the Old Ticket Office, her job, Love Emmy x the business, and her relationship with Tom. The past months had been a whirl of shop opening, Katy secrets, cricket training, and working at the port. Part of Emmy wanted to get off the roundabout of life for a bit. Maybe take a pew and have a little rest. Not much chance of that.

She watched the flames flickering on the far side of the room and thought about it all. Life sure was strange. Not that long ago, she'd been on her own with Callum in a rented cottage with the same old humdrum of life in front of her every single day of the week. Now, life was throwing up challenges left, right, and centre, plus she was living in a completely different location. At least she wasn't bored. There was that. No one could ever say nowadays that Emmy Bardot's life was boring. Sometimes, though, in a funny sort of way, boredom looked fairly appealing when her plate was as full as it was.

Emmy tapped her pen absently against the notebook in her lap, trying to focus on the calculations in front of her as thoughts swirled through her mind. She gazed, lost in thought for a moment, at the lights of Darling twinkling in the night sky outside her window. When she'd first moved to Darling and taken over the little space, she never could have imagined feeling so at home. But now, even the night lights felt as if she knew them, and she truly felt like she belonged on the little island surrounded by fog and hazy blue. Almost as if living on Darling Island in a flat over a shop had always been meant to be.

Her thoughts wound back to when she'd first moved to Darling, arriving in her car alone and wondering at the time what in the world she'd done. She remembered how far she'd come since those early, chaotic days of juggling the renovating with work and Callum's school and cricket training. So much had changed in such a short time. So much had changed in *her* and her life. Emmy Bardot was now in command, driving from the helm, of quite a nice little life.

The faint wail of the foghorn sounding again carried in through the window as she plucked another salted caramel truffle. She sat with her thoughts as her mind drifted to a daydream about something Amy, her sister, had said. Amy had been adamant that Emmy needed a breather from her manic few months. To get away for a week to somewhere warm and sunny. Emmy had to laugh at how Amy naturally thought it was as simple as that. Ping and one could zip off to the sun. Not quite as easy as that. She rolled her eyes. That might be the actual reality in Amy's world, but there was no such luck in Emmy's existence. Popping off to the sun to sip a piña colada hadn't been in the equation for a very long time.

Emmy gave her head a little shake. Holidays were part of the future, hopefully, but for the moment, there were shop orders to fulfil, books to balance, and invoices to send. Holidays to far-off climes were things that happened to someone else in nicer, more perfect lives.

With a little sigh, she turned her focus back to her profit-and-loss sheet. The numbers were looking healthier than expected, but she was hardly in the millionaire stakes, and from her limited skill at projection figures, she wasn't going to make it there anytime soon. She made a few notes, pleased to see her efforts were at least paying off. Her hard work was amounting to something real and tangible, so she couldn't argue with that. She'd actually gone and done it – manifested a beautiful dream that had lived inside her head for a long time. Dreamy sepia-tinted visions that had started in her mind many moons before were now a day-to-day reality in her actual life. Whoopy-doo.

Her eyes flicked to the photographs by her bed and a photo of Callum, gangly and grinning after a cricket match. Emmy's heart caught as she looked at his sweet, young face. He was growing up so quickly it made her feel a bit sick. Life was zooming along at full throttle. She'd struggled often bringing him up on her own and had sometimes almost wished the time away, but now it was the opposite. She regularly wanted to freeze time for a bit and keep everything exactly as it was, especially now. Stay nice and safe.

There were other faces looking back at her from her bedside table, including a picture of her with her two sisters, Amy and Katy. One of her mum and dad on holiday somewhere warm, and now Tom was there at her bedside, too. He looked handsome and a bit broody. Oh, how she liked both of those and the fact that Tom P Carter was now very much a part of her life.

The distant wail of the foghorn again echoed across the water and travelled in through the gap in the window. Emmy finished her chocolate and tried to concentrate on the numbers on her iPad. But she was so tucked up, so warm and cosy, that she could barely keep her eyes open. She'd just close them for a few minutes and have a little rest…

When Emmy blinked awake sometime later, the room was steeped in darkness, only the faintest glow still emanating from the flickering candles on the dresser on the other side of the room. Disoriented, she fumbled for her phone and saw it was past ten. She'd drifted off without even realising it. The paperwork, iPad, and notebook were still strewn haphazardly across her duvet; so much for getting ahead on jobs. They'd bored her so much she'd dropped off to sleep. With a flick of her eyes and a shake of her head, she pushed the duvet off, slid out of bed, pulled her dressing gown on, and went downstairs. Walking into the sitting room, Tom was sitting on the pale blue sofa, and Callum was horizontal on the other one with his phone in his hand. Cricket was playing on the TV, and there were a couple of mugs on the coffee table.

Tom looked over. 'Back in the land of the living, are we?'

'I came up to see if you wanted a cup of tea, and you were comatose,' Callum said without looking up from his phone.

'Ahh, you should have woken me. I must have dropped off.'

'You're joking. No way I was going to do that.' Callum laughed. 'You were dead to the world.'

Tom nodded. 'You obviously needed it.'

'I never was that good at figures. These days they actually put me to sleep,' Emmy said with a chuckle.

'Not surprised,' Callum replied. 'I hate maths.'

'I missed out on the tea then,' Emmy stated.

'You did,' Tom said. 'Want me to make you some supper?'

Tom had read her thoughts. 'Wouldn't say no.'

Tom jumped up. 'Cal?'

'Yeah, please,' Callum said and also got up and headed towards his room. 'Back in a sec.'

Emmy sat on the opposite end of the sofa from where Tom had been sitting and mindlessly watched the men in white clothes on the TV screen throwing balls at each other. When Tom came back, he was carrying three mugs of tea and a plate. Emmy reached forward and took one of the mugs. 'Lemon polenta cake before bed. I stuffed a load of those truffles before I fell asleep. Not the healthiest of evenings.'

'Those truffles are lethal.'

'I know. Tell me about it.'

'They're sleep-inducing,' Tom joked.

'I can't believe I dropped off like that.'

Tom sat down, took a piece of cake, and made himself comfortable. 'The last few months must be catching up with you,' Tom noted. 'Amy said you needed a holiday.'

Emmy rolled her eyes. 'Nah. I'm fine. Just a bit busy this week.'

'You *have* been doing a lot. Also, you say that every week.'

'So have you. So has everyone. Isn't it the way of the world?'

'I guess so. Sometimes when I see what you do in your day, you make me feel tired, though, especially when you do double shifts.'

Emmy dismissed Tom's concern with a flick of her hand. 'I'm used to it.'

'At least you've got your glow back.' Tom lowered his voice. 'Since you came clean about the Katy business. You look so much better,' Tom said, referring to the fact that Emmy had told him that she was back in contact with her estranged sister, Katy.

Emmy whispered back, 'I feel so much better about it having told you. Funny how it works like that. A problem shared and all that.'

'How has she been?'

'Fine.'

'Nothing further on potentially opening the communication with your mum and dad?'

Emmy shook her head and took a sip of her tea. 'Nope. She's adamant she doesn't want to speak to them.'

'Oh well, not a lot you can do then.'

'No. I can't spend too much time worrying about it, to be quite honest. I got myself in a right two and eight about it before. I'm not going there again. Nope, no way.'

'You're telling me. No, you can't worry about it; you'll just end up caught up in a web of lies again.'

Emmy whispered, 'And we don't want that.'

'Nope.'

'Life seems to be full at the moment. I don't need to be thinking about what Katy is or isn't going to do. She's an adult. I'm just going to leave it at that,' Emmy stated. 'It is what it is.'

'Hmm, it would be good if Amy knew, though. I thought that the other day when you two went to the pub. She's not going to be happy when she does find out.'

'I know, but what can I do? I'll cross that bridge when I come to it.'

'There's not a lot else you can do.'

'If only life were simple,' Emmy said.

Tom raised his eyebrows. 'It never *ever* is.'

2

E mmy drove into the back lane behind The Old Ticket Office and parked in her usual spot. As she gathered up her things, a grey sports car pulled in behind her, got way too close to her bumper for her liking, and switched off its engine. Emmy tutted. The lane was a pain for parking, as was Darling as a whole. Visitors without residents' permits often thought that because the lane was tucked out of the way, they could park and get away with it. Emmy would often come out of the gate to find herself nearly blocked in. It looked like today, the grey car was going to do the same thing.

Before she could fully register how close the car was, the driver's side door swung open. Emmy just blinked for a second as she stood in a bit of a trance, staring. It appeared that a movie star had just stepped out of the grey car. She added a gulp to the blinking. Niceeee. In jeans and a casual jumper, the man getting out of the car immediately struck her: handsome, bordering on pretty, mostly gorgeous. She was about to tell him that he couldn't park where he had, but she didn't get a chance.

'Hey.' The man smiled and held up his hand. He charmed and then some.

Emmy had to stop herself from blowing out a stream of hot air. The man didn't just look good, let's put it this way: he sounded good too. Smooth came to mind. Or maybe suave. Definitely lush.

'Hello,' she returned, a bit flustered.

The man approached amiably. He'd dialled the smile up to dazzling. Confident, shiny, and oh-so handsome. Didn't he know it. 'Russell.'

Emmy blinked again, thrown temporarily off balance by just about everything about Russell. Why was this exceedingly handsome man, firstly, in her lane and, secondly, introducing himself to her? She didn't say anything – sort of stunned and wrong-footed at the same time.

He waved his hand towards the back of the buildings by way of explanation. 'Two doors down, I think, if you're who I think you are.' Russell flicked his eyes to Emmy's car and the gate to The Old Ticket Office.

Emmy frowned, not quite sure what he meant. 'Oh, right, okay.'

'We haven't met. Russell.' He extended a hand, which Emmy shook bemusedly.

They had not met, he was absolutely right. There was no way Emmy would have forgotten this man. Vague memories of Xian from the bakery mentioning the man who owned a few shops on Darling filtered through her mind. This must be him. 'Emmy Bardot.'

'Nice to meet you at last. Suits you perfectly, I must say.' Russell's tone was syrupy sweet.

'Likewise.' Emmy felt a slight heat rushing up her neck. Was Russell flirting with her? Surely not. She made a funny, chirpy, squeaky laugh before she spoke. 'I was just about to tell you there's no parking down this lane.'

'I would have been in trouble, would I?' Russell's eyes ran down Emmy's body and back up again. All of a sudden, Russell wasn't quite as nice. Russell made a face which made Emmy squirm a bit.

'Yep.'

'You look like the sort of chick who gets people in trouble.'

Emmy baulked inside. She did not like the way this Russell person called her 'chick.' The last time she checked, she wasn't a baby chicken. 'Ha.'

Russell raised his eyebrows suggestively and definitely looked at Emmy's chest. His eyes lingered there for a second. 'You were going to tell me off about parking in the lane, were you?'

This bloke was really laying it on thick, Emmy thought, with an internal eye roll. She wasn't quite sure what to think, do, or say, so she just stood there awkwardly, sort of staring. 'Ha! Yes.'

'Scary. Wouldn't want to meet you in a dark alley.' Russell then actually winked twice. Emmy gulped. 'Or in a dark lane behind a row of old shops, ha.'

Emmy's creep antennae went ballistic. 'Well, it's nice to meet you, err, Russell.'

Russell suddenly moved closer and casually leant an arm on the roof of Emmy's car. Emmy hesitated, not sure how to behave. Something was weird about this Russell and the way he was behaving. She knew she wasn't happy about it. Emmy smiled and pointed to Russell's car. 'No permit?'

'Not yet. New car and not much time. I've been busy.'

'Right.'

Russell still didn't move his arm from the roof of Emmy's car. 'I hear it's all fully online now.'

Emmy felt uncomfortable but heard herself trundling on with the conversation. She gave him the rundown about what she'd had to do to get her car permit. As she chatted, her brain click clicked away to itself, taking him in. The very expensive watch teamed with his casual but plush attire. His fancy accent. His easy, confident, what he thought was charm. Her brain assessed the way it did when she was looking at passengers in the queue at work. Emmy evaluated him in seconds. She'd spent years and years doing it and was quite the expert. This man was top league. The way he dressed by pretending he hadn't put any effort in, the quiet yet exponentially expensive clothes, the hair, the jaw. All of it put him right up there as clear as day. She could read it a mile off. As she read his body language, something about him also made her feel *very* uneasy. A bright red intuition flag was waving somewhere, telling her to back away. Far, far away.

'Well, thanks again for the insider scoop with the latest on the Municipality of Darling,' Russell said after she'd finished explaining the process. 'Glad I introduced myself to someone who's just been through the whole rigmarole.'

Emmy flashed a polite smile. 'No problem. Happy to help.'

She expected their brief parking tête-à-tête to end there, but Russell showed no signs of moving.

'So, how are you finding Darling and Darling-ites?' Russell asked sort of lazily. There was a quick flick of his eyes down to her chest again.

Emmy nodded noncommittally. 'I love it. The community's been lovely.'

'So you've opened now, have you?'

Emmy had no real clue who this Russell was, but she was no longer alarmed that someone on Darling knew about her when she knew nothing about them. It had happened to her enough times already. She played along. 'I have, yep. '

'I'll have to stop in – all about shopping local, me.' Russell's eyes ran her up and down for about the fifth time.

'That would be nice,' she replied in a tone aiming for politely distant. 'Anyway, I should probably head in and get some work done. Let me know if you need anything else regarding the permits and such. Not that you'd need me to help if you know the ins and outs of how Darling works.' Emmy chuckled a bit self-consciously, wishing she hadn't said what she'd just said about offering help.

'Of course. Don't let me keep you from important business matters.'

Was he being condescending? He was. Definitely. Emmy simply smiled blandly and turned towards the back gate.

Russell didn't leave it at that. 'Hope to see you around, Emmy,' he called lightly after her. 'I have a feeling we'll be bumping into each other frequently as neighbours.'

Emmy glanced back, hoping her expression conveyed detached politeness. *I blooming well hope not.* 'I'll let you get settled in. Enjoy!'

Without waiting for a response, she slipped inside the gate, closing it firmly. Well, that had certainly been an experience. Shaking her head, Emmy put it out of her mind and headed upstairs. She had jewellery orders to sort and dinner to make. But after she'd changed and been to the loo, she couldn't entirely forget the scene in the lane. Overtly friendly, definitely flirty, absolutely good-looking. Smarmy. Possibly a bit scary. Not very Darling at all.

Later on, after sorting out Love Emmy x orders and making a curry, Emmy hadn't thought about it too much. As she'd got on with cleaning the kitchen and getting her work stuff ready, Tom came in at the same time as Callum.

Callum kissed her on the cheek and jerked his thumb out towards the lane. 'Nice car out there behind yours.'

'Yep.'

'Whose is it? Do you know?' Callum questioned.

'From a few doors down.'

Tom frowned. 'Russell? Oh, right, he's back. I wonder how long he'll be staying this time. He's got a new car, has he? I thought as much. Did you meet him?'

'I did.'

'Wouldn't mind his car,' Callum joked as he walked down the hallway to his bedroom.

Emmy decided to mention the encounter she'd had with Russell. She kept it light. 'He parked behind me earlier as I came in.'

'What did you think?'

'He introduced himself with a lot of, shall we say, gusto.'

Tom's eyebrows shot up. 'Can't say I'm surprised. What do you mean?'

Emmy decided against making a mountain out of a molehill. Russell hadn't done anything wrong. It was more that her intuition had spiked a bit. 'Oh, nothing really.' She raced to think of something to keep it breezy. 'Seemed fine.'

Though she spoke casually, Tom's eyes narrowed a fraction. 'You sure?'

'Yep.' Emmy smiled. 'All good.' But she wasn't really. Something was telling her that this Russell was far from good. A voice was telling her that she certainly wouldn't want to come across him in the dark in the lane.

3

A couple of days later, Emmy was in the shop. It had been a busy day, but as the afternoon got later, customers had tailed off, and she was sitting behind the old ticket counter working on adding new products to her online store. She looked up as the door opened and the shop bell tinkled.

'Knock knock!' Russell was standing in the door. He sounded smarmily cheerful.

Emmy fixed a polite smile on her face, moving around the counter to say hello to him. She'd give him credit – he was definitely not shy in coming forward. 'Ah, Russell, nice to see you again,' she lied as smoothly as he spoke.

'This really is such a *sweet* little place,' Russell remarked, leaning casually against a display case and glancing around. 'Just like you, I imagine. Understated but still eye-catching.'

Blech. Emmy wanted to vomit. Here she was in her own business premises, right on the end of a thinly veiled chat-up line with what felt like quite sinister undertones. She hadn't had such a revolting chat-up encounter for years. She'd thought she was too old for them. They hadn't been missed in any shape or form. Yuck. She busied herself wiping down the already pristine counter. 'Thanks.'

'Are you doing anything after you close up shop? I thought a friendly neighbourly drink might be in order.'

Yeah, that would be a no. Two words, mate, the second one is off. 'That's kind of you to offer, but I already have plans this evening. I'm usually quite busy outside of work hours.'

Russell didn't even have the grace to look disappointed. If anything, his eyes glinted as though he enjoyed the challenge of persisting where clearly unwanted. Again, Emmy felt sick as her stomach churned. 'No worries, we'll find time another night,' he said breezily.

Emmy bit her tongue from telling him to sling his hook. 'Mmm.'

Russell flashed a dazzling smile. He really was strikingly attractive on the outside. Strange that it was so at odds with what he was really like from what she'd seen so far. 'I suppose I should let you close up. Don't want to keep you.' With an infuriating double wink, Russell strolled towards the door, leaving Emmy clenching her jaw and shaking her head.

Just after Russell strolled out the door, the shop bell jangled again. Emmy looked up to see her sister Amy breeze in with a quizzical expression on her face.

'Who on earth was that?' Amy asked with wide eyes. 'I came through the front because I couldn't find a space, and I bump into... Who even was he?'

Emmy sighed, coming around the counter to give Amy a quick hug. 'That was the new-to-me neighbour, Russell,' Emmy said in an irritated voice.

Amy's eyebrows shot up as she picked up on Emmy's tone immediately. 'You're not keen?'

Emmy made a little grimacing face. 'That would be a no from what I've seen so far.'

'He certainly seemed charming.'

'Charming is one word for it,' Emmy muttered.

'So what's the deal with him, then?' Amy pressed.

Emmy rolled her eyes. 'Nothing. He's been away overseas since I've been here. I met him in the lane the other day. He gives me the creeps for some reason. He just came in to smarm. I've tried discouraging him, but subtlety is lost on the man from what I can see. Thinks he's God's gift. Tom said he comes and goes on Darling so, hopefully, he won't stick around for long.'

'Just overly friendly?' Amy put her fingers up to sign quotation marks around the word friendly.

'So far. He's just got my creep radar twitching.'

'Right. Shame. He's not too tough to look at.'

'I know. That's where it ends.'

'Pity. Sounds like someone needs boundaries,' Amy said. 'Have you told Tom?'

Emmy winced slightly. 'Nothing to tell. Yet.'

Amy gave her a knowing look. 'Grr. How come we have to navigate this in life?'

'I know.'

'Just steer clear.'

'Yep.' Emmy sighed. 'I'm sure he's harmless.'

Amy nodded. 'I hope so. Tom will have your back.'

'Yeah.'

'Right. So what's on the agenda? Where's Cal? Cricket then Mum's?'

'Yes, as planned.'

'Excellent.' Amy clapped her hands together. 'So it's just you and me and the special evening at Darlings.'

'It is indeed.'

'I'm *so* looking forward to it,' Amy gushed.

'Same.'

'You can fill me in more on all that's been going on in your life.'

Apart from the secret I've been keeping from you about our sister

Katy, Emmy said to herself with a grimace. *Apart from the fact that you don't know I've been seeing Katy and I've been lying to you almost constantly.* 'Yep. You can do the same.'

~

E mmy locked the shop door, and she and Amy then made their way out the back gate towards the lane. As they exited the gate, Amy immediately zoned in on the flashy grey sports car parked too close behind Emmy's little hatchback.

'Well, well, let me guess,' Amy remarked, hands on hips as she eyed Russell's car.

Emmy raised her eyebrows. 'Tell me about it. I'm lucky not to be blocked in. He's been parking like that since he's been here. Hopefully he'll go back to wherever he came from soon.'

'Not exactly considerate to other drivers.'

'Nup.'

'You'd barely be able to open the boot if you wanted to.'

'Totally inconsiderate,' Emmy said dryly.

'I'm surprised he's allowed to live on Darling,' Amy joked. 'How come he got a permit? Who let him cross over on the floating bridge?'

'I know.'

Amy joked. 'He shouldn't have even been allowed to step foot on Darling.'

'Nope.'

'Trouble in paradise.'

'Nah. I have no qualms about telling him to jog on if I need to.'

'He wants to try.'

Emmy had to laugh at Amy's fiercely protective tone. 'Hopefully, it won't come to anything,' Emmy said, giving Amy's arm a squeeze. 'Right. Enough of that. Let's just enjoy our night out and not let anything ruin it.'

'Too right.' Amy agreed. 'Now, what's first on the agenda when we get to Darlings?'

'Bubbles,' Emmy replied. A chilled glass of champagne was precisely what she needed to shake off the week.

'Sounds good. Then you can tell me what's changed with you,' Amy said half-seriously.

Emmy shuddered inside. Nothing got past Amy. Emmy had thought she'd been so clever, too. 'What do you mean?'

'Ems, you were *really* weird and *really* distant for ages, and now we've got the old Emmy back. Clearly, something was going on. I just want to find out what it was.'

Emmy went cold; she thought she'd been so good at hiding the Katy secret, but Amy didn't miss a trick. Time for more lies on the Katy front if she wasn't careful. As they approached Darlings café, the sky was a deep black, and there were no signs whatsoever of the resident Darling fog. The front of the shop twinkled in fairy lights, the 'Darlings' sign glinted, and a row of bikes alongside the door caught the light. A few tiny café tables and chairs sat underneath outdoor heaters, blankets were folded onto the backs of chairs, the tables were laid with gingham tablecloths, and little bottles were filled with flowers. Loads of lanterns with tea lights hung from the trees, and there was a sound of jazz music, happiness, and chatter floating across the air.

'Wait until you see inside,' Emmy said. 'You'll love it. It's magical.'

Emmy was right, and when she opened the door for Amy, Amy raised her eyebrows and opened her eyes wide. A mass of tea lights flickered inside jam jars on the tables, lanterns hung from the ceiling, hundreds of candles were dotted on the floor-to-ceiling shelving, and the place was abuzz with conversation.

Amy whispered, 'Oh my goodness, Ems. It *is* magical. You're so right.'

'Told you. That first night I came here with Tom, I couldn't believe it.'

Amy gaped as she looked around. 'I can't believe how many people are packed in here.'

'It's like a Darling tradition. The tickets for these evenings sell out really quickly.'

'Not surprised.'

Amy gazed around as they were led to a small table tucked cosily in the corner. Emmy smiled at the gorgeous candlelit atmosphere, and Amy sat down and then leant forward across the table. 'And I thought this place was nice in the day. Wow. It's so pretty in here. I can see why it's so popular.'

'I know, it's like stepping into a storybook,' Emmy agreed as she scanned her eyes down the menu. 'Plus, the food is amazing.'

Amy was quiet for a minute or two as she looked at the menu. 'Baked Brie with cranberry compote works for me.'

After they were served drinks, Amy clinked their flutes together. 'To sisters and magical nights out. To coming here again the next time, too.'

Emmy didn't want to toast sisters considering what was going on with their other sister Katy. She heard herself toasting. 'Cheers.' She crossed her fingers that Katy wouldn't come up in conversation.

Amy leant forward and turned her head to the side. 'So, are you going to come clean about what's really been going on with you these past months? Don't think I've forgotten. You were so distant and distracted for ages. Now you're *so* much brighter. As if a weight's been lifted or something.'

Emmy's stomach dropped. She managed to keep her expression neutral. Trust Amy not to let it go. Her sister could read her like a book. 'It was just, you know, a lot of stress with the shop,' she said, fiddling with her napkin.

Amy shot back super quickly. 'You've said that. More than once.'

'Getting everything ready for opening while still working. I guess it took a toll I didn't even realise.'

Amy looked *really* sceptical. 'See, I don't quite buy that. You've always thrived under stress and pressure. Look at what happened with the Kevin thing, and you rose to it. Something else was definitely going on. We all have busy lives and get on with it. You were different. I know you, Ems.'

Emmy scrambled for a plausible deflection. She hated deceiving Amy, but telling the truth about reconnecting with Katy wasn't an option. Not yet, anyway. She grasped at straws. 'I had a lot on my plate, Ames. You yourself have said that. Just the other day you said I needed a holiday.'

Amy's expression changed. 'True. I did say that.'

Emmy managed a chuckle. 'I guess I was in my own head about it, thought I could handle everything when it was a lot to take on.'

'That's the understatement of the year,' Amy retorted. She laughed. 'Just blame Kevin, shall we?'

Emmy was relieved Amy was laughing. 'He gets the brunt of everything. Or, at least, he used to.'

She said a silent prayer that the conversation would stay away from what was really going on. Her stomach knotted with guilt. Thankfully, Amy changed the subject. 'So things with you and Tom are all good now? No more weird tension or distance?'

Emmy nodded, very relieved for the topic change. 'We're great. On the same page.'

'It really seemed like something bigger was going on. But if you say it's resolved...' Amy let her sentence dangle in the air between them.

Emmy squirmed inside. 'You know how ups and downs are part of it. We had our first quarrel.'

'Fair enough.'

'It means we're a real couple now,' Emmy joked.

Amy didn't seem *entirely* convinced, but Emmy felt as if she'd covered herself. She swiftly turned the conversation to Callum and a few problems he was having at school. By the time a sharing platter of mini macarons with clotted cream arrived for dessert, the chat had moved far, far away from family, Tom, or the possibility of anything to do with Katy. Emmy was having a lovely time just chatting about nothing and decompressing from her week.

By the time they left Darlings and were outside in the night air, Emmy was very full, relaxed and happy. It felt good. The lovely feeling of a night just being with Amy and having a laugh surrounded her. Linking her arm through Amy's, she tried not to let Katy anywhere near her thoughts. They strolled away from Darlings, laughing and chatting. Emmy filled her lungs with the cold sea air. 'This was exactly what I needed. Things have been nonstop lately. Nice to force myself to slow down and just go out for dinner, you know?'

'I worry about you taking on too much. You're *so* busy all the time,' Amy noted.

'Don't fuss, Ames. I'm fine.'

'I know you're fine, that's not what I said. I said I worry.'

Emmy felt the guilt about Katy race up through her neck and land on her cheeks. 'You don't need to worry about me. Honestly, I'm fine.'

'Well, I do. That's what sisters do for each other, Ems.'

Emmy gulped and yet again made a deliberate attempt to change the subject. As they got to the back lane, Amy pointed behind Emmy's car. 'Looks like matey boy has gone.'

'Good,' Emmy remarked as she unlocked the back gate and then added. 'Good riddance, more like.'

'From what you've said, the less we see of him around here, the better.'

'Yes, indeed. Tom said he comes and goes constantly, so he'll probs be gone again soon.' Emmy grimaced. 'I do not need a Russell in my life at this stage of the game.'

Amy rolled her eyes. 'Does anyone ever?'

4

A few days later – in jeans, an oversized jumper, and with her hair scraped up on top of her head in a clip – Emmy stood by the back door of the shop with a cup of tea in her hand, looking up at the weather. Wisps of fog rolled in from the sea, and the sky above the old brick walls swirled in a thick grey-white haze. The same as when she'd first arrived on Darling Island, Emmy was still captivated by the unique Darling fog when it came in, and she watched as it swirled around a lamppost in the lane. The air felt thick as she breathed deeply, taking in the cool dampness around her. There was something strangely comforting about being enveloped in the Darling fog as it softened the world's edges, or maybe she was just weird. She was.

Emmy watched, mesmerised by the fog for a bit, then stepped out onto the pavers and peered contemplatively around at the small, bricked yard behind The Old Ticket Office. The yard and the state of it had been niggling at her ever since she'd moved in, but in the grand scheme of things, it had been pretty much at the bottom of her list of things to do. Every time she walked in from the car, she'd tutt to herself, promise that she'd start doing something about it, and then another week would go by full of much more important things than making over the backyard. More important things like keeping a roof over her head.

However, now her determination to get herself in gear and stop making excuses about not having time had taken hold. She'd been inspired when she'd been to pick up the sofa she'd seen on Marketplace from a woman called Jane. Emmy had swooned pathetically at Jane's house. Not only that, she'd experienced full-on life envy and a girl crush at the same time. Since then, Jane's pretty as a picture garden had sprung to mind every single time Emmy had come in the back gate of The Old Ticket Office. She'd been so inspired by Jane, Jane's life, Jane's house, Jane's gorgeous garden, indeed everything Jane, that she'd been itching to give the neglected space a makeover. She'd wanted to move in the circles of Jane's World.

That all sounded very good, and more or less doable, but faced with the reality, she sighed as she looked around. In theory, it was fairly easy, wasn't it? Especially if she said it quickly. They did it on the makeover shows on the telly almost with their eyes closed. In reality, it was a whole different ball game altogether. The area was more than dreary, enclosed by Victorian brick walls. Random weeds poked up between cracked paving stones, a half-shed didn't leave much to be desired, and piles of old crates and empty pots cluttered the corners. Moss. So much moss. The gate to the lane was faded and a bit wonky, a couple of window boxes by the storeroom window dangled precariously from brackets, the path had seen better days, and one side of the wall was completely covered in ivy and more moss. Not that nice. Not in Jane's World at all.

Emmy tilted her head, picturing possibilities for sprucing it up. She cast her mind back to Jane's garden, where somehow everything had been just right. There'd been a little table and chair alfresco area, a small deck, and everything had looked pretty and thriving. At the back of The Old Ticket office, thriving it most certainly was *not*. Depressing more like. With a wrinkled forehead, she surveyed the area – the time-worn brick, the weathered back door, the old guttering. She tried to imagine it, as her mum had said, filled with nicer things. It was *such* a tough ask. She squinted, attempted to remain positive and thought about actual live plants in the window boxes, pots brimming with herbs, shrubs in the beds, a little table, and a seating area. It was doable but a lot of hard work. Was Emmy Bardot over hard work? Had she had enough of it for one lifetime? Possibly.

She sucked it up and stood looking from one corner to the next for ages. Her mind went from brimming with ideas to give the forgotten space new life to calling it a day and going to make a cup of tea. Once she'd got a bee in her bonnet about it, though, she wasn't going to give up. The very least she could do would be to have a good old tidy-up and tap into the delights of her dad's jetwash. She made a little mental plan; first, she'd clear away the clutter of crates and junk from the previous owners that were still haphazardly piled in the far corner. Then she'd wire brush the moss suffocating the walls, jetwash the path, and do something about the window boxes. Give the shed a lick of paint, put in a few shrubs, and hang some hanging baskets – all with not a lot of time and even less budget.

Emmy's mind buzzed with how she was going to do it without spending much money. She could repurpose some of the old bricks as edging for the beds, string up some of the left-over fairy lights from the shop, and scour Marketplace for plants. She recalled the conversation with her mum, who had been all over the potential of a makeover like a rash, had offered to help, and had already started buying and planning. Emmy felt an instant rush of guilt at the thought of her mum. Yet again, her mum was helping her while she herself was keeping secrets. It did not feel nice.

24

As she stood and looked and her mind calculated, she knew one thing for an absolute fact: despite its non-aesthetically pleasing state, she was so grateful that the space was hers. All brick by moss-covered brick *hers*. Years in the rental trap had meant she'd never really been able to settle into anything and make changes. Never been able to call anything her own. Now, she could do exactly as she pleased. Hoo-blooming-ray. It had taken long enough.

She strolled to the gate and shed and stood staring at them for a bit. Both were mottled with age, but the bones were solid and workable. With a fresh coat of paint, it *could* all be lovely. The sea breeze whipped around, and she could hear a trundle from the trams on the other side of the building. She turned around and let her gaze travel slowly up the brick edifice of the back of the shop and the flat above it. All of it, completely and utterly, hers.

Emmy marvelled at how far she'd come already in the relatively short span since first crossing over on the ferry to make a new life on Darling. Then she'd brought with her a head full of plans, running alongside a feeling of more or less paralysing terror at what she'd done. Those early chaotic days of tackling renovations whilst setting up shop now seemed almost a distant memory. Here she was, standing solidly on her own two feet after years of simply trying to stay afloat as a single mum. Not only surviving but definitely thriving. Finally able to catch her breath.

Staring up at the back of the old building, she sighed, nodded, and smiled at the same time. She'd fallen in love instantly with the rambling character of the old place, along with the trams and ferry, and the promise of what came with a coastal life. Now being actually part of it, she cherished everything – the shop, the community, the street, the ferry, and Tom. She stood up straight as she gazed up at her bedroom window and suddenly felt ten feet tall. It had to be said that Emmy Bardot was doing rather well.

$$\sim$$

A few hours later, Emmy was kicking herself for not having made the effort with the backyard earlier. It hadn't taken much to make a vast improvement in a short amount of time, and as she heaved things around, she wondered why it had taken her so long to get going on it. The odd piles of moss-covered bricks were now neatly stacked up on the far side of the shed. Discarded fold-up chairs had been heaved around, stacked up, and hidden in the shed, and a pile of what must have, at one point, been pots of indoor houseplants had been emptied out and stacked by the shed door, waiting to be refilled. She'd cleared what felt like a million cobwebs from just about everywhere, and the pavers were swept and looking so much better. Overall, a couple of hours of work had given dramatic results.

She was standing with the gate open, peering up at it, recalling how when she'd first moved in, it had not wanted to budge. It had been in the very early days, and she'd had so much on her plate that when the gate had stuck, it had felt like the end of the world. She remembered barging the gate with her shoulder, it not moving, and looking up to see Tom standing looking on in amusement. She smiled at her memories as she recalled how Tom had made her fizz right from the get-go. Now, he was simply part of her life. How deliciously nice. With the gate pinned back against the wall, she was standing on the verge, looking back into the yard and assessing her progress, when a car zoomed up the lane too fast and pulled in just down from where she was standing. Russell got out of the car, and before she could nip in the gate and shut it, he was strolling towards her.

Emmy inwardly cringed as Russell sauntered up, his eyes roving over her gardening attire. She suddenly felt very exposed. She did not like him *at all*. Part of her felt super mean – she hardly even knew the man. Yeah, he was a bit smarmy, but overall, technically, he'd not really done anything wrong. Yet.

'Hey, Emmy,' Russell drawled, getting out of the car, clicking the remote with a flourish and leaning an arm casually against the brick wall. 'Fancy running into you out here.'

Emmy squirmed. There was no doubt about the fact that he looked down at her top. She folded her arms. 'Hi. Just doing a bit of tidying up back here. It was long overdue.'

'Looks like you could use an extra pair of hands,' Russell said, glancing around. 'Happy to help out if you need it. I'll always help out a damsel in distress.'

Blech. Over my dead body. 'All good, thanks.'

Russell shifted closer, lowering his voice. 'You know, I was thinking we really should have that drink sometime. Get to know each other properly.'

That would be a no from me. 'I'm pretty busy these days between the shop and family.' She forced a polite smile. 'I should really get back to it…'

'No rest for the wicked, eh?' Russell said. His voice was smarmier by the second.

Emmy's skin prickled. Something about his vibe was so off. Just then, Tom's voice came from the other direction on the lane. 'Ems.'

Emmy almost sagged in relief as Tom appeared. He paused, eyebrows raising at the sight of Russell hovering entirely too close to Emmy.

'Russell,' Tom said coolly with a curt nod.

'Tom,' Russell returned, his tone overly friendly.

'I was just telling Russell about the backyard makeover,' Emmy explained.

Tom stood very close to Emmy, his eyes never leaving Russell. 'You've done loads already.'

'All on her own, too,' Russell said snidely. 'See you guys later.' He sauntered back to his flashy car and towards his flat.

Emmy turned to Tom. 'He is really up himself.'

'Uncomfortable?'

Emmy brushed it off. 'Nah, nothing I can't handle.'

Tom frowned. 'Bit of a creep.'

Emmy sighed. 'Trust me, the world is full of them.'

'Really?'

'Yep, I've been dealing with them all my life,' Emmy stated resignedly.

'Do you want me to have a word?'

'Nope. Best thing with him is to keep him at arm's length. Hopefully he'll get the message. I've seen it all before, unfortunately.'

Somehow, though, Emmy doubted Russell was the type to give up easily, but there was no way she was going to tell Tom that. The best strategy with blokes like Russell was to ignore them first of all. If that didn't work, she'd regroup and move on to the big guns after that. Hopefully, she wouldn't have to because she'd learnt that Russell never stayed on Darling for long, but you never could tell. The Russells of the world sometimes didn't give up.

5

It was a few days later and Emmy's phone buzzed with a new notification as she sat at the counter in her little shop. She scrolled to her DMs and frowned at a new message from someone she didn't recognise. A DM from someone going by the name of Peaches. This person, Peaches, was gushing over the shop pictures and the story Emmy had shared of the opening when Louisa, the harpist, had been playing in the corner. Emmy tapped on Peaches' profile and did a double take; it seemed that Peaches was not any old influencer but one who had over five million followers. Emmy's eyes went wide with surprise; she wondered if the follower count was fake or not, and then asked herself what someone so popular might want with her tiny little business? Probably just a scam.

She read the message further and shook her head.

Peaches: *I'm headed to Darling soon for content creation and would love to swing by your shop for some photos and/or videos. I think my followers would go crazy for the cosy vibes. If I do and you are happy for me to come by, and if it's not too cheeky, any chance you have a discount code I could share? If it's a yes, I'll get my assistant to liaise. Hugs. Peaches* x

The message was followed by a string of pale pink hearts. Emmy had to read the message three times and check the profile twice more before it sunk in. She knew nothing really about influencers, but something was telling her this was huge, and being contacted by someone like Peaches could be massive for Love Emmy x. Part of Emmy felt wary. Probably too good to be true. She'd heard so much about online scams and suchlike, and there was no way Love Emmy x could afford any sort of payment for digital sponsored posts. She tapped on the profile again and scrolled down. Loads and loads of likes and loads and loads of engagement. It seemed the profile, at least, was real. Peaches sure liked the camera, and the camera absolutely adored her back. Peaches was in possession of the perfect Insta life.

Emmy wasn't really sure what to do. What was the go-to when receiving a message like that? After a bit more scrolling, she decided that the potential rewards outweighed any risks and that nothing would come of it anyway. She typed out a friendly response.

Emmy: *Hi Peaches! I'm so flattered you love the shop. Absolutely, I can set up a discount code for you to share with your followers for their first purchase if you like. When are you coming to Darling? Let me know how I can help make your visit special. We'd love to have you. Emmy.*

Emmy hit send before she could overthink it anymore. While business had been okay, and despite the fabulous coastal location of the shop, people weren't exactly knocking down her door to come into the shop and part with their money. She'd, for sure, take any help that came her way. She was well aware there was a serious cost-of-living crisis, and she was also aware of the time of year, both of which meant that business was steady but *very* slow. She'd planned for that – she had her job at the port and her website would continue to make up the majority amount of her revenue. Secretly, though, she'd hoped that the shop had taken off like a rocket from day one. It simply hadn't done that in any shape or form. It was borderline the opposite. But Peaches' visit could potentially be a game-changer. Even a fraction of her millions of followers shopping with a discount code or just following Emmy's socials would be a lovely boost to the small business journey Emmy found herself on.

Emmy busied herself tidying up the shop and mulled it over, letting her mind wander to what a good bit of publicity could do for Love Emmy x. After dusting the antique display unit and cleaning the mirrored drawers, she got another notification on her phone. It chimed away merrily to itself from the old ticket counter.

Peaches: *Hey Emmy. Wow, thank you so much for the offer of a code. That's so kind of you. I'd love to film if I can, too. I think my followers would love it. I'm always looking for content and new places – I'm going to be doing a few different things on Darling Island. My assistant will be in touch. Her name is Gemma x.*

Emmy: *Oh, wow, that's great. Thanks. I'll wait to hear from your assistant.*

Emmy tapped Peaches' profile picture and then scrolled down through many posts. She then opened her photos and went through some videos of the shop she'd not put up on her own account. Not really thinking about it in too much detail, she sent them to Peaches.

Peaches: *It's all so sweet and pretty. The flowers outside would be perfect for one of my shoots! Would it be possible to do some filming outside?*

Emmy had no clue whether or not that would be okay with the powers that be on Darling. She'd cross that bridge when she came to it.

Emmy: *Of course.*

Peaches: *I can't wait to share that discount code – you're going to get so many new customers!*

Emmy beamed from her end. That worked for her.

She sent a quick text to Amy.

Emmy: *You're not going to believe this!*

Amy: *Oh no. Not Kev???? What now?*

Emmy: *Nope. Have you heard of Peaches, that influencer on Instagram?*

Amy: *Who hasn't???*

Emmy: *I hadn't.*

Amy: *What?*

Emmy: *She's coming to the shop!!!!!!*

Amy: *OMFG. When??????*

Emmy: *Soon. She wanted a discount code.*

Amy: *WTAF.*

Emmy: *I know!*

Amy: *You do know this is going to go off, right?*

Emmy: *Really?!??!!*

Amy: *Just a bit! Look it up.*

Emmy: *Wow, my little shop is going to get a boost.*

Amy: *I should say so. What an amazing surprise!*

Emmy: *I need surprises like this in my life, Ames!!!!!*

Running her hands over the front counter, Emmy took a deep breath. She couldn't believe it. Her little boutique that had lived as a dream in her head for so long could turn into a success story if she played her cards right. She wouldn't hold her breath. One DM message was not a given, but she was cautiously hopeful. Just as she was closing the shop door and heading for the stairs, she looked out to see Tom coming along the back path. She could hardly contain her excitement.

'You're never going to believe who messaged me today.'

Tom raised his eyebrows. 'Judging by the look on your face, I'm guessing someone good?'

'Someone amazing!' Emmy gushed. 'Only Peaches, as in *the* Peaches, that influencer with like five million followers.'

'Who?' Tom shook his head. 'No idea.'

'No. I didn't know either, but Amy said she's absolutely massive.'

'Interesting. What does she want with you?'

Emmy quickly gave Tom the rundown. 'It all seems genuine. She was so nice! She's coming here. I'm going to set up a discount code so she can share it with anyone who wants to shop. Ahh!'

Tom shook his head. 'Sorry, did you say five million?'

Emmy fiddled with her phone and turned her screen around to face Tom. 'Yeah, look.'

'This is huge! If even a tiny fraction of her followers visit the shop or use the code, it could totally turn things around. Like, a lot.'

Emmy nodded. 'I know! I'm trying not to get my hopes up too much; it's just a message at the end of the day. This could be an opportunity, though.'

'What if this takes you to world-famous Instagram hotspot overnight?' Tom joked.

Emmy laughed. 'Okay, let's not get carried away. I'm stoked, though.'

'It might just put us on the map.'

'Peaches has so much influence by the looks of it!'

'It could be business-changing,' Tom acknowledged.

'I really hope you're right. It would be great to get some luck for once in my life.'

Tom gave her shoulder a squeeze. 'We need to drink to this.'

Emmy couldn't get the smile off her face as she followed Tom into the kitchen. She was buzzing with optimism. For the first time since opening the shop, Emmy felt not only as if she was living the dream in a sweet little town by the sea, but also that The Old Ticket Office's fate was looking bright. She so wanted more of that.

6

Emmy stood next to Tom in the tram shelter over the road from her shop. With her head cocked to the side, she let her eyes run over the little details of the exterior of The Old Ticket Office and gave herself a bit of a mental pat on the back. She smiled as she remembered the work involved with the installation of the flowers going up over the top of the windows and around the door. It really did look very pretty, so it had been worth the elbow grease and investment in both her money and her brain power. It had all turned out rather well.

She waved to Callum, who was standing in the flat window above watching them down below. Callum had taken to Darling Island like a duck to water, and Emmy loved the fact that moving to Darling had been the right thing for both of them. Callum had made a few local friends via the school run on the ferry, and he seemed to be enjoying having his very own space just as much as Emmy was. Not that Callum had realised before how big a deal it was being stuck in the rental trap, because Emmy had done her best to protect him from that, but now they were in the flat, things just felt more permanent and settled. It appeared that Callum was thriving just as much as Emmy was, and as a parent, that made her feel as if she was at least doing something right.

She stood and watched as the blue and white livery of the tram glinted in the patchy sunshine filtering down through a cloudy sky. The tram trundled and rumbled as it got closer and finally came to a stop just in front of the tram shelter where they were waiting. The conductor, Shelly, called out the stop name from the back of the tram, a couple of people got off, and as Tom and Emmy got on and made their way to the front, Shelly called out hello.

Emmy wriggled across one of the timber seats until she was sitting by the window, and Tom sat down beside her, put his hand on her leg, and both of them sat in silence for a bit as Shelly yanked the rope on the huge bell, called out the tram's destination, and it started again on its journey. Emmy sat back, made herself comfortable and gazed at all the familiar sights of Darling going past the window. She felt swathes of gratefulness whoosh over her that the gorgeous little place was her home. Darling Island was now part of not only a dream she'd had for a very long time but part of her internal woodwork. Almost as if all along it had been where she'd been meant to be. She loved how that made her feel cosy inside.

Tom seemed to read her thoughts. 'Nice living here and being on the tram, isn't it?'

'Yeah, I was just this second thinking it. I love it here.'

'I thought you were.'

'And earlier, too, when I waved to Callum. He's settled well. We both have,' Emmy said with a smile.

'It's a good place to live, and you're good people, so you fit in. Woe betide you if you're not - you're soon made unwelcome,' Tom remarked.

Emmy wrinkled up her nose. 'See, that's weird because I've

heard that about the not fitting in on Darling thing, but how come someone like Russell stays? It doesn't make sense.'

Tom contemplated for a second. 'Why, has he done something you don't like?'

'Well, yes and no, nothing serious, but he's just, well, not very Darling-ish if you see what I mean.'

Tom narrowed his eyes. 'I know exactly what you mean. There are two reasons. Firstly, his parents bought their way in thirty-odd years ago, and secondly, he really isn't here very often so he gets away with it. He's normally around for a month or so, and then he's off again hobnobbing around the world via the money he sponges from his super-rich parents. That's what people say anyway.'

Emmy hoped Russell would be gone again soon. His presence wasn't making her happy. She couldn't wait to see the back of him. 'I see. I suppose that makes sense then.'

'So, yeah, he won't be around long, meaning push never really comes to shove with him.'

'What does he actually *do*?'

'Something in the entertainment industry. No one really knows. There were some rumours about him a few years ago. He got found out for doing some dodgy deals. I can't for the life of me think what they were. Anyway, just steer clear.'

'Yeah, don't worry, I've already got the memo on that.'

'Good.'

'Amy bumped into him on the way into the shop before when we went to Darlings for the evening, and I told her then I wasn't sure about him.'

'Right, yep, you just need to give him a wide berth. Speaking of Amy, anything further on telling her about Katy?'

'No, nothing other than more guilt for me. She's not stupid and she knows something was up before I came clean with you.'

Tom pressed his lips together. 'Very tricky situation.'

Emmy let out a ginormous sigh. 'I know. I feel terrible.'

'This is at some point going to come to a head, though, you *do* realise that, right?'

Emmy shivered and shook her head. She tried not to think about it. She really didn't want to know. 'Yes, I suppose at some point it will.'

7

E mmy smoothed her hands over her black, silky trousers and took a deep breath as she paced and surveyed the shop, ensuring every last detail was perfect. She was really nervous, but pretending she wasn't at all. Peaches, alongside what she had called her 'A Team', was due to arrive for a photo-shoot and video at Love Emmy x. Emmy wasn't really sure what to do, how to behave, or what to expect. The world of influencers wasn't in her vicinity at all. She was more au fait with lost passports and complaining passengers than celebrities.

She'd spent the better part of the day before sprucing up the already pristine shop space. She'd dusted every surface, arranged displays just so, and added extra flowers both around the shop and to the floral installation going over the outside of the shop. She had a carefully selected and much thought-out combination of aromatherapy oils pumping out from various hidden diffusers, and the whole place was flickering in soft light. A high street run-of-the-mill jewellery store it was not.

In the corner, Louisa sat poised with her harp. Peaches, or rather her assistant, Gemma, had specifically asked if Louisa could be in situ for the shoot. That had been the first glimpse

Emmy had seen that Peaches was not planning to pop in and have a quick mooch around the shop and be done with it. Peaches and her team were rather planning everything down to the last earring Peaches was going to pick up. Emmy had totally seen another side of what went on in the world of influencers and then some. It was not for the faint of heart. The briefing sheet alone beggared belief, and when she was instructed on what cushions to put on the chair that Peaches would be sitting on, Emmy had realised that the whole thing was more or less make-believe. Love Emmy x had a new role in the world; it was a set for a show.

Emmy checked the time on her phone, then resumed pacing. She wasn't really sure how the day was going to go. She wasn't sure if she was excited, nervous, or what. She *did* know that she was finding it very hard to stand still. This was the biggest opportunity her fledgling business had seen and possibly would *ever* see. She desperately wanted everything to go well. Since Peaches had first been in touch, she'd done a bit of digging and googling and had quickly come to the conclusion that one big influencer mentioning a product could change small businesses forever. She so wanted some of that. She had her fingers, toes, and everything else crossed that it was all going to go well.

The shop bell jingled, and Emmy whirled around to see Callum and Tom, who'd come to have a quick nose.

'No sign of her yet?' Tom asked, glancing around the empty space.

Emmy shook her head, blowing out a tense breath. 'Nope. Any minute now.'

Callum eyed the fancy refreshment table Emmy had set up with curiosity. 'Free food, though? Score.'

He made a beeline for the table, and Emmy swatted his hand away lightly. 'Do not even think about it!'

Callum frowned. 'What's she going to do with all that anyway? She looks like she eats air for breakfast.'

'Callum! Don't be rude, and do not ever say anything about how a someone looks, please. You can have one of those vanilla whirls.'

Callum happily grabbed one and stuck it in his mouth.

'You've done so well, Ems,' Tom said. 'She's going to love it.'

'I hope so. I just want it all to go smoothly after all the back-and-forth emails and suchlike.'

'Who would have thought there was so much preplanning for someone like her to come into a little shop like this,' Tom mused.

'Tell me about it. I've sent more emails about this than anything else.'

As they were joking about the fact that the light had to be a certain way for Peaches, the shop bell jangled again. Emmy's stomach swooped as she saw three women entering the store. It was definitely Peaches and her assistants. She shooed Tom and Callum out through the storeroom and bustled over the shop. She fixed a bright smile on her face as she went to greet them. 'Hi! Lovely to see you. You must be Peaches.'

'That's me!' Peaches singsonged. 'And you must be Emmy! Oh my gosh, it's so nice to finally meet you!'

Up close, Peaches looked similar to how she did in her photos – chestnut hair, cat-eye make-up, and perfectly turned out. Though without a filter, she looked just a little less perfect. As she walked in wearing matte gold leggings and a soft pink cropped sweatshirt, her high ponytail curled at the ends and bounced. The look screamed casual, but with half a brain cell, anyone could see there'd been a lot of thought to put together the thrown-on-dressed-down look. The label on Peaches' trainers told Emmy they'd been a considerable purchase.

'I'm Gemma, Peaches' assistant,' the second woman introduced herself, shaking Emmy's hand politely. Gemma didn't steal any of Peaches' thunder. She had neat blonde hair in a tidy updo, black capri pants, a silky black shirt, and glasses perched on her nose.

'So lovely to have you,' Emmy heard herself gush. 'Come in, make yourselves at home. Can I get you anything? Cup of tea?'

'Ooh yum, don't mind if I do.' Peaches helped herself to a fancy cupcake from the table and started to pick tiny bits off and pop them into her mouth.

Gemma smiled. 'No thanks. I avoid gluten and processed sugar if I can.'

Peaches laughed. 'Of course, sorry! My Gemma's so health-conscious, not like me with my sweet tooth.'

Emmy showed them around, the butterflies in her stomach going full force. 'Ha! Yes, me too. Love a bit of sugar.'

Peaches bit into a cinnamon bun. 'Wow! What are these?'

Emmy smiled. 'Cinnamon buns.'

'Yes, obvs, but I've never tasted one like this before. This is some cinnamon bun. The icing!'

Emmy shook her head. 'I know. There's a bakery just down the road here, and they make them in-house. Everything in there is amazing.'

Peaches turned to Gemma and pointed. 'Put the bakery on the list.' She turned back to Emmy. 'Darling Island's not quite the backwater we thought it was going to be, eh?'

Emmy wasn't sure what to think of that comment. She tried to beam in response, but it came out more as a sort of watery smile. She made a non-committal sort of sound. 'Mmm.'

As she showed Peaches around, Peaches oohed and ahhed appreciatively in all the right places. 'Oh my gosh, Emmy, every-thing is *so* lovely,' she gushed. 'I just love, love, love the feel. What a fabulous place. Absolutely divine. So my vibe, yes, so my vibe.'

Emmy flushed. Peaches seemed genuinely impressed, if very full of herself. 'Thank you. I do my best.'

Peaches nodded enthusiastically. 'Lovely.' She held up a pair of drop rose gold earrings. 'Oh, and I adore these! You have such a good eye. So good. Surprising, really.'

The growl inside Emmy's head thankfully stayed where it was. On the outside, she remained more than amiable, but Peaches seemed to have a bit of an edge to her. At least Peaches seemed to be genuinely enthusiastic about Love Emmy x. Peaches appeared nice enough, but with Emmy's vast experience and knowledge of dealing with the general public, she could tell Peaches would be the sort to turn in a split second. Peaches nodded and then pointed over to Louisa, the harpist, in the corner. 'Oh my gosh, she's amazing.'

'Yes, that's Louisa. It's so nice to have her.'

'Are you kidding? More than nice! I am *obsessed*!' Peaches trilled. She turned back to Gemma and pointed around the shop. 'We need to get some shots with the harpist, but in the background, you know? As if I spend my days floating around to music. Do you think she knows any Abba stuff?'

Gemma pushed her glasses back up to the bridge of her nose and nodded, already tapping away on her tablet. 'Yes, that would make for great visuals with the branding.'

Peaches clasped her hands together eagerly and looked at Gemma with raised eyebrows and wide eyes. 'Okay, well, I'm ready when you are. We'll need hundreds of shots to get one good one. You know the score. The video filters need to be en pointe today.'

Emmy blinked, almost overwhelmed by Peaches' confidence, or was it arrogance? 'Um, I thought you could start with some shots outside and the flower installation.'

Peaches' face dropped. Clearly suggesting anything to her was not the done thing. Peaches screwed her nose up, and the rest of her face then followed suit. 'We have a run sheet of exactly what we're doing when. You should have been sent it.'

Emmy clearly wasn't welcome to propose anything. She

flicked her hand dismissively. 'Righto, yep, just do whatever you like. Let me know if you need anything.'

Peaches frowned and then shook her head as if in clarification. 'Sorry, you have kept the store exclusive for me for the morning as discussed?' Peaches raised the end of her sentence questioningly. 'With the option to move on into the afternoon if we need to. Yes?'

'Yes, yes,' Emmy said quickly.

Gemma bustled around and started unzipping a garment bag. Emmy had to stop her chin from dropping to her chest as accessorised hangers and clothes were pulled from a huge bag. 'We have a few options for outfits.' She turned her wrist over to look at her watch. 'The hair and make-up artist should be here any second.'

Emmy wasn't sure how much more make-up could fit on Peaches' face. 'Great.'

Gemma raised her eyebrows in question. 'As per my email, she'll need somewhere to change.'

Emmy said a silent prayer that she'd set up a changing area in the storeroom. Now, she really wished she'd done a much better job. Peaches clearly thought she was a very big deal. 'Yep, through here.'

All of them trooped in, just as a make-up artist with two hard silver roll-along suitcases and a gigantic tote bag over each arm arrived. Emmy settled them all in the corner of the storeroom, offered to make tea, and once she was back downstairs with the tea, left them to it and stood chatting to Louisa in the corner. Peaches emerged a short while later in a flowing floral maxi dress and wedges. The casual clothes from earlier were but a distant memory. Peaches obviously just arrived at places in those. Gemma helped artfully arrange Peaches' hair over one shoulder whilst a girl with a huge light bouncing disc lurked in the background.

Peaches shook her head and addressed Emmy. 'Hair and

make-up are not going too well today, but we're just going to go for it. Hopefully, the lighting in here will hide it.'

Emmy wasn't really sure what to think. Peaches was nice enough, but the whole thing was quite the eye-opener. Peaches was one hundred and fifty per cent focused on herself, and everything was fully staged down to the last false eyelash on Peaches' top lid. It was almost in direct contrast to what was broadcast on the Instagram squares. Emmy kept squinting and shaking her head, trying to marry the two up in her mind. Peaches ran a manicured finger with a jewel on the nail down an iPad as Gemma passed her a phone with a Peaches logo on the cover. Peaches read out the various scenes and poses in front of the displays they were going to go through. A second assistant held a camera with a microphone on the top and mirrored Peaches as she walked around. Peaches took a sip from a pale pink cup, flipped her hair, and then stood as if she was in serious contemplation over a pair of earrings in Emmy's antique display unit.

Every few minutes, while Louisa played the harp in the background and Gemma watched on from beside the camera, Peaches changed up angles and poses. The camera stopped and started, and in between poses, the make-up artist butted in and fluffed Peaches here and there. Peaches' hair was adjusted, and she was handed a basket as a prop.

'Yes, love the basket!' Peaches said as she leant on the antique display case. 'Ooh, can we get some with the neon sign in the background?'

Emmy wasn't quite sure how to act around this woman who was behaving as if she were in a full-on Hollywood production. Emmy was clearly way behind the times and way out of her depth. She tried not to roll her eyes, kept in mind the millions of followers, and steeled herself to indulge Peaches' every whim. The influencer knew her angles and how to work the camera. Every pose seemed effortless, but it was obvious that it had been practised and perfected many times. Every single little thing was staged.

Gemma approached Emmy with a smile. She gestured out to Darling Street. 'You said in your email about parking in the lane if there was a spot. Otherwise, I need to put another ticket on the car.'

'Yes.' Emmy pointed to the back of the shop. 'If you go all the way around, you should be able to park by the gate here at this time of day.'

'Will I get a ticket?'

'You shouldn't. Though officially you need a permit.'

'Right. I might just chance it then.' Gemma rummaged for her car keys in her bag and put her phone in her pocket. 'If there's a spot, I'll grab it. Peaches prefers not to have to walk too far after a shooting day. I'll be back in a jiffy.'

About ten minutes later, Gemma came in via the back door from moving her car to the lane. Emmy frowned at the look going across Gemma's face as Gemma grabbed her bag and put her keys away. 'Everything okay? Did you get a spot in the lane?'

'Err, yep.'

'Are you okay?'

'I think so. Sorry, yes, I'm fine.'

Emmy narrowed her eyes. 'Did something happen in the lane? Did someone say something to you about not having a permit?'

'No, no, it's fine.'

'Are you sure? Did you find a space?'

'I did.'

'You squeezed in okay?'

'Behind a grey sports car.' Gemma shook her head and closed her eyes for a split second. 'There was a, err, a man getting out of it.'

Emmy immediately realised what had happened in the lane.

Russell. Say no more. 'Oh, right, yes, I see.' She lowered her voice. 'Sorry, that's the, umm, neighbour.'

Gemma clocked the look on Emmy's face. 'What a creep. Poor you.' She tutted and shook her head. 'I haven't had to deal with that for ages. He totally undressed me with his eyes.'

Emmy felt *so* embarrassed. 'God, I'm so sorry.'

'It's nothing I can't handle. I just don't believe people still get away with behaving like that these days.'

'I know.'

Gemma dismissed it and made her way over to Peaches, who was having photos done with Louisa strategically playing away in the background. After exhaustive photos and videos all through the interior, they stepped outside to make use of the exterior and the flower arch around the door. There was an outfit change where Peaches changed into jeans and a cropped boxy blouse, swapped the basket for a Chanel bag and platform shoes. She then posed by the flower arch as the camera assistant held up her phone and shot content for stories over and over again. As Emmy watched on, she smiled to herself as she remembered her dad, Bob's, extensive YouTube watching of flower installation tutorials. Never in either of their wildest dreams did they think the flower installation would be used as a backdrop prop for one of the biggest influencers in the UK. Both Gemma and the videographer kept shooting photos at a rapid pace while Peaches vamped and preened. The make-up artist constantly re-fluffed Peaches' artfully mussed hair when needed and sprayed her from a bottle of peach glow.

Peaches snatched the phone from the camera assistant and stared critically down at the phone with her eyes narrowed. She shook her head repeatedly, tutted, and instructed that the whole scenario needed to start again. Eventually, Peaches was satisfied with the still shots outside the shop, and she was eager to film some video clips of her fake arriving at the store. She practised walking along the pavement a few times, shouting at Gemma, asking her if her stomach was sticking out. Once that scene had been filmed umpteen times, Peaches beamed at Emmy. 'Next on our schedule is one of me walking in and you greeting me at the door.'

I really would rather not, Emmy thought to herself. Emmy was rapidly going off the whole Peaches thing. She'd made the time and effort now, and she'd invested in having Louisa for the day, so she had to suck it up and do it for her business. She put on her work smile. 'Love to.'

The scene was recreated several times until Peaches deemed herself cute enough for Instagram. Next, Peaches wanted close-ups of her gushing over the jewellery and other trinkets in yet another outfit choice. All the while, Louisa sat in the corner playing the harp.

Emmy was instructed to put her hair up and stand behind the display cabinet. She nodded along, providing commentary when prompted as if they were having a genuine conversation. Peaches certainly knew how to work the camera. Her reactions seemed somehow natural and unforced when Emmy knew they must have been rehearsed to high heaven.

After filming around the interior window from the inside, they headed outside again so Peaches could dramatise discovering the shop's window displays for the first time. Emmy watched as Peaches opened the door to the shop; the bell tinkled, and the harp played.

'Oh my gosh, you guys! Look, guys, how sweet is this place? Can you even believe it? I find the best places for you!' Peaches exclaimed as she opened the door and stepped outside. She ran her fingers along the window, gushing about how obsessed she was and what a hidden gem she'd found. Gemma followed Peaches with the phone camera as she flitted around. Emmy marvelled quietly at how effortless Peaches made it all look and how she was now privy to the information that just about everything on Peaches' socials was a curated snatch of a made-up existence. She'd be scrolling through her socials from now on with very different eyes.

After hours more of the same thing over and over again but with different outfits, finally, Peaches deemed they had enough footage. 'Well! I think that's a wrap,' she said, checking herself in her phone camera yet again. 'We might get a couple of posts out of that if we're lucky.'

Emmy was almost weak with relief. She was exhausted just from watching. Sod being an influencer for a laugh. And people thought it was a passive income! She tried to still sound enthusiastic as a little part of her inside wanted to shoo Peaches and her entourage out the door as quickly as she could. 'That was amazing, Peaches. Thank you so much for coming. It's been great.'

'Of course!' Peaches said as she pulled Emmy into a bubbly, over-the-top hug. 'I can't wait to get this footage edited for the Gram and see if we get anything out of it. I hope so.'

Gemma handed Emmy a business card with Peaches' social media handles. 'We'll be sure to tag you if and when the content goes up.'

If and when? Emmy felt her stomach sink as she thought about how much she'd spent on Louisa, the refreshments, and how much time she'd spent cleaning and getting the shop ready. She'd thought the social media mention was a given. How wrong she was. She was clearly such an amateur in this world. Peaches and her crew had spent hours filming in her tiny shop, and they were thinking they might get one or two posts out of it or maybe not. You live and learn.

Emmy tried to remain positive as she helped clear up the Peaches' props, chatted to Louisa and Gemma, and they all waited for Peaches to get changed. Once they were out the door, Emmy stood in the sudden quiet, watching them walk down the path towards Peaches' car. The old walls of the shop themselves seemed to exhale. A normal day felt almost dull in comparison.

Just as Emmy was gathering up her phone and locking one of the display cabinets, Tom came through the back and poked his head around the shop door. 'Hey. How'd it go?'

Emmy raised her eyebrows. 'Err, I don't actually know. Put it this way, it was an eye-opener.'

'Not what you expected?'

'What you see on the squares and reels is not what goes on behind the scenes. Outfit changes, so many iterations of the same things, so much fluff and ponce. She totally had her own hair and make-up artist.'

'Interesting. I bet you loved that. Not.'

'Ha! You know me too well.'

'Bit of a prima donna?'

'She was, but nice too, sort of,' Emmy agreed. 'I'm so curious to see how the videos turn out. Peaches didn't seem convinced that they'd turned out that well.'

'Oh, right, okay.'

'She was fawning all over everything, though, and she said the shop looked amazing.' Emmy sighed and shook her head, 'What a lot of work.'

'I'm sure she'll get something from it.'

'I hope so. It was so nerve-racking. I totally underestimated what goes into it. Like totally and utterly.'

Tom wrapped an arm around her shoulders. 'You look shattered.'

Emmy sighed. 'I am.' She felt drained and unsure what to feel about the day. She just hoped that after the money she'd spent on Louisa that Peaches would mention The Old Ticket Office and give Love Emmy x a boost. She hoped Peaches and her following might take Love Emmy x to the next level. After all the work she'd put in, she was going to pray her ship was finally coming in. But after the show she'd seen put on that day, she certainly wasn't going to hold her breath.

8

It was a week or so after Peaches' photoshoot extravaganza at Love Emmy x. Emmy was with her sister Katy, dishing about the influencer's much-anticipated visit. The visit had been the weirdest thing for Emmy, almost like an out-of-body experience that had actually happened to somebody else. Emmy had come down from it with a bit of a bump and was now thinking that the whole thing had been a dream. Or a nightmare. She was sitting with Katy in the kiosk café in the park around the corner from Katy's house, watching Elodie play with a puzzle on the children's table in front of them.

Emmy took a sip of her coffee and relayed the day to Katy. 'She was so bubbly and enthusiastic, but at the same time sort of mean, almost. No, not mean, I don't know what it was. I can't put into words how she was in real life compared to what you see on her socials,' Emmy mused as she sat with Katy. 'She's even more confident than she seems in her videos, but very calculated, if you know what I mean.'

Katy took a sip of her latte, eyes wide. 'I still can't believe Peaches was actually there, in the flesh, at your little shop. I've been following her for years. I'm talking since the old, old days when she had a couple of thousand followers. Actually, maybe less than that. Way before she went viral. When she still called herself Kim.'

'You and me both on not believing it. It was odd having a star in the shop,' Emmy said with a shake of her head. 'The whole thing was surreal.'

'What did she do then?'

'What didn't she do? She was so good at posing for the camera and making things look natural when they were the complete and total opposite. It was so, so staged. There were assistants and run sheets and all sorts. Talk about a surprise. It's so not what you see on your phone screen. Nothing like it.'

'Well, she is a professional, I suppose,' Katy pointed out. 'It's her job, and she makes a shed load of money out of it. They all do.'

'Yup. I guess you're right. Why would I expect her to be anything other than professional?'

'Exactly. So, how long was she actually there shooting?'

Emmy huffed out a breath, thinking back over the marathon photoshoot. Just thinking about it made her tired. 'Honestly? Like six hours or more. She went way over the time allocated. She did shots all through the store, then went outside, too. There were so many outfit changes. I was exhausted just watching.'

Katy's eyebrows shot up. 'Six hours? Wow! She really put you through it for the Gram, eh?'

'No kidding. I was running around like the rest of them, following her instructions. Meanwhile, she just glided through one perfect pose after another, telling everyone exactly how things had to go.'

Katy laughed. 'So she seemed to like the stuff then?'

'She seemed to. She was gushing over everything, saying

how obsessed she was with the Love Emmy x vibes and how it all had my personal flair. Which made me chuckle. What even is my personal flair? Last time I checked, I didn't have one. Ha!'

'Look at you go, turning influencers into fans,' Katy joked.

'She even took a few things with her afterwards. Paid full price and everything.'

'Even better!'

'I know. I couldn't believe it,' Emmy said. 'She was just so… what's the word? Full-on. Yes, that's the word. "Emmy, this is so adorable, I'm obsessed!"' Emmy said, mimicking Peaches' over-the-top tone.

Katy grinned. 'I can totally picture it. I know that voice she does nowadays. She didn't start like that. And she's tagged you, has she?'

Emmy shook her head. She'd been stalking her notifications, but so far, Peaches had not tagged Love Emmy x or posted anything. 'Nope. Not a sausage yet.'

'Oh, right, that's disappointing.'

'Tell me about it.'

'So when do you think she'll actually post the content she shot?' Katy asked.

'No idea,' Emmy admitted. 'That's the thing I'm now realising. There wasn't any actual agreement. It was all a bit fluffy. Could be today, could be weeks from now. Her assistant said they'd let me know.'

'Let's hope it's sooner rather than later. This could be huge if she shares it with all her followers.'

'We'll see. I won't hold my breath, I don't think,' Emmy joked. But secretly, Emmy was on pins and needles, waiting to see what Peaches decided to post and when. The influencer's seal of approval could potentially turn her small business around.

'Gosh, right. So you don't even know. There wasn't any formal agreement or anything. Yikes.'

Emmy sighed. 'Nope. It was like she was doing me a favour. Apparently, according to her assistant, the regular charge for a post is loads, but she wanted my shop for content that no one else had posted yet.'

'Right. Makes sense.'

'I can't stop checking my phone! Every notification gets my hopes up, thinking it might be Peaches. But so far, nothing. At least I didn't pay, I suppose.'

'The waiting will be torture,' Katy noted.

'I know.' Emmy groaned. 'I wish she could have just posted something right away while the excitement was fresh. Now I'm over-analysing everything. I guess you live and learn with things like this.'

'Yeah, I would be too. I suppose you can't do much about it now.'

'No. What if she didn't like the shop as much as she acted like she did? What if the pics don't come out good enough to post?' Emmy laughed and rolled her eyes. 'Ugh, I'm driving myself crazy.'

Katy contemplated for a bit. 'I'm sure she got loads of great content. Her followers are going to love it from what I've seen, and she's correct: Love Emmy x is right up her street.'

'I hope so.'

'The place looked amazing in your stories. Her followers will be drooling over it once she posts. I'm certain of it, Ems.'

Emmy smiled. 'Fingers crossed. Hopefully, if and when she does, the algorithm blesses the content and pushes it out wide. I could do with a boost.'

Katy nodded. 'I'll leave offerings to the algorithm gods. But honestly, Ems, you should be proud; you got your dream business up and running and now have influencers wanting to collab with you. That in itself is huge!'

Emmy hadn't thought about it like that. 'When you put it like that, you're right. Anyway, at least it's going in the right direction.'

'Exactly.'

'I should just be patient and enjoy the ride.'

Katy lifted her cup in a toast. 'And whoever doesn't appreciate Love Emmy x is clearly not seeing what I'm seeing from your socials.'

'Cheers to that.' Emmy laughed, clinking her cup to Katy's. Emmy just hoped that something amazing was going to be the result of all the effort, time, and money she'd spent.

E mmy was back home after the coffee with Katy. She'd spent a couple of hours doing housework, cleaning the bathroom, and getting her work uniform ready for the following days. As she'd pottered and cleaned, she'd constantly checked her phone for notifications from Peaches. Crickets. Absolute crickets. Not even a sniff of a post, by the looks of it.

She tapped on Peaches' profile to see the latest post. It was a single photo of Peaches pouting at the camera. Emmy couldn't believe it when she realised that the photo was one of the ones in the shop. Peaches was wearing a floral maxi dress, her hair was pulled over her shoulder, and she was looking right into the camera. There was no tag about the shop or where Peaches was. Emmy blinked down at her phone, exponentially deflated. After the mammoth hours of shooting, she'd hoped for more than a single selfie without the shop even tagged. A post focusing on Peaches' make-up palette was so disappointing it was untrue. The caption focused entirely on how much Peaches loved the dress and the coordinating eyeshadow. She scanned the text on the post three times. It hadn't mentioned Love Emmy x in the slightest. Emmy tried not to feel disappointed as she shook her head and sighed.

She consoled herself that perhaps Peaches was just spacing out the content, building anticipation before sharing the full photoshoot. Emmy sent up a silent prayer that Peaches was going to do a special feature on The Old Ticket Office and that her time and investment hadn't been a complete and utter waste. As the day went on, it looked as if that was absolutely going to be the case. Emmy anxiously checked Peaches' feed multiple times, and the crickets continued on their merry way. There were plenty of new stories hitting Instagram, just none of Love Emmy x. Emmy felt so *pathetically* disappointed it was untrue. Her hopes dimmed further as she tapped on the stories going along the top of her phone. It seemed Peaches had moved on after getting her make-up selfie, and that was going to be that. Emmy felt as if she had been taken for a ride. Not time well spent.

She'd hoped the collab would boost her business, but it appeared to have stalled before it had even taken off. She made a funny little growling noise and shook her head. She hadn't even liked the stupid collab word in the first place. The whole thing had been a *monumental* waste of time. She shook her head as she sat on the sofa in the sitting room on the phone with Amy.

'I just don't understand. She seemed so excited during the shoot. Her assistant was very positive too. Why hasn't she shared any of it? Grr. I'm such an idiot. Ames!'

'I know, it's weird. Who can understand the mysterious minds of influencers, though? Maybe she's just waiting for some reason. I don't know.'

'Or maybe she decided it wasn't worth posting after all,' Emmy said morosely.

'Don't think like that. Remain positive. Manifest it.'

Emmy gave a half-hearted smile down the phone, wishing she shared Amy's confidence. It felt as if it had been ages since Peaches' visit and nothing had come of it, and she was starting to lose faith that anything would. She shook her head. She'd learnt one thing that she knew for sure – if there was a next time, she'd be getting things in writing from the get-go. She wasn't ever going to be taken for a ride by the influencers of the world ever again.

9

Emmy sank down onto one of the plastic chairs in the canteen at the port with a dejected sigh and poked half-heartedly at her salad. She was on her lunch break, but she didn't have much of an appetite. All morning, her mood had been deflated, unable to stop dwelling on her disappointment over the Peaches collab that had come to zilch. She berated herself for thinking too much about it in the first place. Why in the name of goodness had she let herself get caught up in it in all? Influencer my left foot. She'd imagined Love Emmy x taking off all over the show. That hadn't happened in the slightest. Nothing like it, in fact.

'Why the long face?' Jessie asked as she sat down at the table next to Emmy a few minutes later with her own lunch. 'Workday blues? Because if you have them, I definitely have.'

'More like influencer letdown blues,' Emmy stated with a roll of her eyes. She then launched into an explanation of the photo-shoot with Peaches, relaying to Jessie how excited she'd been for the potential exposure, only to have nothing much come of it so far.

Jessie listened as she took bites of her sandwich. 'Wow, so

she spent ages shooting at your place but hasn't posted any of it?'

'Just one lousy photo about her stupid eyeshadow which she didn't tag, so it was pointless for me,' Emmy said glumly. She turned her phone screen to Jessie, showing Peaches' recent posts.

Jessie scrolled back through Peaches' feed. 'That's so weird. She shares like ten photos a day from whatever juice cleanse retreat she's at. Why just the one from your shop?'

'Exactly! She acted *so* into it at the time. I don't get it either.'

'Maybe the vibe didn't really fit her aesthetic after all?'

Emmy's face fell. She'd considered the same thing but hated to hear it said out loud. 'I guess so.'

Jessie quickly backtracked. 'Or who knows, maybe she's got a content calendar, or she's going to build suspense or something.'

Emmy stabbed at a tomato half-heartedly. 'At this rate, there won't be any suspense left. It's been a while already.'

'That's crazy that she'd dedicate all that time and effort to it and then not post anything.'

Emmy had thought the same thing many times. 'Yup.'

'I mean, I'd have been spamming posts for days if I'd been let loose in your shop,' Jessie said with a giggle.

'I just don't get it. I feel like I've been strung along,' Emmy said as she tapped her phone and checked Peaches' Instagram stories for the tenth time that day. She shook her head. 'I guess she got the selfie she wanted and lost interest. I don't know. Who knows in this game?'

'Bit bad of her, though.'

'I'm trying not to take it personally. You live and learn, right?'

'Anyone would be disappointed in your shoes. You went way out of your way to accommodate her. The least she could do is throw you some decent exposure in return.'

'That was my thought exactly,' Emmy said resignedly.

'Sort of rude too. *Very* rude, actually.'

'I guess when you're Insta famous with millions of followers, you don't have to play by the usual polite rules the rest of us in the normal world have to adhere to,' Emmy said with raised eyebrows.

'No kidding.'

'Oh, well.'

'It's still early days. Maybe she'll surprise you with a massive feature – stories, reels, the lot. You'll go viral, Ems.'

'Gosh, I hope so. I've been glued to my analytics, waiting for any uptick. It's *so* not happening at the moment.'

'Fingers crossed! If she ghosts you completely, then she's even shallower than she looks.'

'Too right. I'll try to stay hopeful.'

Jessie continued to chat, but Emmy was only half in the conversation. Her thoughts kept circling back to Peaches, and she had to force herself to stay focused. Her eyes strayed constantly to her phone, willing it to light up with a notification from Peaches. Her phone remained dark. What a horrible, disappointing, *total* waste of time.

By the time Emmy's shift ended, there had been zero new posts from Peaches, and Emmy had given up hope. Exhaustion from her double shift and complaining passengers had also really finished off her day. Her mind kept going over the Peaches thing again and again. Not only was she fed up about the money and time she'd spent, but she also felt as if Peaches' silence was a snub at Love Emmy x itself. A colossal rejection and a snub she took very, very personally. Silly little Emmy Bardot and her silly little jewellery shop.

As she drove home to Darling, she vacillated between over-thinking the whole big waste of time to forcing herself to stop letting it be front and centre of her mind. She thought about when Gemma had first contacted her, and she'd gone through Peaches' posts. She'd seen how the lucky few small brands granted the golden seal of approval had seen a huge boost. It made her feel horrible that Love Emmy x wasn't good enough. Her shop and she herself had not performed. Emmy Bardot was just not good enough. The feeling that she had somehow missed the mark ate away at her as she steered her car onto the floating bridge. Just as she put the brake on and leaned her head back against the headrest, her phone buzzed.

'Hey,' she said to Amy.

'How was your long day?'

Emmy let out an elongated whoosh of air. 'Long mostly, but not too bad.'

'You sound fed up.'

'I am. You got that right.'

'What's up?'

'The Peaches thing.'

'What about it?'

'She's not posted anything, and it's made me feel *awful*. She must have realised Love Emmy x is rubbish.'

'Aww, yeah, it's pretty bad after all you did. I guess you just have to stop thinking about it and let it go.'

Emmy knew that was the answer, but she didn't want to do that. 'I can't help it.'

'There's a million reasons why she could be sitting on those photos,' Amy reasoned.

'Name one,' Emmy challenged glumly.

'Okay, um, maybe a big campaign or project she was contracted for had to take priority over her own content.'

'Or maybe she just thought my stuff was awful in the end. That's what I'm gleaning from it.'

'Don't even go there. The shop is beautiful and you know it. Any sane person can see what a gem it is.'

'Just not the one with five million followers,' Emmy added a laugh, but inside, the whole thing had knocked her for six. She felt like an idiot.

'Honestly, don't let one flaky influencer mess with your self-confidence. You've created something amazing, Ems. You know it, I know it, we all know it.'

'You really think so? I'm doubting everything.'

'I know so. You've done so well. Just keep plugging away. Slow and steady wins the race, as Dad always says.'

Emmy grimaced but tried to take Amy's words on board. She was having a massive case of self-esteem failure. She couldn't let go of the fact that Peaches' silence shouted that Emmy's shop just didn't measure up. Not special enough. Not stylish enough. Not worthy of being spotlighted before millions of followers hanging on Peaches' every last word for their queen's next tip. Emmy flicked her head, trying to get rid of the negative self-talk. The logical part of her brain told her to ignore the niggling, the other part swallowed her whole. She felt frustrated tears pricking at the edges of her eyes. She hated how Peaches and her stupid shoot had unravelled her completely. She was now questioning why she had bothered chasing the Love Emmy x pipe dream at all.

'You okay?'

Emmy quickly straightened up and tugged at the skin at the corner of her right eye. 'Sorry. Yeah. I'm just a bit tired of it. It's been such hard work.'

'Yeah, it has. I did say you needed a holiday…'

Emmy's lower lip wobbled. 'It's so stupid to let this upset me. So much for being strong, eh?'

'I'd be disappointed, to be honest,' Amy noted.

Emmy nodded. 'I'm overthinking it, though. Kitchen-sinking it for sure. I always do that.'

'Don't we all? You just have to put it behind you.'

'Yeah.' Emmy sighed. 'I do.'

'Don't let some online nitwit make you question yourself. Look how far you've come. Shall we talk about the rental trap you were in?'

Emmy smiled and puffed out an ironic little swish of air. 'Ha.'

'You took a dream that lived inside your head for years and turned it into a reality all on your own. You made that happen, Ems! Not me or Mum and Dad or anyone else – just you with your vision. And let me tell you, along the way, you met the dashing Tom P Carter,' Amy joked and chuckled.

Emmy smiled but felt tears well up at the same time.

'If Little Miss Influencer can't see that, it's her loss. Don't you dare let it make you question for one second the amazing thing you've created. I'm not having it.'

Emmy wiped her eyes. 'Thanks. You're right,' she said in a small voice. 'I just lost perspective for a bit, I suppose.'

'Uh yeah, I'll say. You had a dream and made it happen on your terms. Don't lose sight of how huge that is.'

Emmy nodded. 'I did.'

Amy was on a roll. She continued her lecturing. 'Don't let the Peaches of the world dim that light. Not even for a second.'

'Thank you, Ames.'

Amy joked, 'I've a good mind to send her a DM.'

Emmy laughed, imagining Amy giving Peaches a talking-to.

'Forget Peaches,' Amy added airily. 'We'll make our own viral videos.'

Emmy grinned. 'Yeah.'

'Right, I have to go. Chin up.'

'Thanks, Ames. I needed that.'

As Emmy tapped her phone, she sat and stared out the window. As usual, Amy was always there for her, batting on her side. She felt the same pang of guilt she'd had since Katy had come back into her life. Amy was her chief cheerleader, and here she was keeping things from her. Just as it had initially done, the feeling made her want to heave. It didn't feel nice at all. How was it all going to end up?

10

A brisk wind nipped at Emmy's cheeks as she stood leaning on the broom in the backyard of The Old Ticket Office and looked up at a grey and blustery sky. In an attempt to put thoughts of the Peaches disaster behind her, she'd decided to get out in the backyard and get on with its makeover, and her mum was coming over to give her a hand. She'd forget about Peaches if it was the last thing she did. She'd decided to put it down to a lesson in life and how not to put too much hope into something she couldn't control. She gazed thoughtfully at the tired old space around her, shivered at the cold wind coming in from the sea, and tucked her hands into her cardigan pockets.

She'd done a lot of clearing up in the backyard, but it was far from where she wanted it to be and a long way from the inspiration she'd seen in Jane's garden. Cracked pavers dotted with weeds still stretched away from her, piles of empty pots and bags of soil were ready for some kind of gardening miracle, and there were still signs of the building's previous life as an unloved insurance office every which way she turned. The weathered half-shed was slumped in the corner, paint peeling around the door frame, the window boxes flanking the exterior wall, though now weed-free, were not looking particularly cheerful, and there was still moss growing across one whole section of the wall. All in all, it was depressing.

But in her mind's eye, Emmy was buoyed by pushing on with making her new place somewhere she loved. She envisioned the potential and was determined that by the time spring rolled around, she'd be able to sit outside with a cup of tea and enjoy the Darling sunshine. As she looked around, feeling a bit deflated, she tried to remind herself that Rome wasn't built in a day. She pictured flowers spilling from the replanted window boxes, the beds beside the shrubs on the right, and the shed sporting a fresh coat of paint. Maybe a bistro table tucked over by the wall where she'd now learnt that the light lasted longest in the evenings, and perhaps a fire pit or a chiminea might go down well. To be quite frank, any little bit of foofing would be an improvement.

She was well aware of what a bit of vision and elbow grease could do to transform a space. She'd done it in the poky flat she'd first lived in after Kevin, and she'd made the best of the rental cottage. The problem was that she now had a lot on her plate, the weather wasn't particularly lovely, and her overall enthusiasm was waning. But the eyesore that greeted her every time she walked in from work needed to improve, that much was obvious. She was no longer prepared to put up with it. Despite the nippy air and the fact that she had enough jobs on her list to keep her busy, she wanted to push on with the makeover. She told herself that she was lucky to have an outdoor space that was her own, whatever it looked like, and that people would give their right arm to have what she did. She'd zip her mouth up of whinging, pull on her big girl pants, and get on with it.

Shaking off the chilly air, she gripped the broom handle and continued vigorously sweeping leaves and debris from between the pavers until there was a pile in the corner. Just as the first time she'd worked on the yard, the more she worked to clear and sweep, the more she began to see hope emerge in front of her. Oh-so-satisfying to see the place taking shape.

She'd just stepped back to survey her progress when the gate latch rattled behind her. Emmy turned to see her mum on the path, absolutely laden down with bulging shopping bags.

'Hello, darling!' Cherry called out brightly, somehow balancing the overloaded bags as she wrestled the gate closed again. 'I come bearing supplies, and there are loads more in the car. *Loads.* Don't tell your dad, though. I had some of it kept for me at the shop. I stopped in there on my way here and picked it up. Happy days!'

'Mum!' Grinning at the sight of Cherry overloaded with stuff, Emmy propped the broom against the shed and rushed over to relieve Cherry of some of the bags. 'What in the world have you bought?'

Bustling past Emmy towards the back door, Cherry paused on the step, looked around, and handed Emmy a couple of bags. 'It looks different already.' She rubbed her hands together. 'Ooh, I've been thinking about this for weeks. Let me at it. You know how much I love a makeover or six. In my element, for sure.'

Laughing, Emmy put the bags down by the back door. 'Thanks for coming.'

Cherry tutted as if offended. 'You don't need to thank me. You know that. Now come on then, let's get a cup of tea, and then I'll finish getting stuff from the car. How are things with you?'

'Yeah, good.' Emmy winced inside about the Katy situation. She tried to put it to the back of her mind as they went upstairs and waited for the kettle to boil. Once the tea was made, Emmy leant back against the worktop, letting the warmth from the mug seep into her fingers as she watched Cherry bustle about with a few of the bags.

'I found the most lovely firepit at the garden centre,' her

mum gushed. 'And I've got a load of plants in the back of the car. Honestly, you're not going to look back. It's all about the details.'

Emmy grimaced at her gardening skills, which amounted to exactly zero. 'Hopefully, I can keep the plants alive. I've never been that good at gardening.'

'It's hardly gardening, darling. I've got a couple of hanging baskets full of pansies, too, all done and dusted. They just need hanging up. The pop of colour is what it needs.'

Emmy smiled in her mug at her mum's enthusiasm. She'd always been the same way with any creative project – brimming with ideas and utterly immune to doubts. Her mum was a grafter; she steamed on in and got things done. Emmy envied the way Cherry dove into challenges head first without over-thinking. It went through Emmy's mind as her mum rattled on how Cherry took charge and very much liked to be in control. It made her realise that Katy wasn't wrong about Cherry liking things to be done her way. She tried to push the thoughts aside. 'Thank you. You've been hitting the shops hard by the looks of it. Hopefully, it will be transformed down there.'

'That's the plan. You just have to do what I say, and it will be looking lovely in no time.' Cherry rubbed her hands together eagerly.

'I'll follow your lead, don't worry.'

Cherry continued, not pausing for breath, 'The shed? I was thinking a nice robin's egg blue.' She held up two nearly iden-tical paint swatches. 'Which one do you think?'

Emmy pursed her lips, squinting at the shades of blue. Clearly, she was having a blue shed – it didn't look like she had much say in the matter. 'The one on the left.'

'Perfect choice. I had a feeling you'd say that,' Cherry declared. 'That's the one I got, so you're lucky.'

Emmy just shook her head. She actually hadn't had a choice in the matter at all. She finished the last sip of her tea. 'Well, the shed isn't going to paint itself. Shall we get stuck in?'

'Yes indeed. Let's glow-up this garden, darling. I can't wait to get my teeth into it,' Cherry said as she rinsed her mug under the tap and then put it in the dishwasher. 'Cherry Bardot to the rescue!'

～

The next few hours went by in a flash, and Emmy's back was certainly feeling it. Fuelled by cups of tea, Cherry's multitude of supplies, and her enthusiasm, as the day wore on, the yard was slowly but surely looking like a different place altogether.

Emmy put her hands into the small of her back and rolled her head from left to right. She looked over at her mum, wondering how her mum wasn't exhausted. Cherry was nothing of the sort. She hummed happily as she pulled weeds from between the pavers with gusto and then began to fill the sad-looking beds down the right-hand side of the path with the plants she'd bought from the garden centre. Emmy shook her head, wondering where her mum got her energy from. Her mum was going hell for leather, digging in plants and unpacking new pots as if her life depended on it. As Cherry gave Emmy the task of rubbing down the exterior of the shed, a look of disbelief crossed Emmy's face as her mum continued to buzz around as fit as a fiddle. Sometimes Emmy wondered if she was actually Cherry's flesh and blood. Cherry was the literal embodiment of energy, while she felt like a wrung-out dishrag most of the time. She took her orders from her mum, picked up a hand sander, and started to push it back and forth over the old shed.

By early afternoon, not only had the wind died down, but a weak but not unwelcome sun had come out. The first coat of pale blue covered the shed, and the hanging baskets Cherry had bought were hanging on the back of the building. Cherry was still zipping around doing things at nineteen to the dozen.

Emmy stood back to appraise their handiwork. She put her hands on her hips and nodded. 'We've made progress at least. It's freshened things up already,' she said as she glanced around, taking it all in. With the work she'd previously put in, plus her mum's planting and directing, plus the shed's mini makeover, the place looked like a different space entirely.

Cherry stood beside her, beaming at the now blue shed. 'Doesn't it just brighten the whole place up? You see, I knew the blue was the only way to go,' she enthused. 'I can already picture some window boxes on the windows. I'll get your dad onto that.'

Guilt swarmed Emmy's body, well aware that her mum knew nothing about Emmy being in contact with Katy. 'I don't know what I'd do without you on projects like this. You're so good at it.'

'Oh, stop.' Cherry waved off the praise. 'It's nothing. Remember the time I decided to redo the back garden path at home and ended up re-landscaping half the lawn too? I just love it. I really am in my element, being in charge of things like this. Only if I'm in charge, though, you know how I am!'

Laughing, Emmy nodded. 'How could I forget? It looked amazing when you were finished, but you nearly drove Dad mad in the middle of it all.'

'Well, you know how particular I can get once I've set my mind on something.' Cherry shrugged. 'But it turned out lovely in the end, did it not?'

'It really did,' Emmy replied, whilst wondering what Katy would say about their mum having her mind set on things. She went a bit cold inside. Katy had a point about a lot of things to do with Cherry. The rest of them just chose to shove it under the carpet. Unfortunately, Katy hadn't, and that was where her problems had started.

By late afternoon, the sun had dipped, and it was not warm.

Emmy kept shaking her head as she looked around at the difference. Cherry might be a control freak and liked to be in charge, but she certainly knew how to turn something around. 'I reckon we should call it a day and head inside. We're losing the light anyway, and it's turned really chilly.'

'Good idea, darling. I'm about all gardened out for one day,' Cherry replied as she gave the replanted window boxes a pat as they made for the back door. 'Not a bad job, eh?'

'Thanks so much for doing all this,' Emmy said.

'Won't it be lovely seeing everything in bloom here come spring?'

'It really will.'

Cherry chuckled. 'What would you do without me, eh?'

Emmy writhed inside, hoping she wouldn't find out how she would cope without her mum. Goodness knows what would happen when Cherry finally learnt the truth that Katy was back on the scene and had been for a while. Emmy *did* know that it wasn't going to be nice.

~

A couple of hours later, Emmy was sitting in the kitchen with her mum, Callum was in the sitting room on the PlayStation, and a chilli was bubbling away on the hob. Emmy took a bottle of red wine out of the pantry cupboard and raised her eyebrows in question to her mum.

'Don't mind if I do. Nothing like a nice glass of wine to round off the day,' Cherry said. 'Only a very small one, though, please, Ems.'

Emmy passed her mum a glass and pottered around the kitchen. As they chatted, she put the chilli into a huge serving dish, scooped rice from the rice cooker into a bowl, Callum came in and got a plate, and Emmy sat down with her mum at the table. Cherry dug in and ladled chilli and rice onto her plate. Emmy followed suit.

'Mmm. This hits the spot perfectly,' Cherry noted. 'You always were a good cook, Ems.'

'Was I? I can cook a few basic things well,' Emmy said as she reached over to the worktop to grab the wine to top up their wine glasses.

Cherry continued to tuck in and chat. 'How are things going with you and Tom?'

'We're good,' Emmy said as she fiddled with her fork. 'I really like him. But you know, just taking things slowly.'

Cherry smiled. 'I'm just so pleased for you, darling. It's clear as day how happy you are. I love seeing it. You seem happier now after that little blip you had when you weren't yourself.'

Emmy didn't even want to think about the fact that Cherry had previously picked up on the fact that Emmy had been stressed because of the secret about Katy. 'He's pretty good. I lucked out finding someone who just fits, you know? Like we were meant to be in each other's lives. We just get on.'

'Oh, the heady days of romance! You deserve it after Kevin.' Cherry chuckled.

Emmy laughed. 'Just blame Kevin.'

'He still gets the blame for everything. Even now.'

Emmy smiled. She loved being with her mum and loved that they were so close. But were they really? The Katy thing had made her question bits and bobs, here and there, about whether their relationship really was that close after all. Was it close because it was always on Cherry's terms? Katy would say that. Plus, of course, Emmy had to deal with the now ever-present underlying layer of guilt. Katy complicated things, and the fact that Tom knew and Cherry did *not* filled Emmy with angst. Emmy wrestled with almost constant pangs of guilt over keeping it from her family. On top of that, she wasn't stupid and nor was her mum; it was only a matter of time before it all came out in the open. And she had been the one who had lied.

Emmy gulped down a mouthful of wine as she thought about Katy. Her mind raced back to memories of bitter arguments and slammed doors when Katy had left. She shoved it to the back of her mind as her mum chatted away about a woman at golf who had broken her ankle and they finished the chilli. After clearing up, loading the dishwasher, and wiping down the sides, Cherry made moves to go. Cherry popped her head around the sitting room door to talk to Callum, and then Emmy walked her out to the lane to her car.

'Thanks again for all your help, Mum.'

'Of course, darling. My pleasure. Always here for you, darling, you know that. Always was and always will be.'

Emmy beamed on the outside even though inside she felt dreadful. That was the thing. No matter what Katy or anyone said, her mum *had* always been there for her. She'd supported Emmy through ups and downs, thick and thin, and Emmy hadn't even told her that one of her daughters was safe and sound. Emmy Bardot gulped. Not the best feeling of her life at all.

11

It was a few days or so later, and Emmy pedalled leisurely down one of the cobbled Darling back streets, the salty sea breeze bracing on her cheeks. It was a very Darling day, with a foggy full sky and droplets of mist in the air. As she cycled along one of the back roads running behind the bakery, she breathed deeply, inhaling the smell of freshly baked bread wafting across the street.

She was pedalling along in a world of her own, with the wicker basket attached to the front of her bike jammed full of small Love Emmy x parcels and envelopes. Since the actual physical store had opened, the business had slowly but surely trucked along. Business wasn't exactly coming out of her ears, and she was very glad she'd kept her job at the port. Just as she had in the early days, though, when Love Emmy x had been just a tiny few things in an Etsy store, she adored it and had high hopes for its future. It was just a shame the Peaches thing had come to nothing. She tutted to herself but put it down to experience; she wouldn't be letting any old person on social media use her hard-earned shop as a backdrop for content anytime soon. Especially not one named Kim.

As she looked down at the parcels in the bike basket and coasted towards the post office, she focused on the customers she *did* have and smiled at the thought of her parcels arriving up and down the country. They were beautifully wrapped, carefully chosen, and sent with a lot of thought and care. That had to go a long way in life.

Up ahead, the blue and white striped awnings of the various shops at the far end of Darling Street came into view. Emmy took it all in with a smile – she always felt as if she'd cycled back in time when she was pedalling around Darling. Without any big chain stores or high street franchises marring the Darling landscape, it all felt pretty special and very unique. Passing various shops in the Darling uniform colours, she thanked her lucky stars that she'd found The Old Ticket Office, and sometimes she indulged in the old Darling superstition that actually the little island had found her.

Slowing her bike, Emmy peered into the shops' windows as she whizzed by. Someone raised their eyebrows at her in recognition, and Leo the Australian, whom she'd met through Tom, waved and called out hello from the other side of the street. She loved being part of the Darling woodwork and how it made her both feel settled and that she belonged. It had been a long time coming in her life.

Arriving at the post office, she wedged her bike into the rack outside, unhooked her wicker basket full of parcels from the front, and pushed open the door. A queue of people stood lined up at the counter. Emmy now knew a few faces and smiled as she spotted Jane, the woman from whom she'd bought the sofa, at the top of the queue. She watched as Jane finished up at the counter and then stepped to the side and turned around to head back out the door. On seeing Emmy, Jane stopped.

'Hey. Fancy bumping into you here.'

Emmy girl crushed like crazy. 'Jane, hi! How are you?'

'I'm really good,' Jane replied breezily. 'More work than I can keep up with, but it keeps me out of trouble.'

'Well, you certainly look well.'

'I am, actually. I had a bit of a run of being unwell, but I've finally got it under control, thank goodness.'

'Ahh, yes, you did say that before. Good to hear you're better.'

Jane turned her head, surveying the basket by Emmy's feet in the queue. 'By the looks of you, you're busy too. Business must be doing well.'

'It's ticking along. Finally feels like things are starting to fall into place. The shop was a lot to take on. I underestimated it a bit. Yeah, but things are going well, if a bit slow.'

'So happy to hear it. Oh, and how's the sofa?'

'Yeah, lovely. Thanks again for that. It's great.'

'No worries.'

'Actually inspired by you, I've been working on the area behind the shop. It was very unloved, and I just kept putting it off and putting it off. You know how it is. Never enough time in the day.'

'Oh, right. I bet that's not an easy job,' Jane noted.

'Ahh. It's not too bad. My mum has been helping me a lot. She's into makeovers, god love her.'

'I might have to get her round,' Jane joked.

'I've told her she should start a little enterprise. Anyway, I think I've broken the back of it now, you know? That's half the battle sometimes.'

'Oh, I do know, for sure. My place was awful when I moved in. The thing with gardens is they take a bit of time, too.'

Emmy nodded. 'Yep, true. Actually, though, you'd be surprised how much just sweeping and clearing it out has done.'

'I bet!'

'Mum gave me some hanging baskets full of pansies, which are brightening the place up.'

'Oh yes, they always do.' Jane squinted and held her head to the right for a second. 'I'm just remembering something someone told me in the bakery. Did I hear you had some big influencer in the shop recently?' Jane asked. 'Or have I completely made that up?'

Emmy raised her eyebrows. She hadn't really told anyone much about Peaches, but things went around on Darling whether you told anyone or not. 'I did. That was an eye-opener.'

'Right. By the look on your face, it wasn't great.'

'Nope. *Never* again.'

'Oh why? That's a shame.'

Emmy let out a long sigh. 'She's not even mentioned the shop. I invested in a lot of stuff for it, too.'

Jane shook her head. 'Aww, that's a bit off! Oh well, you live and learn.'

'You certainly do.'

'We don't behave like that on Darling.' Jane laughed.

Emmy played along. 'No, maybe I've already forgotten what it's like in the real world.'

'Long may it last on this little island where people treat each other as they did in the old days.'

'Yep, hopefully.'

Jane shifted her basket on her shoulder and made as if to go. 'Oh well, let's hope at some point she mentions you. You never know.'

'Hope so.'

Jane squinted. 'Didn't someone say there were like a million followers or something? That's right, isn't it?'

'Five million,' Emmy stated.

'Oh, wow! So it would have been huge if she mentioned you. *Really* huge.'

'Yes, like business-changing.'

'I'll say a prayer for you,' Jane joked.

'Yep. I need all the prayers I can get,' Emmy bantered.

'Righto, well, see you later. Good luck with the shop. Don't hold your breath on the influencer.'

Emmy smiled as Jane walked away. She'd put way too much weight on the Peaches thing in the first place. Time for her to put it behind her and move on to other things. She smiled at the little interaction with the lovely Jane and thought about how nice it was to feel like she belonged. She had a feeling she would be okay; Darling Island would have her back.

12

Emmy had spent most of the rest of the day doing boring life things; she'd tidied up the airing cupboard, ordered Callum some new school shirts, and cleaned the flat from top to bottom. As she finished buffing the kitchen worktops, she thought about her conversation with Jane and subsequently, just out of interest, pulled her phone out of her bag where it had been sitting all day. She tapped on Instagram and typed Peaches' name into the search bar, and the influencer's pretty pastel reel feed showed all manner of loveliness. Peaches really did have a very nice life indeed. Emmy then tapped along the stories on the top, taking in Peaches' stories. Suddenly, Emmy stopped and held her finger down on the story filling her phone screen. Then she nearly dropped her phone. Then she squealed a little bit. The Old Ticket Office was staring back at her. The next screen showed Peaches holding a pair of earrings up to the camera while Louisa played the harp in the background. Hardly daring to breathe, Emmy pressed again. A gorgeously edited story of Love Emmy x filled her screen. Clips of Peaches admiring the window played. The shop looked so, so, *so* good. Emmy read the caption about six times.

Obsessed with this hidden little gem of a boutique. Owner Emmy curates the most amazing finds. You are going to die. Shop with code in bio!!

Emmy then tapped on the little squares to see Peaches' posts. There was one of her shop. The post already had many, many likes and *loads* of comments. Emmy slapped a hand over her mouth as she took it in. She pressed the green app for her online shop on her phone and shook her head as she realised that she had new orders and masses of visitors. Peaches' endorsement was sending her store into overdrive. For ages, Emmy went back and forth from watching the stories six times over to watching the live visitors on her shop dashboard. She could barely absorb any of it and was flabbergasted at the number of comments and likes on the post. It was going to be huge for her, that she could already see. She grimaced at the fact that that very morning, she'd written Peaches off as a 'no hope' to Jane in the post office. She swallowed at the things she'd thought about Peaches in her head.

She didn't quite know what to do with herself as she sat at the kitchen table in the flat and watched as the visitor numbers on her shop went way past a hundred. Ping, ping, ping went her phone. She couldn't stop herself from smiling, almost as if she'd won the lottery. She tapped on her sales again – she'd sold more in a few hours than she normally did in weeks. She continued to stare at her phone in a state of disbelief, opened her laptop as if to convince herself that it really was true, and then made herself a celebratory cup of tea.

With her mug of tea in her hand, she went downstairs to the shop and just stood there for a while, leaned an elbow on the old ticket counter, and just breathed. She closed her eyes and said a thank you to the Instagram gods, and to Peaches, and to anyone else who fancied a listen, and then checked her phone again. She half wondered if the sales had happened only in her imagination. It hadn't – they were there and coming in thick and fast.

She had no idea what the sudden rush meant for her little shop's future or how long it would last, but she did know that she was so blimming well grateful. Even a handful of new customers felt like a win-win to Emmy. She pressed her hands together so hard in prayer pose, they wiggled back and forth. She was having good luck, and she wasn't messing things up. She pumped her fist to the ceiling and squeezed her eyes closed. *Yes, yes, yes!* Hoo-blooming-ray.

Once Emmy had stopped punching the air, she called Amy. Amy answered in a couple of rings. 'Ames! Get on Insta! You're not going to believe it.' Emmy heard her own voice sounding near-hysterical.

'What?'

'Peaches finally posted, and it's blowing up!' Emmy swore.

Emmy's phone was silent for a bit while Amy looked. 'Oh my goodness! What the actual? There are so many likes!'

'I know. That collaboration seems like a lifetime ago.'

Amy screeched. 'The comments are asking what the shop is and where they can find it! Peaches has tagged it and linked. Oh my god, it's all over her stories. Like every single one!'

'I know! Ames, I've had loads of orders already.' Emmy couldn't quite believe it. The long-awaited Peaches bump had arrived. Peaches' glowing endorsement was sending her followers racing to Love Emmy x. Emmy was going to strap herself in and enjoy the ride.

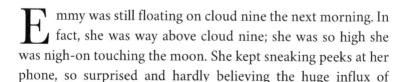

E mmy was still floating on cloud nine the next morning. In fact, she was way above cloud nine; she was so high she was nigh-on touching the moon. She kept sneaking peeks at her phone, so surprised and hardly believing the huge influx of orders that had flooded in overnight after Peaches' reel had hit her followers. She was in the storeroom making a dent on the orders when Tom, dressed for work, poked his head around the back door. He did a double take at the stacks of packages piled up. 'Blimey, you're already swamped! That Peaches effect is no joke. And there we were slagging her off.'

'I know. We thought it was a lot yesterday.' Emmy shook her head. 'It's gone bonkers almost overnight. I can barely keep up. I'm getting orders from America! She's posted another reel!'

Tom beamed. 'I know what I'm doing later.'

Emmy laughed. 'I'll be doing this all day. I am *not* complaining!'

'We said we thought it would be huge. That many followers aren't to be sniffed at.'

'I know. I just didn't really believe it. I just hope I can maintain some of the momentum after the initial frenzy dies down.'

'Making hay while the sun shines, Ems.'

Emmy beamed. 'I intend to. I'll make hay anywhere I have to. Amy is on her way to give me a hand.'

As if she'd heard them speaking, Amy came up the path. 'The cavalry has arrived,' Amy joked.

'Thank goodness,' Tom said. 'It's gone mad overnight.'

Emmy felt herself flush as Amy and Tom stood chatting. She was over the moon with what Peaches had done. She'd thought and planned and schemed for years about Love Emmy x, but there was no way she would ever have been able to secure the sort of promotion that had come her way.

It was all very chaotic and a bit mad, but definitely a wonderful reality. She adored Love Emmy x and was so happy someone else not connected to her thought the same, too. Not her mum or dad, or Amy or Tom, but someone who genuinely seemed to approve. That feeling alone felt special. Love Emmy x was her baby, the physical embodiment of everything she'd imagined in her head for years and years. Having other people love it too felt almost too good to be true. As Tom and Amy chatted, for a second, she just stared at the shop dashboard open on her laptop. She made a point to take it all in as she stood beside her plastic storage tubs in a bit of a daze. A really nice and *very surprising* big old dollop of luck had come Emmy Bardot's way. She was going to milk it for all it was worth.

13

It was the Saturday after Peaches posted on her socials. Emmy bustled around the shop, hardly able to keep up with the customers continually coming through the door. After a long time of radio silence, Peaches had not only shared a reel on Love Emmy x, she'd shared loads more on her stories, and had showcased a video on the flower installation out the front of the shop too. Much to Emmy's complete and utter amazement, the reel had gone viral, and Emmy was feeling the effects of it *big time*. Peaches had sent millions of her followers racing to see Love Emmy x, and Emmy couldn't keep up with things fast enough. It was all so surreal to be in the centre of it all that to Emmy, it felt like a bit of a dream.

Overnight, the little shop on Darling Street had been transformed from sleepy with a few customers every now and then if Emmy was lucky to being busy. At one point, Emmy'd had to lock the door as visitors eager to experience the influencer-approved boutique for themselves had tried to pile in. Emmy had not dreamt in her wildest dreams that Peaches' recommendation would have had not only massive clout but that it would be almost instant. That was the weirdest thing about it all. Since the reels, Love Emmy x, both the online and in-person versions, had had a constant stream of visitors. Bring that right on.

Emmy looked around the shop from behind the counter, unsure, really, as to what to think about it all; a pair of teenagers gushed as they took selfies in front of the neon Love Emmy x sign, boyfriends sat looking bored by the coffee machine, and a group of women in their fifties were trying on necklaces and just about everything and anything they could get their hands on. It was as if someone had flicked a switch on Love Emmy x and finally turned it on. It hadn't come soon enough.

Emmy couldn't believe how big of a deal Peaches' endorsement actually was. In fact, she felt a bit guilty because, despite being more than hospitable to Peaches and her crew, in the back of her mind, she'd pooh-poohed it all a bit. She'd not, in any shape or form, considered that a mention from Peaches would have as much reach as it had. It had, in fact, by the looks of what had happened so far, turned her business around.

It was all a long time coming. As Emmy looked around, she thought about the years it had taken to get Love Emmy x from an idea in the back of her head to what was now playing out in front of her eyes. She'd pottered along with it from its first inception to opening an Etsy shop, to a store online, and now this. She'd dreamt for so long of opening the shop and putting her vision in her head to life. Now, not only was it actually happening, but it was having its own little glorious moment of success. It felt more than good. So, so, so blooming well good.

By noon, she'd helped more customers in one morning than she normally would have done over entire weeks. There'd been an almost frenetic influx of customers, both in the actual store and on her socials, and her online analytics were going gang-busters. Emmy didn't quite know what to do with herself and was finding it hard to catch her breath. She sort of buzzed around in a chaotic, happy fizz. She also kicked herself for not being prepared, not thinking things through, and completely underestimating Peaches' influence altogether. The actual pieces Peaches had bought had long since sold out and her pre-orders were off the scale. She was so annoyed with herself for not having a plan to capitalise on the momentum and a bit embarrassed at what an amateur she clearly was in the online world of influencing. With all those thoughts running around her head and realising that the shop was getting busier and busier, she tapped her phone to call her mum. Her mum answered on the third ring.

'How are you, darling? How is it going today at the shop?'

'Great. I'm actually swamped at the moment, which is why I'm calling. Peaches' post has worked, to say the least.'

'Well, that all sounds wonderful! I'm so pleased for you, darling.'

'Meaning loads of people have turned up here! Mum, can you come and give me a hand?' Emmy said, hoping her mum wasn't intending on going to golf.

'Of course. You know I'd do anything for my girls.'

Emmy sagged in relief. 'I'm run off my feet, and then I've got all the packaging and posting things out later. If you can help, it would be great. Otherwise, I am going to be up all night.'

'I have no plans today. I'm on my way. Cherry to the rescue.'

Emmy exhaled, feeling some of the pressure ease at the same time as wincing at the guilt about her and her mum apparently being so close in light of the mahusive secret. She decided guilt and the secret would have to wait. She didn't have time for continually overthinking and feeling bad when the shop was going nuts right in front of her eyes. 'You're a lifesaver. Thanks, Mum. See you soon.'

As she helped a customer, put a sale through, and assisted someone else, her mind went over her lengthy to-do list at the same time; it got longer and longer and scrolled endlessly through her head as she worked. Once her mum arrived, she'd at least have someone else in the shop, and she'd be able to delegate a few of the urgent online orders for her mum to pack behind the scenes. Her mum couldn't get there fast enough as far as she was concerned.

When Cherry arrived about an hour or so later, Emmy hugged her by the storeroom door, feeling almost weak with relief. 'I'm so glad you're here! It's been absolute madness. I'm just so unprepared.'

Cherry looked into the shop and raised her eyebrows in surprise. 'Not to worry – Mum is here now. Just tell me where you need me.'

After a quick tour of the back room and instructions on the online order packaging process, Emmy left her mum to start on the orders and turned back to help someone who was looking for a special gift for her friend who'd just lost her husband to a heart attack.

The rest of the afternoon flew by in a blur, and Emmy dealt with customer after customer, with her mum helping in between. She'd put the payment dongle through its paces and made so much small talk with so many different people that she was almost numb from the nose down. Cherry went from helping in the shop to packing orders out the back, and by the end of the day, knew her way around both the payment process and how to beautifully pack a Love Emmy x order.

When the shop's foot traffic finally tailed off and closing time had arrived, Emmy turned the sign on the front door to 'Closed' with a long, happy sigh. She slumped back against the door as her feet throbbed, her hips felt tight, and the sides of her cheeks ached from smiling and talking. Cherry appeared from the back room, looking similarly worn out but smiling. 'Well, I must say when you said you needed help, you weren't joking! That was an avalanche! I'm drowning in heart-shaped drop earrings out there.'

Emmy huffed a laugh. 'Tell me about it. I had no idea a quick

Instagram reel could have such an immediate impact on my life and on the soreness of my feet. Ha.'

'I know! When you told me about this Peaches person, I had no idea! Little do I know the way of the world these days.' Cherry chuckled.

'Thanks for rushing over. I never could have handled this solo. It got more and more chaotic as the day moved on, didn't it?'

'Crazy.' Cherry waved off Emmy's gratitude. 'Think nothing of it, darling. That's what I'm here for. Besides, I'm just tickled by all of this. Imagine what Grandma is thinking from up there looking down on us.'

'She'd be happy.'

'You are now reaping the rewards after so much hard work.'

'I've waited long enough.' Emmy nodded as she gathered bits from the top of the antique display unit and put them away.

'I'd say this is the start of good things. Amazing what that post has done.' Cherry pointed to the back room. 'The amount of orders on the website. We're going to be packing for days.'

'It was nonstop, but I did love every minute. Even if my feet may actually fall off now.'

Cherry chuckled, rubbing the back of her neck. 'Occupational hazard, I'm afraid.'

'I'll put up with it. Hopefully, it's not just a fleeting trend.'

'I guess you don't know…'

'Nope. Anyway, wow, what a day.'

Cherry turned her left wrist over and looked at her watch. 'Do you want me to stay for the evening? If you need an extra pair of hands still?'

Emmy bit her lip. Here was her mum, as usual, helping and here she was, not telling her about Katy. Her inner voice chided, screaming that she was a horrid, nasty liar. Emmy pushed the voice away. 'If you're sure you don't mind, that would be amazing.'

'Of course.'

'I definitely feel a bit in over my head at the moment. Who would have thought this would happen?'

'You'll have to recruit Cal, too,' Cherry said with a smile.

Emmy flicked her eyes upwards. 'I think the PlayStation is a lot more interesting than jewellery. I'm not sure I can trust him to pack orders.'

Cherry laughed. 'I think you're right.'

Impulsively, Emmy hugged her mum. 'Thank you. You and Dad are always just here for me, helping me out.'

'We're always in your corner, darling. You know that.'

Emmy did know that, which was precisely why she felt so bad about the Katy secret.

'We've got your back, Ems. However we can help ease the load, we're here.'

Ice slipped down Emmy's spine. 'Thank you, Mum. I really am grateful for that.'

～

Cherry had spent a few more hours in the storeroom with Emmy packing orders. By the end of it, there was a huge pile of them stacked up in the corner. They'd finished off, tidied up as best they could, had a quick cup of tea, and barely able to keep her eyes open, Emmy had walked her mum to the lane and waved her off.

She was sitting on the sofa in the flat with her feet up, finally having a chance to breathe and properly get her head around what had gone on. All because of a social media reel from Peaches, her shop had *exploded*. Emmy shook her head in wonder at the ways of the online world. Tom came in with a cup of tea as Emmy was scrolling through the website analytics in disbelief. She turned her phone around to Tom as he sat down. 'Look at these numbers. I never dreamt an uptick could happen so fast. Orders are up nearly one thousand per cent in just a few days. What the heck?'

Tom whistled. 'Influencers are no joke, by the looks of it. It's a whole other world. Peaches definitely delivered.'

'That's putting it mildly.' Emmy laughed. 'I just hope I can keep up this momentum now that the initial surge is dying down.'

Emmy scrolled to her own profile. 'Wow, I've gained thousands of followers. Thousands. How weird is that?'

Tom joked. 'You have solid social proof now.'

'I do. I wonder if this will last or just die off?'

'I hope it does last. I guess only time will tell whether you get any lasting impact.'

'Hmm. I feel a bit bad. I totally dissed Peaches when she didn't post right away. I was so disappointed. Remember?'

'Yup.'

'Bide your time, eh?'

'Yeah. You've worked for this, though,' Tom noted seriously. 'She didn't just like the place by some random chance. You made the shop happen. Don't lose sight of that.'

Emmy tilted her face up to Tom's as her insides went nuclear. 'Aww, thanks. I couldn't have done it without everyone's help, though.'

'Sure you could,' Tom countered. 'You absolutely could.'

Emmy sent up a prayer of gratitude for what had transpired and for the fact that Tom P Carter had catapulted into her life. The old nagging voice was also beside her, telling her not to get too cosy because something would come along to mess things up. It always did. It always had. The voice continued to taunt. It told her the shop doing well was because of Peaches; the voice sat on the sidelines snidely telling her that she'd never be able to sustain it on her own merit. Emmy tried to silence the inner critic and told herself that her vision all those years ago, when she'd been hoping to buy a present for Amy and had hated the horrible high street jewellery stores, was what had contributed to her success. She tapped on a review of the online Love Emmy x shop and read out its gushing words on a parcel that had arrived, noting how special everything was.

Tom nodded. 'See, Ems. *You* created that, not anyone else. Love Emmy x is just as special as you. It's not just a spot of luck that's happened here.'

Emmy swooned and clung to the 'special' comment. She did indeed like being on the end of that a lot. She needed to remember she was special every day of the week.

14

Emmy hurried along the pavement, her collar flipped up
against a cold, chilly wind. She was late and could do
without going to meet Katy for a coffee. She'd already changed
it twice, so she's had to commit. The cold weather was definitely
making itself known, with leaves swirling across the pavement
and a chill seeping through her jacket. She was certainly feeling
the temperature. She shivered and quickened her pace,
surprised at how quickly the weather had turned. Rounding a
corner, she pulled her jacket tighter as she spied the coffee shop
where she was meeting Katy. As she walked past the window,
the café looked cosy, warm, and busy. She couldn't quite wait to
get inside and get out of the cold, nippy air. The meetings with
Katy had continued to happen since she'd told Tom about Katy.
She'd not been completely happy about keeping the secret, but
she'd felt as if, really, there was little she could do about it. She
still felt awful telling lies, but with Tom now in the know, it was
much easier to navigate, and she just had to hope that when
Amy and her mum and dad did find out, they wouldn't be too
upset.

Stepping into the café, Emmy instantly sighed in relief as the heat hit her and the ambience of the place made her smile – exposed brick walls, lots of little lamps on a huge bookcase toppling with books, worn armchairs, and a deep green velvet sofa along the back wall. Twinkling fairy lights, flickering flames from an open fire, and lush potted plants added to it all. Emmy made a mental note to look out for an armchair for the shop as she peered around for Katy. Unwinding her scarf, she inhaled the smell of coffee beans and baking. She looked around the tables until she saw Katy tucked against the back wall with her head bent to her phone.

Emmy's pulse quickened as it seemed to do every time she met up with Katy. Even after months of slowly rebuilding their relationship, seeing Katy still felt a tiny bit surreal and as if she was doing something wrong. Mostly because she sort of was. She wound through the chairs and tables and beamed as Katy looked up.

Katy stood and hugged her. 'Hi.'

'Hey, brrr, it's chilly today. How are you?'

'Good. I know, it's not warm! I thought the same. Time to get the big coat out.'

'I feel like I've only just put it away,' Emmy said as she took her bag off her shoulder, relishing the warmth from the fire. 'On a day like today, I need a nice, hot, milky coffee.'

Katy nodded in agreement. 'I know, the chill came out of nowhere somehow.' She gestured around at the coffee shop. 'This place is perfect for weather like this.'

Emmy nodded as she looked around. The coffee shop was now familiar to her; it had become her and Katy's regular meet-up spot, which in itself made a whoosh of anxiety about her mum and dad and Amy race through her veins. Whenever they met, they followed the same-ish routine – a table tucked away in the back corner where they could chat without worrying and small talk which mostly kept away from both family and anything in the past. So far it had worked, and Emmy just let it be and hoped that eventually it would lead to their family getting back together. Emmy wished to high heaven that it wasn't her and Katy secretly meeting, but despite how many times Emmy had urged Katy to consider speaking to Cherry, Katy hadn't budged from her views. In fact, Katy remained as staunch as ever that their family was better off not dredging up the past and that Emmy was to keep the secret. Emmy had decided to let it be.

'So, how's your week been?' Katy asked, jolting Emmy back from her thoughts. 'How's the shop? What else has happened now that you're famous? I'm surprised you made it here without an assistant.'

Emmy chuckled. 'Not much because all I've been doing is working. At one point, I had my stuff with me in the car, and I was packing orders in the car park during my lunch break. It's been nuts. Good nuts. It's turned my business around.'

'Hilarious. Happy for you, though. I was looking through Peaches' stories the other day. Have to say the shop looks amazing. She really does have quite the life. How does she look like that all the time?'

'Yeah, it's not real, that's how from what I saw. She looks like that because she has a make-up artist in her employment, and she travels with outfit changes.'

'Unbelievable. I travel with outfit changes in case I get toddler muck on me,' Katy joked.

'Ha! Too funny. So what's been happening with you? How is the lovely Elodie?'

'Chatting away. Ems, my little bubba is growing up.' A wistful smile crossed Katy's face.

'They have a habit of doing that, unfortunately. I have a tall, hairy one now.'

Katy laughed. 'Time flies, doesn't it? Feels like yesterday I was in hospital looking at her, wondering how she was mine. Now she walks and talks and does all sorts of things. Plus, she's totally got me wrapped around her little finger. Who would have thought?'

Emmy traced her thumb around the coffee mug, lost in memories. 'Yep, it certainly does. They always need their mum, though.'

'I hope so.'

Just then, two pieces of cake arrived, and Katy leant forward. 'This cake is sinful but so worth it.'

'I really shouldn't, but I will. Ha ha.'

As Emmy took little pieces of the cake and she listened to Katy chat, she kept thinking about her mum, their mum. She felt terrible that Cherry had helped her for a whole day when the Peaches thing had first happened, all the while Emmy had lied. As they chatted, she was in two minds about whether or not to bring up Cherry again. The decision was taken out of her hands when Katy set down her fork with a decisive clink.

'So, I actually have some news.'

'Oh? What sort of news?'

Katy's face clouded over. 'I went to the GP, and I got some health results back. Nothing too serious yet, but enough that it's on my mind.' She gave a half-shrug. 'Thought I should tell you.'

'Results?' Emmy's thoughts careened wildly. 'Are you okay?'

'It's really nothing confirmed,' Katy said, aiming for a reassuring tone. But Emmy wasn't comforted. 'I had a blood test, and that came back showing low iron. Could be nothing, but I haven't felt right for ages, so I'm having more. I've had this weird pain in my stomach and constantly feel like I need to go to the loo.'

Emmy just stared, mouth dry. She knew Katy, or at least she thought she did. She didn't beat around the bush. For her to voluntarily go to the GP and have tests done meant she must have been really feeling unwell. 'I noticed you seemed really tired the last few times I've seen you...'

Katy waved a dismissive hand. 'Oh, you know how it is.

Elodie's busy schedule keeps me running. Just mum fatigue, I hope, but yeah, I haven't felt right which is why I decided to go and get a checkup.'

'So, you're having more tests?'

'I am, Dr Bardot,' Katy attempted a light-hearted tone.

'Not being funny, Kates, but your health is nothing to mess around with in your position.'

'What does that mean?'

Emmy knew what it was like to be a single parent, and she'd had a lot of support and help behind her. Katy didn't have much at all. She thought better of verbalising her concerns too much. 'Just that with all you've got on your plate, you need to be on top of how you feel.'

'You're probably right.'

'I've had to learn to put myself first sometimes. I also get a lot of help.' Impulsively, she mentioned their mum. 'You should tell Mum. Let her support you.'

Katy stiffened, expression clouding, her tone suddenly sharp. 'Absolutely not. We're not reopening all those old wounds. We've been through this, Ems.'

Emmy mentally kicked herself for pushing. 'I get not wanting to dredge up the past. But she's still our mum. Don't you think she'd want to help?'

'It's *none* of her business, to be quite honest.'

Emmy tried not to get too angry. 'You're as stubborn as ever. Don't you think enough time has passed?'

'No, I don't,' Katy retorted. 'As far as I'm concerned, that ship has sailed.'

Sensing the conversation careening off the rails, Emmy reeled in frustration. 'Sorry. I just hate feeling like I'm keeping secrets from Mum. But you're right – it's your choice what and when to tell them.' *Was it really, though?* Emmy thought. *Where was her opinion in all of this?*

Katy's posture relaxed. But Emmy knew the wall was back

up behind her eyes now. She silently cursed herself. 'Please, just let it go for now.'

'Of course.' Emmy hoped she sounded convincing despite the knot in her chest. She gestured to Katy's half-finished cake with an attempt at a bright smile. 'Cake will make you feel better.'

Katy took the lead right away. 'Chocolate cake helps everything, doesn't it?'

'Yep, chocolate has healing powers, or so they say,' Emmy joked. 'That's what I tell myself. It's my excuse to stuff a whole bar of Dairy Milk in one go on my break at work.'

An hour or so later, Katy paid the bill and then picked up her bag. 'Right. I'd better shoot off.'

'Call me anytime, okay? I mean it. Anytime you need to talk more or just vent, I'm here.'

Emmy sat back down and watched through the front windows as Katy hurried down the street towards the corner. Just before rounding out of view, Katy glanced back and waved.

Emmy raised her hand and smiled. As she sat there with her thoughts, she shut her eyes for a second. Now, on top of her lying to her mum and Amy, there was Katy's health. It was probably nothing, and as Katy had said, more likely that it was because of Elodie and mum tiredness, but what if it wasn't? As the other people chatted and sipped their coffees around her, the cosy background sounds suddenly irritated Emmy. Her thoughts galloped wildly to what would happen if there was something wrong with Katy. Her mind flitted off in all sorts of different directions. Guilt gnawed at her, too – the weight of secrets kept from her mum and Amy making her feel dreadful.

Emmy understood Katy's lingering hurt after so long estranged from their family, but she was also over it in some ways. They all deserved a chance to put it in the past, to come together again. Katy, though, was having none of it. Katy just couldn't or *wouldn't*, more like, let it go. Sitting there with the whole situation swirling around her head, she gulped the last cold dregs of coffee and forced herself to take a couple of deep breaths.

Once she was outside in the fresh air and the bracing wind again, she felt a bit better as people bustled past with their heads down against the cold, and she made her way back to her car. Hands thrust deep into her jacket pockets, she tried not to think about anything at all.

Not thinking didn't work. In fact, all she could think about was what if something was wrong with Katy. Katy being sick threw a whole other dimension into things. It would be so much easier if Emmy could just stop analysing it all and worrying morning, noon, and night. Sometimes, she thought that worry was her middle name. If it wasn't about money, or Callum, or this or that, or the shop, it was what was going to happen about the Katy secret.

Emmy sighed as she clicked the button for her car and got in. For a good five minutes, she just sat with the engine running, waiting for the heater to warm up, and mulled over the conversation in the coffee shop. She then pressed the map app and sighed as three lines of red meant the traffic was not on her side. She saw she had a missed call from Amy. She pressed the button on her steering wheel to put the call through the car system and pressed to call her back. Amy's voice filled the car.

'Hi.'

'Hey. How are you?'

'Fine. Just calling to chat. Where are you?'

'On my way home.'

'Oh, right. Been anywhere nice?'

The lies started. 'Just to pick up some packaging for the shop. I'm going through it at a rate of knots at the moment.'

'Right.'

Amy proceeded to chat about her day. Emmy put her seatbelt on, indicated right, and pulled out onto the road. She half-heartedly listened to Amy, popping in yeps and mmms and reallys here and there to indicate that she was listening when her mind was more on Katy. As she stopped at a traffic light, Emmy felt herself drift off and half-wish she was Amy. Amy's problems always seemed like much easier problems to have. What would Amy have done in the same situation Emmy was now in? Amy would probably have dealt with it much better. Emmy imagined herself being Amy, floating around in her lovely house with no money worries, her nice little job, lovely holidays, and everything just so perfect. Not being a liar.

'So, what do you think I said to her about that?' Emmy heard Amy ask. As the light went green and Emmy eased the car forward following the one in front of her, she scrambled about what to say. She had no idea what Amy had been talking about. Something about the woman at work who was head of outbound sales. She made a sound as if she was contemplating the question. She had no idea.

'You can guess, right?' Amy prompted with a hoot.

Emmy really couldn't. She said something non-committal, added in a jokey tone and hoped for the best. 'Your usual way with words, Ames.'

'Exactly.'

Emmy continued to do what she did best when she was feeling the way she was: listen and try to sound cheerful and hope that Amy, who usually picked up on everything, didn't get wind of Emmy's galloping mind. For once, as Amy trundled on and on about the situation at work, she was so wrapped up in her own world that it worked. For now.

15

A brisk wind nipped at Emmy's cheeks and nose as she strolled hand-in-hand with Tom along the coastal path just past the Darling Island sailing club. Despite the chill, bright sunlight popped between clouds, and little diamonds danced on top of the water. In an oversized cable knit jumper, a huge plaid scarf, and a floppy cream-coloured slouchy beanie, Emmy listened as Tom told her about an altercation that had happened in the lane with someone who had been trying to illegally park.

As they meandered and chatted, Emmy had to pinch herself that this was actually her living her life. It had been a manic time with another reel having gone live via Peaches, and the explosion that had happened to Love Emmy x almost overnight hadn't seen much sign of abating. The resulting influx of visitors from the reel had left Emmy scrambling to keep up with everything in her life. Tom, along with Callum, had been put to work in the storeroom packing parcels, and Emmy had done her best to keep all the balls in the air. It wasn't a bad problem to have.

'Hard to believe it's not been that long since Peaches and

Gemma first got in touch,' Emmy remarked, gazing out at the sea. 'Feels like a lifetime ago already.'

'No kidding.'

'Remember when I was whining that it had all been a waste of time?'

'I do.'

'I swore I would never get in cahoots with an influencer again. Little did I know.'

'Now other influencers are jumping on board,' Tom acknowledged.

Emmy smiled, remembering the thrill when Peaches had finally shared the video of The Old Ticket Office after the silence. The influx of followers placing orders had completely overwhelmed her tiny operation. 'I never could have prepared for how fast things blew up after her post. I still get dizzy thinking about those first few days.'

'I don't know how you survived it. I could hardly walk through the back without tripping over boxes.'

'Pure organised chaos,' Emmy agreed with a laugh. 'I felt like I lived at the post office those first few days. But Mum was a godsend helping me stay afloat.'

Tom shook his head. 'I still can't believe how quickly the word spread after Peaches shared that one video. Who would have thought?'

Emmy inhaled and then let out a long breath. 'I know. Weird really when each morning, I'd wake up to more influencers tagging my shop, wanting to collaborate. My inbox was flooded.'

Emmy still couldn't quite get over how she was still opening her socials to discover she'd been shouted out by accounts with millions of followers. Other people deeming Love Emmy x worthy of attention still stunned her in a very nice way indeed.

'You went from zero influencer collabs to every mega-star

on the platform begging for a piece of the action. I'm surprised you still have anything to do with me,' Tom joked.

'Seriously, it's nuts but I'm so grateful. Never in my wildest dreams did I think going viral was possible.'

'It was bound to get noticed eventually.'

'Aww, thanks, but I didn't think that.'

'Everyone who comes in falls in love with it immediately. That is the key. As I already said, you created something really special, Ems. No one else did that. No one else had that vision.'

'I've had the shop in my head for years. Funny how other people love it too.'

Tom agreed. 'You launched a full-on trend.'

Emmy flushed, remembering the messages rolling in from influencer accounts eager to collaborate. She'd gone from an out-and-out nobody with a handful of followers to fielding offers left, right, and centre. 'Getting that first nod from Peaches seemed to make others interested. Not sure about on-trend, though. I think it's the opposite of that – that's the appeal.' She shook her head, still perplexed by the fickleness of social media.

Tom nodded. 'Whatever the reason, thank goodness it happened. You just have to worry about who you choose to collaborate with next.'

'Not a bad problem to have.'

Emmy gazed out at the sea again, marvelling that mere months before, she'd worried about whether Love Emmy x would ever really take off. She'd not told anyone directly, but she'd let her thoughts wander to it being a failure and having to shut the shop down and perhaps rent the space out to someone else. She shuddered at the investment she'd put in; now it was taking off and then some. 'I'm just relieved, mostly.'

Tom nodded. 'Yep.'

Emmy relished the opportunity that had come via Peaches, even though she wasn't quite sure what to do with it. Her Richard Branson skills weren't her most effusive. 'I had my worries in the beginning about pursuing this, and now look at me.'

'To be fair, I definitely wasn't sure about the Peaches thing. She certainly came up trumps, though.'

Emmy thought back to the early days in the rental cottage when she'd ploughed her money into her first Etsy shop. Every little bit of profit she'd made had gone back into buying more stock. Doubts had plagued her, and in the back of her mind, she'd always thought that she'd mess things up. Then, when she'd moved to Darling, on paper, the whole thing had seemed a teeny bit ludicrous. But deep down, Emmy had felt as if it had been something that she just had to do, whether it worked or not. 'I doubted myself so much.'

Tom put his arm around Emmy's shoulder. 'You were made for this, Ems.'

Emmy went nuclear. Tom had her back and was turning out to be the security blanket that had been missing in her life since she'd found out about Kevin's gambling. It felt amazing to have someone like him cheering her on. 'Thank you. You've had to put up with me through all this, too, though!'

'I may be a bit over listening to packing dilemmas,' Tom joked.

'True relationship problems,' Emmy bantered back.

They continued their stroll as the sun glinted off the sea. Emmy mused how Peaches had posted a reel taken on the ferry. 'It's funny how someone like Peaches got sucked in by the Darling thing.'

'It does that to people.'

'She has so much sway just by posting about places she visits, and when she got here, she must have seen how lovely it is.'

'Yeah, actually, we don't want her to post about it *too* much.'

'No. We should have got Russell onto her. That would have put her off,' Emmy joked.

'Didn't you say the assistant had a run-in with him?'

'Not quite, she just said he was in the lane and he was a creep.'

'Right. I haven't seen him for a while. Have you?'

Emmy shook her head. 'No, thank goodness. Hopefully he's gone back to his hobnobbing.'

'Yeah. Less of him the better.'

Emmy looked out at the water and smiled. The view was good, she was good, and Tom was good. All around good. It felt amazing.

The next morning, Emmy stretched beneath the covers. She could hear Tom pottering quietly in the kitchen down in the flat, making tea. She loved hearing him in the house. It had been a long time since she'd shared random everyday things with someone else apart from Callum. It had been her as the responsible person doing all the adulting things for such a long time that now hearing someone else making the tea (and doing it properly) was worth its weight in gold. Rolling over, she grabbed her phone from her bedside table, checked the BBC, and scrolled idly through a few notifications. An email from another influencer inquiring about collaborating caught her eye. Emmy raised an eyebrow as she read through the woman's lavish praise for Love Emmy x and the curated style of The Old Ticket Office. She quickly typed a polite response, indicating she'd be in touch shortly about partnership options. Who even was she? She had options now, did she? She even had rates. More than fabulous.

Emmy opened Instagram and navigated to the influencer's glossy feed. Just as she expected, the photos showcased an amazing, effortless life of glamorous travel, beauty shots, and impossible poses with unreal backgrounds. The images were so very artfully composed, and the life looked more than fabulous.

Emmy chuckled to herself and rolled her eyes – in the old days, she would have had some serious life envy. But now, with the knowledge of what she'd seen from Peaches and the curation of her perfect Insta life, she felt nowhere near envious. In fact, far from it. Peaches' short reels showcasing her supposedly fabulous lifestyle came with a team of people, a day's worth of filming, a lot of hustle, and a shedload of work. There was absolutely nothing effortless about it whatsoever.

Emmy clicked back to the woman's inquiry email and nodded to herself. She was more than happy to work with the woman if it would mean the sort of exposure that Peaches had given to her fledgling business. Typing away on her phone screen before she'd even stepped out of bed, Emmy wrote a reply message and attached a social media outline about them working together. She hit send, well-pleased with how her business was taking off.

'You're a bit chipper this morning,' Tom remarked as he walked back into the bedroom, balancing two mugs of tea and a plate of cinnamon buns.

'I woke up with a DM from another big influencer. What's not to love?'

'Who's the lucky influencer?'

'She's sort of an up-and-comer compared to someone like Peaches. But her photos are gorgeous. We now know how much work that takes.' Emmy pulled up the profile and handed her phone to Tom. He scrolled and studied the images with wide eyes. 'Wow! Do people really live like that? How many art galleries can one woman visit?'

'Tom!'

Tom shook his head. 'And how many houses covered in wisteria is she going to amble nonchalantly past with a market basket full of flowers over her arm, pretending no one is filming her from the other side of the street? Hilarious.'

Emmy burst out laughing. 'What got into you this morning?'

Tom smirked and shook his head. 'It's just all so fake.'

'Inspiring is the word I'd use.'

'Pah!'

'I don't really care as long she wants in on my stuff.'

'Precisely. A way to expand your reach, one wisteria-covered London house at a time. I bet she made a special day trip there just for that one tiny bit of footage.'

'I'm excited to collab with her.' Emmy held her fingers up in speech marks around collab.

'You definitely have my vote. I'll even love you if you start prancing around with a basket full of flowers over your shoulder as if you've just been to a flower market. I'm not being your cameraman, though.'

Emmy sipped her tea and laughed. 'I don't think there's much chance of me ever doing that.'

'Good. If you do, I'll be dust.'

Emmy swung her legs out of bed. 'Right, well, I'd best get on. There are so many orders to pack again.'

'Do you need a hand?'

'Yep. I'd love one. Why do you think I wanted you to stay over?'

'Wow, and here I was thinking it was for my personality and good looks,' Tom deadpanned.

Laughing, Emmy stretched as she got out of bed and pulled on her dressing gown. She leaned over and kissed Tom. 'Not at all.'

Once Emmy had showered and dressed, she made her way downstairs to the storeroom. She switched on the lights and surveyed the overflowing boxes and shelves all around her. She was grateful for her meticulous storage system and carefully thought through packaging scenario, without which there would have been no way she would have managed to get the avalanche of Peaches' orders out on time.

Tom followed in behind her, holding two steaming cups of

coffee. 'Good job we have caffeine with us to tackle this madness.'

Emmy took one of the mugs. 'You read my mind. I'm going to need litres of tea and coffee to get through this.'

'I still can't believe the volume coming in daily. The Peaches day is paying for itself a hundred times over, that we know for a fact.'

'No kidding. Everyone wants what the Insta babes are raving about. And there I was moaning that I'd wasted money on Louisa the harpist,' Emmy said and gestured ruefully to the plastic boxes surrounding them. 'The thing with it all, though, is that they want everything right here, right now.'

'Good job you've got a system sorted. Might need to look at bringing in help...'

Emmy joked, 'That's why I've got you. Nah, there's no way I'm getting anyone in. I'm a long, long way off that.'

'Never say never.'

Emmy pulled the orders up on her laptop, and they got into a bit of a system. Tom checked the orders and pulled items from the tubs while Emmy packaged them up, printed off the labels, and checked things off. Before she knew it, a few hours had passed with about a trillion cups of tea in between packages. She looked through into the shop and smiled, remembering when she'd first viewed it. Now it was not only looking amazing, but it was successful, too. She couldn't quite believe her luck. 'Can you believe this used to be a dusty old insurance office?'

'Ha, yup, I walked past it every day, so I can believe it.'

Emmy suddenly felt emotional. Lots of things came flooding back to her: the years in the rental cottage, her tiny first sale on her little Etsy shop, juggling her job at the port with setting up Love Emmy x on the side – all of it seemed to swim in front of her eyes. She was at a loss for words. It felt strange to be successful. Strange to be doing so well. Make-believe almost.

Swallowing a lump in her throat, she dragged a huge cardboard box from the side of the room and started to pull off the brown tape. 'We now have to get this lot into those tubs in the right order.'

'I thought we were done!'

'You're joking. This isn't even the half of it.'

'I hope you are going to pay me in something very nice.'

Emmy giggled. 'Of course!'

A few hours later, both Emmy and Tom didn't want to see another little packet of jewellery ever again in their lives. Tom snapped a lid on one of the plastic tubs. He pointed to a toppling pile of parcels ready for the post office. 'Mission accomplished. How does it feel to have this many orders going out?'

'Absolutely knackered, but also unbelievable.'

'Yeah, it's huge.'

Emmy shook her head. 'Thanks for being here through the chaos. I'd have drowned under those boxes long ago without you.'

'You've come far, Ems, and I love you for it. A lot. Like really a lot. You've cracked on and worked hard.'

Emmy swooned. She loved Tom more than he could *ever* love her. She just wasn't going to tell him how much too often, though. Keep that one nice and close to her chest.

16

Emmy hummed along to a playlist as she flitted around tidying up The Old Ticket Office. She sorted out pieces in the antique display unit, sprayed them with glass cleaner, polished them to within an inch of their life, and did the same on the mirrored drawers beside it. She paused for a second to look around at what she had created and allowed herself to feel proud for a second. Letting herself feel that felt weird but oh-so-very good. She revelled in it for a bit, nodding away. She'd done well, yes, yes, and yes again.

With another weekend coming up and an inbox full of DMs informing her that people were intending to visit the shop, she wanted the place to look its best. She'd dragged herself out of bed early to get a head start on all the things to do and was working as fast as she could. She'd dusted every shelf, polished the front windows, and added two huge vases of flowers to the cabinets. She'd raced through things one job at a time, plugged in the vacuum in the storeroom, and started to attack it with gusto.

As she worked, her mind flitted from one thing to the next. She had so many things to think about; it was as if everything in her brain was sitting on a Ferris wheel chair. The wheel continually circled again and again and didn't stop for a second to let her get off. It moved from Katy's health problem to Peaches to a few issues Callum was having at school and then turned inevitably to Tom. Her relationship with him had moved at a bewildering pace – relationship milestones were being reached and fast. It was screeching along so quickly, in fact, that it frightened Emmy a little bit. Ever since the disaster that had been Kevin, she'd been determined and independent and vowed she'd never really rely on or get too close to anyone ever again. She'd kept her heart under lock and key and had been adamant that it was staying that way. However, when Tom P Carter arrived on the scene, all those things went out the window. The eyes had helped, ditto the shoulders. She'd fallen in head first and not really protected herself in any shape or form. It took her breath away how much she loved him. Sometimes she pretended she didn't love him at all just to remove the feelings of being overwhelmed. But there wasn't any getting away from it. She really was in very, very deep. It was so *deliciously* nice and so *revoltingly* scary at the same time that, mostly, she tried not to think about it too much at all.

Since their first major argument and Tom's fiery response to her evading the truth about Katy, Emmy was more in love with him than ever. And therefore, she was more scared that she might, in the long run, get hurt. Despite all those feelings, which she kept completely under wraps, they'd settled into an easy rhythm together that she adored. Right from the word go, Emmy just loved having Tom around. Just loved *him*, really. He offered a sort of unwavering presence and support all the time. When she'd felt a bit lost at sea and felt adrift, he was just there. Tom P Carter made her feel safe. She liked how that made her feel. A lot.

As she pushed the vacuum hose back and forth over and over again, her thoughts strayed to the future. She found herself picturing things with Tom – holidays, properly living together, all sorts. Not getting married or a ring on her finger, though, no, no, she'd never do that again. She now strangely couldn't imagine her life without him around. She'd come a long way from what she now realised was the lonely, sad around the edges woman she'd been in the cottage, always wondering how her life was going to turn out or when it was going to start.

Though they hadn't explicitly defined where things were headed, Emmy knew in her soul she wanted a life with Tom more than anything else. *He* and *her* felt as if it had always been meant to be. Plus, she still fancied the pants off him, which was always a bonus in a relationship. Boy, did she love that. The wide shoulders, the hips, gulp, the everything. Butterflies still swirled in her stomach, remembering the first time she'd seen him in the lane. She smiled to herself and laughed as she remembered when she'd got sunstroke and he'd carried her up the garden path. She'd go through that again any day of the week.

She knew from what Tom had said that he was on the same page, at least, she hoped he was. Sometimes she wondered why. Why would Tom love someone like Emmy Bardot? As she pushed the nozzle of the vacuum over the shelves and across the tops of her plastic storage tubs, she sent up a silent prayer of gratitude for all that was Tom P Carter. She loved having him in her life.

A few hours later, as if Tom had known she'd been thinking about him, right on cue, she looked over to the back door to see him letting himself in. Her insides went nuclear as he smiled from the door. Tom P Carter wasn't looking too shabby.

'Hello. I was just thinking about you. Your ears must be burning.'

Tom chuckled. 'How lovely I am? How lucky you are? Either of those? I don't mind which.'

Emmy rolled her eyes. Little did he know that was about the

nuts and bolts of it. She made it into a joke. Never a truer word said in jest. 'Totally. Both of those.'

'Good. Wow, it's been a day of it already. I need a cup of tea.'

'You and me both.'

'Is Cal here?'

'No, he's at Mum's.'

'I'll put the kettle on then.'

As Emmy followed behind Tom up to the flat, she thanked her lucky stars. Lost in her own little world, thinking about how serious she was about him as she watched Tom making the tea, she wondered where it was all going to end up.

Tom waved in front of her eyes and set a mug down in front of her.

'Welcome back. You were a million miles away just now.'

Emmy flushed and flicked her head back and forth. 'Ahh, sorry.'

'What have you been thinking about?'

Emmy wondered if she should mention that she'd been thinking about their relationship, where it was at and where it was going. 'Just imagining the future.' She made light of it and joked, 'Cheesy stuff like that.'

Tom didn't say anything right away. Emmy felt her already nuclear insides turn molten. Perhaps she shouldn't have brought it up. Tom kept the tone light. 'I happen to love cheesy where you're concerned.'

Emmy felt her cheeks go red. 'Aww.'

'Sorry, what are you saying? Are you saying you want to make things more...' Tom stopped for a second, contemplating what he was going to say, 'Serious?'

Emmy chuckled. 'I thought you didn't *do* serious?'

Tom's tone was still light, but his actual words weren't. 'Again, where you're concerned...'

Emmy tilted her head up. 'Are you flattering me?'

'It seems I am.'

Emmy studied Tom over her mug, wondering if, really deep down, he felt as strongly as she did. She decided to live on the edge and ask him his thoughts on the matter. Test the waters and put it out there. 'Have you thought any more about, well, about us?'

Tom smiled. 'Where is all this coming from?'

'I don't know, actually.' Emmy flicked her hand dismissively. 'I've been thinking about it on and off all day.'

'I'm on the same page as you, at least I think I am – very much here for the long haul.'

Inside, Emmy sort of squirmed. Tom just always seemed so confident and sure of himself. Superior almost, somehow. He was also so handsome she wanted to die. Part of her couldn't quite understand how someone like *him* wanted to be with someone like *her*. 'Right.'

'You know I'm not going anywhere. I've got no choice. I live a few doors down.' Tom again made light of the serious conversation. 'You're stuck with me, Ems.'

'Okay.'

'So, that's settled then?'

'I guess so. It's nice to hear it.'

'You're my future, Ems,' Tom joked. 'Do you want me to tell you that ten times a day?'

Emmy kind of realised that she *did* want just that. Who even was she? So much for the independent I-don't-need-anyone person she'd been. She fired back as quick as a flash. 'Twenty if possible.'

'I love you, Ems.'

'Same.'

'Good. I'm pleased we're settled on that.'

'Yes, right, yes, me too. Absolutely.'

17

Emmy slowly blinked awake, squinting against the light filtering through the blinds. For a moment, she forgot where she was, nestled under the duvet after sleeping like a log. She then remembered precisely where she was as she registered the foghorn going off, the waves in the distance, and the sound of seagulls somewhere outside. She went to get out of bed, realised that it wasn't a workday, wondered why she'd woken up so early, tutted, and tried to go back to sleep. It didn't work, and twenty minutes later, she'd put on her slippers and dressing gown and tiptoed down to the kitchen to make a cup of tea.

She poured hot water into the pot, set out two mugs, one for her and one for Callum, opened the fridge, stared in it for ages wondering if she could be bothered to do a fry-up, decided it was a no, and took out two eggs. After putting them on to boil, pouring the tea and then making egg and soldiers, she sat at the tiny breakfast table in the kitchen looking out over an early morning on Darling Street. The fog was thick and heavy over Darling. It swirled around the rooftops and chimneys on the other side; a couple of trams slid past below, and she watched various Darling-ites here and there scooting along on their way to the ferry.

The weather had definitely turned on Darling Island. The flat felt chilly, even though the Darling fog seemed to wrap everything in a soft, hazy fuzz. Emmy pushed up the old sash window a tiny bit for some fresh air and, as she dipped her soldiers into her egg, she felt a nippy sea breeze racing in the window. Much earlier than usual for a day off, she was surprised when Callum shuffled into the kitchen.

'Good morning.'

'Morning.'

'Sleep well?'

Callum nodded. 'Yep.'

'Were you warm enough? It was cold last night.'

'Yeah, fine. How'd you sleep?'

'Like a baby once my head hit the pillow. I went for that huge bike ride yesterday. The sea air does wonders,' Emmy said as she turned and pointed out the window to the sea in the far distance.

Callum took the mug from the worktop, put it in the microwave, pressed a button and waited for it to ping. 'What are you up to today?'

Emmy stopped herself from rolling her eyes. She'd told Callum at least three times that she was going out for the day with Tom. 'We're going down the coast. I did tell you.'

'Oh yeah, sorry. You're not opening downstairs?'

Emmy had also told him that twice, if not three times. 'No. Just packing orders later, maybe.'

'Right.'

'Do you want to come out with us?' Emmy asked, knowing full well going out for the day with her and Tom was probably right at the bottom of the list of things that Callum might possibly want to do.

Callum didn't take long to make up his mind. 'Nah. Where are you going again?'

'Lovely Bay.'

'Nice,' Callum said, definitely not meaning it. He shook his head. 'Wait, where?'

Emmy again tutted inside. Callum had been with her when Xian, the owner of the bakery, had told her about a place she was scouting out for another one of her chain of bakeries and holiday rental properties. Xian had mentioned a place called Lovely Bay and a property that was for sale there that she and her daughter were hoping to buy. Emmy had loved the sound of it for a day out and had said she'd like to go and have a nose. The whole conversation had clearly gone straight over Callum's head. 'Lovely Bay. Remember the conversation in the bakery the other day when we were chatting?'

Callum made a funny face. 'Not really. Was I there?'

Emmy shook her head. In one ear, out the other. 'Doesn't matter. What are you doing?' Emmy had no doubt that Callum would be on the PlayStation for a lot of the day, or *all* of the day more like if she wasn't there to put a stop to it.

'Dunno.' Callum shrugged.

'Tom has planned a bit of an itinerary for us in Lovely Bay. It's quite nice, apparently.'

Callum appeared completely uninterested. A day out with her and Tom was probably the last thing he would want to do. 'I bet.'

'So you definitely don't want to come?' Emmy wasn't serious but she pretended she was to make Callum squirm.

Callum also pretended and made out that he was considering her offer for a second. 'Ahh, thanks, but I'm good.'

'Rightio.' Emmy pushed her chair out. 'I'm going up to have a shower, then.'

Callum was already engrossed in his phone and didn't really look up. 'Okay.'

An hour later, Emmy was in the passenger seat of Tom's car. He smiled as she looked at a list on his phone. Emmy joked, 'Look at you being all organised. I'm not sure Lovely Bay will be ready for you.'

'I intend to romance you for the day. No packing orders or printing off labels for either of us today, no family drama or teenage dramas either. We are free. Lovely Bay, here we come.'

'What are you after?' Emmy joked.

'You'll find out.'

Emmy swooned inside. Not that she was going to let Tom P Carter know that. She was totally wooed merely by the fact that she was sitting beside him. In fact, she'd pretty much been wooed by him from the moment she'd laid eyes on him. Wooed by his very presence.

Tom put his hand on her leg as he drove along, and Emmy sighed happily. 'What are we doing, then? You spoke to Xian, did you?'

'You said you didn't want to know and to leave it up to me. I didn't speak to Xian, actually. I had a chat with Holly, though, so yeah, just wait and see.'

Laughing, Emmy sat back in her seat and watched the coun-tryside whizz by the window. A while later, they were coasting along on their way to the little town, Lovely Bay, which Xian had mentioned. A lighthouse appeared ahead of them, almost looking as if it was coming out of the top of roofs, and any sign of the morning fog they'd seen on Darling Island had long since burned off. Emmy opened the window a touch to let in some fresh air. 'Ahh, it's so good to have a day off and have nothing to worry about.'

'Yep.'

Emmy looked down at her phone and searched for some info on Lovely Bay. 'It says on the far side of Lovely Bay itself it's home to mudflats, a yearly crabbing competition, meadows, marshes, and it has many birds, otters and deers.'

'Oh, I didn't read that bit.'

Emmy began reading from the Lovely Bay Information Centre's website, 'Lovely and Lovely Bay occupy a prominent position on the South Heritage Coast in a designated Area of Outstanding Natural Beauty. Set around numerous greens, our small town offers a range of boutique shops; our very own renowned Lovely Chowder and Lovely is home to the famous Lovely Brewery and a unique picture palace cinema. Lovely also has a listed train station, two sailing clubs, and the surrounding area is noted for its coastal and countryside walks. Pop down for the day. We guarantee you'll love it.'

As they got further into the town and drove along through the centre of Lovely Bay, Emmy couldn't get enough of it. Pretty shops lined the sides of the road, beautiful stripy blue and white bunting layered across the streets, and despite the chilly but sunny weather, Lovely Bay was bustling with locals going about their business.

'Not too bad, eh? Xian wasn't wrong. Apparently the whole place centres around little greens and bridges.'

Emmy peered out the window. 'It lives up to its namesake,' Emmy agreed. 'It really is *lovely*. No Darling fog either.'

'Now to find somewhere to park,' Tom said.

A few minutes or so later, they'd found a parking space on a side road just along from a green, and Emmy oohed and ahhed at the houses lining the street. Lovely Bay sure gave Darling a run for its money. She lost herself in tall Victorian villas, higgledy-piggledy roofs, and pretty gardens as she walked along. A man on a ladder was hanging up baskets full of brightly coloured pansies, a couple of women in big jumpers were standing with mugs of coffee chatting by a front gate, and a sweet Labrador sitting in a tiny patch of sun on a porch lazily opened one eye as Emmy and Tom strolled past.

They passed along down the side of the River Lovely, where a few different people were walking dogs, a woman with a basket full of shopping raised her eyebrows in greeting, and a couple of runners were clearly heading to the beach for a jog. Emmy inhaled deep breaths of crisp air and couldn't quite articulate how pleased she was to be having a day off.

As they ambled to the road they'd first driven down on the way in, they pottered in and out of shops, bought a coffee, and meandered from one end to the other. They stopped outside a flower shop bursting with bouquets and gigantic galvanised tubs of flowers, peered in the window of a boutique with a pale pink cruiser bike out the front, and spent ages perusing the menu board for Lovely Bay Fish Bar. Emmy linked her arm through Tom's as they walked along, going over a little bridge and strolling alongside a green slowly taking everything in. Eventually, they got to the beach hut-lined prom and stood by a railing for a while, lost in a seemingly endless blue sky and chilly billowing sea air. Just as they were musing what to do next, an old vintage boat chugged by from the right, and they watched as it went past.

Tom followed Emmy's gaze. 'Wow, nice.'

'Yep. A girl could get used to this lifestyle and having days out. Here's to lots more days off pottering around a pretty town doing nothing but mooch around. It's *so* nice to have a day off,' Emmy admitted.

'Nothing but the best for you,' Tom joked.

'It's so *cheerful* here, or am I imagining it?' Emmy noted as she looked around.

'The weather helps and all the little greens. Cold but sunny.'

Emmy's stomach rumbled, and Tom laughed. 'Right on cue,' he said as he checked his watch. 'If we walk over to the other side of Lovely Bay, there's a café on the water I thought we could try. The Google reviews are outstanding. Holly mentioned it – she looked at a holiday home for their property business near it. Apparently we have to try the Lovely Chowder while we're here.'

'Yeah, I read that about having chowder. They have a property business as well as a string of bakeries - who would have guessed?'

'Apparently so – those two are dark horses, I think, with fingers in many pies.'

About fifteen minutes or so later, Emmy and Tom were standing outside a café overlooking a small, but packed harbour. Emmy turned her mouth upside down and nodded at the same time. 'Hmm, looks nice enough.'

'You can't come to Lovely Bay without the chowder in this place, according to the reviews.'

'I'm not sure I've even ever had chowder.'

'Yup. It's a local tradition.' Tom read from his phone. 'This place, according to the information here on Tripadvisor, is known as a must-stop destination located in the heart of Lovely Bay.'

'I read something about secret chowders too – did you read that?'

'Ha ha, yep, speakeasy places not open to the likes of us where you get a local chowder – I did read about that. Sounds a bit weird and very underground.'

Tom pushed open the door; Emmy followed him inside, gasped, died, and went to heaven. Inside a small timber-clad lobby area with fishing basket pendant light fittings, an oversized distressed teal dresser held an old tub for umbrellas, gigantic bottle green pots showcased exotic-looking plants, antique fishing rods repurposed as coat hooks housed a jumble of coats, and a long line of shelving on the left was stacked with shells and things collected from the beach. Emmy inhaled and held her breath for a minute as divine smells enveloped her – food, essential oils, and flowers all mixed with the scent of the River Lovely swirling not far from the door. Emmy took her coat off and hung it on one of the hooks on the fishing rod. She beamed as she followed Tom, and for a second,, she just stood taking in the decor. On the left-hand side, a wood burner was perched in between tables where old-fashioned green Bentwood chairs were tucked underneath tables, a huge old battered leather Chesterfield sat along the wall on the other side, and old weathered shutters ran all the way from left to right on the windows looking out towards the sea. Dumb waiters perched here and there were piled with vintage dishes and huge water jugs.

Emmy was mentally taking notes for The Old Ticket Office as fast as she could whilst feeling like a total shopkeeping amateur. The place was stunning; tasselled fabric-covered lamps stood on surfaces, huge Kilner jars of sea glass were dotted around, and gigantic bunches of dried flowers and herbs spilt from wicker baskets attached to the walls. Layers of shelving were lined with a mismatch of old photos showing Lovely Bay from days gone by, piles of local history books were dotted here and there, and little baskets chock-full of mismatched fabric napkins graced the tables. Tiny glass bottles held sprigs of greenery, sweetie jars were jammed with faded driftwood, and by the coffee machine, masses of pots holding a jumble of greenery and ferns looked ready to topple.

A woman in a tan butcher's apron, a white shirt with the collar turned up, and glossy hair smiled. 'Hello. I can sit you over there in the corner if you like. Just along from the wood burner there, or how about squeezing on the end of the Chesterfield if you don't mind a sharing table?'

Emmy made a quick decision. 'The Chesterfield would be fabulous. Thanks,' Emmy said as they squeezed in and out of tables and passed the roaring wood burner. Emmy sat down, tucked her bag under the table, settled in, and shook her head as she looked around. The sweeping views of the sea and waves outside added to the ambience, and she couldn't quite get enough. The café was warm, cosy, bustling, and just oh-so lovely. Emmy was in her element as she sat with her chin on her hand and squinted at a chalkboard menu propped up against the wall. She scanned the choices and flicked her eyes over towards the counter and coffee machine, where a display unit was chock-full of sandwiches, wraps, pastries, and cakes. Another big chalkboard sign dangled from a rope on the ceiling, detailing a seafood chowder of the day. Emmy's eyes were wide as she leaned over the table and whispered, 'How on earth did you find this place tucked away around here? I want to live here. I may have to move in. I won't be coming back to Darling with you, soz.'

Tom looked at the chalkboard menu. 'I am now understanding the five-star reviews. I've been in worse establishments,' Tom remarked, clearly pleased with both himself and his find.

'I'll say,' Emmy agreed. 'Best spot ever.'

As Emmy sat with her head cocked to the right, analysing the seaside paraphernalia displayed on gigantic rustic open shelves and wondering if she could totally steal a few ideas for Love Emmy x, the woman came back to the table. 'Rightio. We get you to order at the counter over there, you'll get a number, and then we'll bring your food over.'

Emmy nodded. 'Thank you.' She gestured to the chalkboard. 'This is it, is it?'

The woman pointed to the counter and the coffee machine. 'Yep, plus sandwiches and wraps. Oh, and of course, the chowder. Most people have that. It comes with sourdough. You'll love it.'

'Great, thanks. I'll go and have a look.'

The woman beamed. 'Gorgeous day for a visit to Lovely Bay. It's chilly but sunny out there on the river today.'

Emmy nodded. 'Yes, the sun came out for us.'

Just as the girl was about to turn away, Tom pointed to a couple at the next table. 'Is that on the menu? What they're having?'

The woman followed where Tom was looking. She turned back, and a funny look crossed her face. 'No, no, that's not on the menu, that one, no.'

Tom frowned. 'Where do we order that then? Is there a specials board at the counter or something?'

The woman looked a bit flustered. 'Nope. What you see on that menu there and then what's in the cabinets is what we have. The sourdough today is lovely, and the wraps too.'

'Oh, okay. So that one isn't available? It's a chowder, is it?'

The woman stumbled over her words a little bit. 'No, no, that's for, umm… That's all gone now.'

Tom lifted his chin. 'Okay, thanks.'

As she walked away, Tom frowned. 'What was going on with that?'

'No idea. Bit weird.'

'Must have been that secret chowder thing.'

'You reckon?'

A couple of minutes later, Emmy was standing looking into the display unit, trying to decide on a sandwich. Tom was by her side. The sandwiches were huge, old school, delicious-looking. Another woman smiled and chatted. 'The cheese, ham, beetroot, and salad are nice. Homegrown beetroot from just down the road here, same with the ham and cheese.'

'Yep. I'll have that, please,' Emmy said.

Tom pointed to the board. 'I'll have the seafood chowder.'

'Any tea or drinks?' The woman gestured to a shelf where there was an array of glass ceramic-topped bottles. 'We have our own lemonade if you fancy trying it. Lovely Bay lemonade is our bestseller, but they're all nice as it goes. I would say that though, ha!'

Tom nodded. 'Done. Too easy. Yep. We'll have a bottle of that. That would be great, thanks.'

'No worries,' the woman said as she tapped things into an iPad and turned it around. 'There you go.'

'Great, thanks,' Emmy said as she tapped her card on the top.

The woman then handed Emmy a small timber sign with a hand-painted number, and they headed back towards the Chesterfield. As Emmy sat opposite Tom, her mind tumbled with styling ideas she could steal from the little café. She had to pinch herself when she heard herself discussing whether or not Tom thought Bob would be able to hang a chalkboard over the earring section of The Old Ticket Office and whether she could do secret jewellery only available to certain customers. Here she was, Emmy Bardot, sitting in a café for a day out with a partner, her own small business, her actual own home, and good things happening in her life. She almost fizzed with appreciation for it all. Life was quite good. Or so she thought.

18

Emmy's day had been long, busy, and mostly good. The two days a week she opened Love Emmy x, the actual shop, were turning out to be time well spent. Thanks to digital media, rather than opening the shop doors on any given day and waiting for random customers to walk in, her shop hours were focused, and the majority of time encompassed a stream of customers. She glanced at the clock as she tidied up the shop counter, noting it was almost time for Katy to call.

She hadn't seen Katy since the chilly day when they'd met and had chocolate cake in the coffee shop, but they'd spoken on the phone a couple of times. Katy had been back to the doctor and had another blood test. The bloods had again shown up the low-iron problem, which was already in the throes of being fixed. The tests, however, had done nothing to explain the pain in Katy's stomach, the constant feeling of her needing to go to the loo, and the general overall feeling of her just *not being right*. Katy'd had another appointment booked and had promised she would phone once she'd got back home from the appointment to let Emmy know exactly what was going on. Emmy was concerned. Underneath everything else going on in her life, ever since Katy first mentioned feeling unwell, Emmy had a constant worry gnawing at her about the situation.

Something inside was telling Emmy that Katy wasn't okay. She'd tried to shove it under the carpet as much as possible and not think about it too much. Not that doing that had really worked. She'd reasoned with herself that Katy was just suffering from mum fatigue like every other mum with small children on the planet. Katy was doing the majority of caring for a young child, holding down a job, and basically soldiering along on her own, doing all the adult things in life without a break. A niggly little feeling, though, was telling Emmy that wasn't the half of it. Katy had done quite a good job at downplaying it, but if Emmy knew anything, it was that Katy was as tough as old boots, and for Katy to be going to the doctor and going back again meant things were not great.

After flipping the old-fashioned shop sign on the door to 'Closed' right at 5 pm, Emmy hurried up the steep stairs to the flat, put the kettle on, sat down at the kitchen table, and scrolled mindlessly through her phone. As she waited for Katy to text or call, she shook her head at the ever-present guilt about talking to her sister when no one else in her family knew. Not only was she in secret communication with Katy, but now there was a problem that could be quite serious. The lingering guilt over keeping their reconciliation secret from the rest of the family wasn't getting any better. In fact, it just kept on getting *worse*.

Katy had still been absolutely adamant about not changing her mind about telling Cherry and Bob. She'd made it abundantly clear that she wanted no contact with their parents whatsoever. In Katy's mind, Bob and Cherry were different people from the ones Emmy had in her life, and Katy's wounds were raw even after years of no contact. But from Emmy's side of the fence, omitting the truth wasn't getting any easier anytime soon. She constantly wavered between respecting Katy's boundaries and hating the secrecy with a passion. Most of the time, she felt as if she was stepping on eggshells. Right now, with the health issue, the eggshells were very close to getting cracked.

Emmy's phone buzzed with an incoming video call from Katy. Emmy quickly finished pouring out her tea, took three chocolate Hobnobs out of the biscuit tin at the same time as pressing the green button on her phone, and then propped her phone up on the kitchen table.

'Hi. How are you feeling?' Emmy asked.

Katy shrugged. 'Oh, you know, the usual. Just trying to keep my head above water.'

Katy looked pale and drawn. She looked even more drained than their last call, if possible.

'What did the doctor say?'

'I need to go and have some scans.'

'Right. That's it? Nothing more?'

'Yeah. You know what it's like at the GP. They're just the gatekeeper.'

'True.' Emmy bit her lip. 'Hopefully, the tests will provide some answers. The waiting won't be nice, though.'

'You can say that again. I'm trying not to let my thoughts spiral.'

'So what were the results of the latest blood tests?'

'My iron has gone up with the supplements, so that's good.'

'Have you been able to rest more? You said you were going to go to bed earlier and force yourself to put your feet up,' Emmy asked with a concerned look on her face.

'Pah! I wish! I don't know where the time goes, you know?'

Emmy chuckled wryly. 'I *do* know. I'm concerned about you, though. You look really pale and off-colour.'

Katy waved her hand. 'I'm fine. Hopefully just the normal mum juggling act trying to keep the tiny human alive and all that. I would like an answer, though. I can't quite seem to keep all the balls in the air at the moment.' Katy smiled.

Emmy noticed, though, that Katy's smile didn't quite reach her eyes. Emmy's worry spiked. She knew Katy must be feeling awful to voluntarily admit even that much weakness. 'Yep.'

'Honestly, I'll be fine. Let's talk about it after the scan.'

Emmy could almost hear the battle raging in Katy's mind between self-reliance and reaching out for support. Emmy changed tack. 'How's Elodie doing then?'

'Busy as a bee, as per usual. I swear I don't know where she gets the constant energy from.'

'They are at that age.'

'At least she sleeps well now.' Katy laughed.

'That's half the battle.'

'I just worry...' Katy's voice caught. 'If something's wrong with me, what am I going to do, Ems?' Katy swore.

Emmy felt her stomach churn. Katy was voicing what Emmy hadn't yet. 'I'll be here. It'll be okay.'

There was a wobbly pause from Katy's end. 'I don't want to let her down.'

'Oh, Kates. Trust me. You won't.'

Katy looked choked up and awful. 'I've not felt right for ages, and now I'm worrying.'

'I can tell.'

'The appointment just really took it out of me. It's the lack of sleep worrying about it making me overly emotional, too. Sorry. What a nightmare.'

Emmy didn't know what to say for the best. 'You're allowed to be emotional.'

Katy managed a shaky smile at that. 'Some days it's just a lot trying to keep everything together solo.'

'I'm good for venting. I have an Olympic gold medal in it.'

Katy laughed and swiped under her eyes. 'Ha.'

Before Emmy had thought about it or even realised, as had happened before, she heard herself bringing up Cherry. 'Maybe now would be a good time to consider letting Mum know? She'd want to support you.'

The air went painfully silent. Emmy kicked herself and bit her lip. Bringing their mum up always felt like navigating a minefield with Katy. Katy shook her head. 'I just can't, Ems. Even if she wanted to help, which I doubt, too much has happened.'

Emmy's heart sank. She didn't press on. There wasn't any point. 'Okay. I get it.' She wanted to get it. She nodded as if she did. She *so* didn't.

Katy exhaled. 'Thanks.'

Emmy had to swallow the lump in her throat. She thought about the lost years. She tried not to dwell on what-ifs and should-haves. She steered the conversation away from Cherry. 'So what's been going on with Elodie at childcare?'

'Sensory play has been the gig this week. I'm glad they get to do that there and I don't have the mess here,' Katy said with a roll of her eyes.

'Yeah, ha, too funny.'

Katy turned around towards the sitting room. 'Look, actually, I'm going to have to go. She's had screen time since we got back, and I need to get tea on.'

'Okay. Look, call me as soon as you know anything. Let me know if you need anything, too. If you want me to come over. Text me anytime before, after, whenever you need.'

'Yeah, thanks for listening. I will. See you later.'

'See you.'

Emmy sat staring at the blank screen for a long time after the call had finished. She felt all over the show and mostly helpless. She mulled over the conversation and couldn't lose sight of the strain of holding everything together that was written clearly across Katy's face. Trying to take her mind off it, she went up to her bathroom, yanked stuff out of the laundry basket, scouted around Callum's bedroom for dirty clothes on the floor, started a load of laundry, and tidied up the sitting room. When that didn't work, she grabbed her jacket, wrapped a scarf around her neck, pulled on her trainers, and headed out to see if a walk would do her any good. Emmy headed for the sea as her mind decompressed from the conversation with Katy. The whole thing was turning into a nightmare. The sea breeze helped clear her mind a tad as she wandered down to the water-front, but mostly everything felt off-kilter about the situation with Katy. She couldn't stop thinking that if something was seriously wrong, she was going to have to tell Cherry and Bob.

Finding an empty bench by the water, she sat for ages, just staring at the waves as they crashed one after another onto the beach. It was as if the secrecy was turning her crazy. As she thought about morose things, her stomach clenched, and her mind raced wildly. She closed her eyes and forced herself to stop dramatising. Sagging against the bench slats, she gazed up at the darkening sky. Hues of grey, purple, blue, and fuzzy white whizzed by above the sea. She let out a huge sigh. Things did not bode well. She could feel it in her bones.

19

It was a week or so later, and with a mug of chamomile tea in her hands, Emmy was curled up on the sofa in cosy leggings and an oversized fluffy-lined jumper. Wind absolutely howled outside, the foghorn had gone off a few times, and driving rain spattered against the darkened windows of the flat. Little tea lights were dotted along the windowsill and on the coffee table, she had a jazz playlist on, and a tub of salted caramel truffles was open in front of her. It was a chilly, blustery evening after a long, tiring week, and Emmy was more than happy to stay bundled indoors beside the fire.

Sipping her chamomile tea, she sat surrounded by notebooks, a book she was binge-reading, her iPad, three pens, random sheets of paper, and her laptop. She was sitting listening to the rain and mulling over business strategies and ideas. Ever since Peaches' mind-blowing endorsement of The Old Ticket Office, which had skyrocketed Emmy's business almost overnight, she was keen to find ways to get more influencers on board. The initial customer surge had definitely slowed down, that was a fact, but rather than a trickle, it had mellowed to a slow but sure stream of income plopping in her store every day. She could so cope with that and wanted it to continue.

Peaches' reach had been a revelation to Emmy, and she wanted to build on the boutique's social media momentum and cement its visibility as much as she could. The small business entrepreneurial fires that had been taking up space in her head since she was a little girl had been stoked by her first taste of real, *tangible* success. She didn't want it to be a fleeting dream, but on the other hand, sucking up and chasing influencers whose egos were not small sort of made her want to scratch her eyeballs out. Sucking up wasn't quite one of Emmy Bardot's best skills. It had to be done, though, and hence she was brainstorming ways to get influencers to buy into the Love Emmy x world.

Glancing at the time on her phone, Emmy wondered idly when Tom would be home. She'd spoken to him just as he'd come out of a meeting, and he'd been walking back to his car in the pouring rain. He was also shattered after a long work week, so Emmy had ordered a takeaway and told him they were doing nothing other than putting their feet up and brainstorming a few ideas for Love Emmy x.

Bouncing around concepts with Tom would help her to see where and how to take her little business to the next level, hopefully without too much sucking up to anyone at all. Just as she was thinking about him, she heard the back door go and then his footsteps up the stairs to the flat. Tom breezed in, looking a bit weary. A smile crinkled his eyes as he came over to the sofa and kissed Emmy on the cheek. He pulled off his tie and chucked it on the chair.

'Hi. How's your day been?' Emmy asked.

'Not bad. You?'

'Manic. Then I got stuck for ages on the motorway because of the rain. The ferry was bad, too. It was absolutely chucking it down. I'm glad to be home. How'd your meetings go?'

'Oh, the usual madness, but productive overall.'

'Same.' Emmy launched into a quick recap of her day – a shift at the port, loads of customer problems, terrible traffic, a website update, and talking Amy down from a ledge regarding someone who had annoyed her at work. Emmy rolled her head from back right to back left, trying to ease a knot of stress she'd been carrying around with her all week.

'Sounds like you've got loads on the go as always,' Tom noted.

Emmy smiled. 'Yep. I love being busy, though, and I love coming home here. You can't beat it.'

Tom gestured to the piles of things surrounding Emmy on the sofa. 'We're still on for brainstorming ways to get influencers and their gigantic egos to the shop without having to resort to pandering to social media queens?'

Emmy raised her eyebrows and joked. 'Yup. I need your expertise in wooing people. From what I've seen, it's your skill set. It worked for me anyway.'

'Happy to be of service.'

'I'll go and get the food. It's keeping warm in the oven.'

Ten minutes later, they were chatting about Love Emmy x and tucking into a curry as the rain continued pattering against the windows. Emmy had been mulling over ideas all week. 'So. How am I going to get more of these social media queens to my shop? Ideas?'

Tom nodded. 'Tempt them somehow.'

'Right. But how?'

'Get them here for an experience to *feel* the shop. That's what sells it. Like us the other day in that place in Lovely Bay.'

'Hardly ground-breaking. I reckon they get invited to stuff willy-nilly.'

Tom wrinkled up his lips and then took a swig from a bottle of beer. 'How about an event where they can preview your stuff, but it's like a limited edition and a bit secret? Like what we read about the secret Lovely chowder thing. Something like that...'

'Yeah. Would they come, though? It's a long way and a faff with the ferry and everything.'

'If you made it exclusive, it could work.'

'How'd you mean?' Emmy questioned with a frown.

'Like sell *super* limited tickets and make it all hush-hush. Turn it into a premier experience. Almost more of a networking event than a shop day. Don't know. Could work...'

Emmy tried to picture what Tom had said. 'Yeah. Make it more exclusive. I like that.'

'Get Peaches to endorse it. The influencer version of those pop-up shops brands do. I saw one on my way to the office the other day. People were actually queuing up for it before it opened.'

'Yes, hmm, could work. Would anyone really come, though?'

'A genius way to take advantage of what Peaches, unknowingly to us, started.'

'Hmm.'

Tom went on. 'Bring them all to you in a hit, rather than chasing one-offs and having to do the same thing with each of them over and over again.'

'Right, yeah. Strike while the iron is hot and they are interested.'

'Seriously, Ems, I think it could be huge. Imagine if they all post at once. We've already seen what one single reel can do.'

'Wow. Yeah, when you say it like that. Sort of stack it up so it comes at the same time. I'd have to be really ready, though. I sold out of so much stuff last time. There was a lot of wasted opportunity there.'

'It's a winner out of the gate. Those influencers will probably start a bidding war for tickets from what we've seen so far with the messages about that necklace with the flower that sold out because Peaches bought it.'

Emmy's thoughts raced. 'I'd need somewhere to put them.'

'The storeroom.'

'That'd need help! It's hardly Instagram-able at the moment.'

'Yep.'

'It's easy to get carried away imagining the possibilities. A lot harder to actually make it *happen* in reality, as you know with that blimming flower installation.'

'Doable, though.'

'I won't get ahead of myself. Getting buy-in from the influencers will make or break it. But maybe if I start putting out feelers...' Emmy trailed off, thoughts already galloping ahead. The logistics would be endless, but if she didn't have a go, she wouldn't know.

'No harm in testing the waters, as they say,' Tom noted. 'I can't see it can do any harm. There's not a lot of cost involved, just organisation. You've already got this place.'

'Ahh, it's so good having someone to just mull things over with,' Emmy said and then went to say something about her ex Kevin and stopped herself. No one wanted to hear about him. It was boring old news. Kevin was toast. 'Thank you for letting me ramble.'

'Your sounding board, brainstorm partner. All of the above,' Tom joked.

'Thanks, honestly.'

'Soon full-time event coordinator once this takes off. No doubt I'll be assigned a job to do.'

'I'll need you for manual labour.' Emmy giggled. 'Making all the Love Emmy x dreams happen one day at a time.'

Even though on the outside Emmy was laughing and joking, on the inside she felt emotional. It was such a *huge* deal for her to have Tom. No one really understood that, despite Amy thinking that she did. No one had been there on the nights in the rental cottage when she'd swum around in a sea of one monotonous day of doing all the things after another. Images of late nights sitting hunched over her laptop, trying to figure out how to get a website up and running, and trying to do everything on a shoestring budget flashed through her mind. She had to look down for a second, unexpectedly overcome.

Tom picked up his beer bottle and clinked it on Emmy's glass of tonic water. 'To your vision coming to life.'

'To the Emmy and Tom brainstorming sessions more like.'

Tom chuckled. 'Every day of the week.'

'So we're doing this, are we?' Emmy bit her lip. 'I'll probably lose money initially, but if it generates even one viral post...' She tried not to second-guess herself but found herself doing it anyway. 'What if the investment of time and money flops?'

'It's scary putting yourself out there. You thought that about Peaches though and the harpist, and look what happened there in the end.'

'It would be quite a bit of money and a gamble. Embarrassing too if no one is interested.'

'What, you mean more of a gamble than picking up your life and moving it to an island only accessible by ferry where you know no one and buying an old insurance office?'

Emmy giggled. 'There is that.'

Tom gestured around the flat. 'This is the proof of how far you've come already.'

'You always know exactly what to say. How do you do that?'

'You just need reminding sometimes.'

Emmy exhaled and laughed, but she needed to remember that what Tom said was true. She would get on with what they'd brainstormed and set up an influencer event in the storeroom at the shop. She also realised that she needed to bolster herself a bit more. No more second-guessing. She'd come a long way, and not only that, she needed to say yes to the fact that Emmy Bardot was now doing well and in control of a very good life. It just all somehow felt quite odd and as if it belonged to someone else.

20

It was a week or so later and the day Katy got her scan results. Emmy paced the flat, phone wedged in her pocket as she waited for Katy to call. Glancing at the time, Emmy chewed her thumbnail anxiously as a thousand dire scenarios raced through her mind. She forced herself to breathe, trying not to worry. She had a horrible feeling of dread rising like bile in her throat. It was the secrecy that was making her completely overreact and blow things out of proportion. She tried to remain calm. Spiralling useless thoughts around and around wasn't anybody's friend and certainly not hers.

Finally, after what felt like hours of waiting, Emmy's phone began vibrating in her pocket. She fumbled in her haste to answer, dropped her phone on the floor, swore, picked it up, and pressed to answer. 'Hi. How was it?'

Katy sounded flat. 'Sorry, I know I said I'd ring right after the appointment. It was just a lot to digest.'

Emmy dug the nails of her right hand into her left wrist. Katy didn't sound good. She forced an even, calm tone. 'It's okay, I'm just glad you called.' She moved to perch on the edge of the sofa and waited.

'Well, at least we have an answer. The scans showed a mass. Or actually, several masses. It seems it's fine, though.'

Emmy felt a whoosh go around her stomach. She closed her eyes. Oh god. She felt her jaw clench. 'What sort of masses? What does that mean?'

'I need a few more tests to make sure what we're dealing with before deciding on the next steps, but I have fibroids. So, yeah, a bit of a surprise.'

Emmy closed her eyes for a long second and then opened them and stared out the window. 'Benign?'

'The doctor didn't want to speculate much, but yes. She said it's extremely rare for a fibroid to be cancerous.'

Emmy squeezed her eyes shut again. 'Thank goodness.'

Katy's voice sounded strained. 'I'm so relieved.'

'Me too.'

Katy was speaking quickly. 'One of them is *very* big. Like the size of a mini pumpkin. It's what's causing the pain, etcetera. It's why I'm constantly needing to go to the loo. She's recommending surgery.'

'Oh, right, I see. Okay.'

Katy didn't sound good. 'I'm scared, Ems. Even though I'm relieved, obviously. I know people deal with much worse than this, but…'

'Yeah, you must be. At least it's not, well, I was thinking all sorts.'

'I know. Fibroids, though, at my age – surprising.'

'So, is the wait long for this sort of thing?'

'I can get it through my insurance. So, no.'

'Oh, right, okay. That's good.'

'I get the insurance cover through work. The benefits are great. It's one of the reasons I stay there.'

Emmy felt more relief. 'You're going to go down that route?'

'Yeah. It all seemed quite routine.'

'Still surgery at the end of the day,' Emmy noted.

'Yes.'

'What will you do about Elodie?'

'It shouldn't be too much of a problem. I've already spoken to her dad.'

'So it's good news then. I can't tell you how relieved I am.' Emmy let out a huge sigh of relief. 'Fibroids sound manageable compared to the alternative. I've been thinking all sorts.'

'I know. I feel like I can breathe again. The not knowing was awful.'

'Absolutely. So what's the next step then?' Emmy asked.

'Just wait. I need another scan and then to discuss when to schedule the operation if that is indeed the way I go,' Katy explained.

'Right. And recovery time?'

'Depends on the procedure, but could be anywhere from not much at all to like a good few weeks, I think.'

Emmy whistled. 'Blimey. You'll need help looking after Elodie.'

'I know it's not ideal timing, but it is what it is. Elodie's dad is amazing. He can have her for however long I need to recover. Or just come here. I don't know, I'll cross that bridge when I come to it.'

'Well, that's something. Obviously, I'll come and help.'

Katy made a noncommittal 'hmm' noise. 'Thanks, Ems, that's really sweet of you to offer. I'll see how I feel. Hopefully, I'll bounce back quickly, I hate feeling useless.'

Emmy snorted. 'Yes, you've never been one to sit still for long. But you've got to look after yourself too. No rushing your recovery.'

'Really though, thank you. I appreciate you looking out for me even when I'm being stubborn.'

Emmy felt a rush of emotion. 'Of course.'

The tension that had been between them since Katy had been going to the doctor seemed to have dissipated somewhat. Emmy felt so much better. Though fibroids were no picnic by the sounds of it, and she was totally going to google the heck out of it, Emmy was relieved. She was also *highly* emotional. She also didn't know what was coming next.

21

Emmy secured her bike on the ferry railing and leaned her forearms against it, gazing out across the shimmering estuary. The breeze whipped strands of hair across her face as she watched the Darling Island coastline get further and further away. Beside her, Tom mirrored her posture and stared out at the water. His shoulder was leaning against hers as they both looked across the sea. Emmy's thoughts swirled, and she smiled at Tom. 'Thanks for dragging me out on this ride.'

'Yeah, it's good to be outside. Cold though!'

'I've been cooped up indoors too much. Oh, so many parcels and emails. The perils of a small business taking off. Ha.'

'Yep.'

'Shame we had to bump into Russell coming out of the lane earlier,' Emmy said, referring to when they'd turned at the bottom of the lane to see Russell, their creepy neighbour, coming the other way. Russell had made small talk with Tom and at the same time had somehow managed to rove his eyes up and down Emmy a few times. Emmy wasn't sure whether or not Tom had clocked it.

He totally had. 'Yeah, I ignored it.'

No flies on Tom, that was for sure. 'Oh, I wasn't sure if you saw it.'

'He wants to try.'

Emmy swooned and, unsure what to say, didn't say anything further. Huddled against the railing as the ferry gate clanged shut and the ferry dropped down into the water, they fell into companionable silence. Emmy breathed deeply, filling her lungs with the cold air and holding her face up to the sky. Once they'd reached the other side, they wheeled their bikes down the ramp behind the queue of foot passengers. When they'd proceeded away from the ferry, they hopped on their bikes and cycled along. Emmy felt the wind in her hair and was so glad she'd decided to leave Love Emmy x stuff, a very teenage Callum, and the housework needing doing behind. She trailed behind Tom along a bike path snaking away from the ferry and felt her jumbled head full of too much to do slowly start to decompress. Tom had suggested they go out for a bike ride and just cycle and see where they ended up with no destination in mind. It worked for her, as she pedalled, got lost in the view, and looked over at Darling on the other side.

From the other side, Darling Island looked very quaint. She could see the sailing club by the water and a row of tall white houses looking out across the estuary. Flags on top of one of the houses flapped madly in the wind, and bright sunlight glinted off their whitewashed backs. As they pedalled along, salt-tinged coastal air filled Emmy's nose, seagulls wheeled overhead, and a much more professional-looking cyclist than her lifted his head in acknowledgement as he whizzed past coming the other way.

The bike path morphed through trees to more of a bridleway running not far from the water's edge. Mostly empty except for a few dog walkers, Emmy pedalled beside Tom, and they chatted about an issue that had come up at the Darling Chamber of Commerce. After a half hour or so of cycling with no destination in mind, they pulled up to an old jetty and propped their bikes up on their stands. Emmy laid a thick tartan picnic blanket on a bench and pulled a flask from her bike basket. Taking the lid cups off, she plopped in two tea bags, poured on hot water, splashed in milk from a little jam jar that had been in a cool bag, and pulled out two small baskets.

Tom raised his eyebrows. 'What? You sneaked these in! When did you go to Darlings?'

'This morning. Before you came over.'

'You must have been up early.'

Emmy *had* been up early. Worrying about the Katy situation. 'I was. I thought a Darlings basket might go down well on our bike ride.'

'Lovely,' Tom said as he took the basket Emmy was handing him and untied the blue and white gingham cloth on the top. He delved inside and smiled.

'What are the delights on offer today?' Emmy asked.

Tom opened a package of greaseproof paper. 'What in the world? I have a small loaf.' He wrinkled his nose up.

Emmy followed suit, opening her package. Inside was what appeared to be a mini cottage loaf. Beside it sat a large wedge of cheese, a small pot filled with oversized pickled onions, and slices of red apple. In a little lidded pot, a dark Branston-style relish was wedged into the side of the basket. A note said the apples were from the farm on the far side of Darling and the cottage loaf from Holly's. 'Ploughman's Darlings style.'

'How did Evie know we'd be needing this on a bike ride on a brisk day?' Tom laughed.

'No idea, but she got it right.'

Tom tucked in. 'Simple.'

'So nice, eh? How do they do it in there and always get it right?'

'No idea.'

'If I shoved a bit of cheese in a cool bag next to slices of apple and some Branston, it wouldn't taste like this. Callum would moan for England if he had this in his lunchbox.'

'Ha. Said the woman who is an expert at styling.'

Emmy picked up the white basket. 'What, you reckon it's all about the presentation?'

'Yup. Plus the fact that it's all sourced locally and is the best.'

'Right, yeah.'

'Evie was way ahead of her time,' Tom noted as he flicked out the blue napkin. 'I mean, look at this idea. So simple. You collect it in the morning or whenever and everything has been thought through and provided. Then you hand it back in. Rinse and repeat. Too easy.'

'Hmm. Yeah. It *is* a good idea.'

'Nearly all of it is recyclable.'

Emmy nodded. 'So true.' She shuddered. 'Just think about all that plastic in one of those supermarket meal deals. Those horrible little plastic forks with a tub of chemical-tasting salad.' Emmy made a faux vomit sound.

'Yeah, totally should be banned. We all spend our lives being lectured about the environment, but big businesses get to do what they like. Then you get somewhere like Darlings doing their little bit for the environment, and they have been for a long time.'

Emmy giggled. 'Hark at you. Tom Carter for PM.'

'I've probably got a chance. We change PMs every few months now, don't we?'

Emmy laughed and popped one of the pickled onions into her mouth whole. 'I'd vote for you.'

'That's one vote then.'

'Yeah, might be your only one.'

'What's Callum been up to this week?'

'Going fishing with my dad later.'

'Right. Are you dropping him over there?'

'I'd really rather not.'

'Why?'

Emmy made a wincing face. 'I'm sort of avoiding them a bit.'

'What, because of the Katy thing?'

'Totally.' Emmy felt Tom's body language change. She bristled. 'It's all been really concerning.'

'Yeah, I bet the waiting and uncertainty wasn't nice for her.'

'No.'

Emmy's thoughts shifted to the other dilemma gnawing at her – whether or not to finally tell her mum about reconnecting with Katy. She chewed her lower lip, wishing the ethics were simple. 'I just don't know if I can keep lying to Mum while all this is happening. It feels so wrong to exclude her like this. What do you think?'

Tom nodded slowly. 'I can see both sides.'

'Yep.'

'Thing is, Ems, I don't want to speak out of turn...'

Emmy interrupted him. She hated it when people said that as if it excused them for what they were going to say. 'But?'

Tom screwed his face up. 'But I think it's time you told your mum or at least Amy.'

Emmy sighed. 'Do you?'

'To tell you the truth, I think it's pretty lame on your side not to tell Amy. You're *supposedly* so close.'

Emmy's back went up immediately. 'Oh, right. Say it how it is, why don't you?'

'Sorry, but someone has to say something. It's not just Katy's feelings now, it's Amy's too.'

Emmy stared down at her lap for a second. He was right – they both knew it, but she didn't want to have to deal with it. 'I've been so focused on the blow-up I'm dreading, I didn't consider her enough.'

'It's none of my business, but I don't really agree with the secret anymore. You *did* ask me what I thought, so I'm telling you.'

143

Emmy felt herself getting both emotional and a little bit angry with Tom. As far as she was concerned, it wasn't his business. The other rational part of her brain was telling her she couldn't have it both ways in her relationship with him. She wanted a partner and someone to love her blah, blah, blah, but she didn't want to be told when he had an opinion. It didn't quite work like that out in the real world. She stopped herself from getting annoyed. 'No, it's not really your business.'

'You're avoiding your parents, Callum is affected, and you're not seeing Amy. Something's got to give here, Ems. As an outsider looking in, I can see it as clear as day. You're just too *in* it to see it clearly.'

Emmy felt herself getting riled up. She bristled at Tom's words. She knew he made some fair points, but she wasn't ready to hear them, truth be told. 'I know, it's just that this is really complicated. It's been a long time since Katy left. I can't just waltz in and announce we've reconnected out of the blue.'

Tom held up his hands. 'You're right. Sorry. I don't fully grasp the history. I just think secrets have a habit of blowing up, that's all. I mean, look what happened with us.'

Emmy gave a begrudging nod. She knew he was right. 'I hear you. I do want to tell Mum and Amy eventually. But Katy expressly asked me not to say anything yet. I have to respect that.'

'What about your dad, though? He does loads for you, and you're lying to him pretty much twenty-four-seven.'

'Tom!'

'Sorry, Ems. It's true. I'm calling a spade a spade here.'

Emmy sighed heavily, her shoulders slumping. 'Ahh. I just can't handle it. I know Mum is going to be *so* angry. She's so harsh and unforgiving about Katy. She'll say something like "going behind their backs" or something. I am pathetic.'

Tom screwed up his face. 'Your mum? Really? You think

she'd react like that? She also does loads for you. I mean, look at the backyard alone.'

Emmy sighed. Just as Katy had said, there was another side to Cherry. It rarely came out, and no one really saw it, but this was one of the situations where it would rear its head. 'Possibly. That's what I mean about this being complicated. The Katy thing is a touchy subject. Hence, why I find myself in this mess.'

Tom tapped her arm. 'But isn't avoiding them going behind their backs in a way?'

'Ugh, I know.' Emmy groaned and dropped her head into her hands. She swore more than once. 'Honestly, I'm just scared of their reactions. Dad will be worried. Mum will get all emotional and also be worried, but she'll be angry too. She'll have a million questions. Ahh.'

'Tricky one.'

'I want to wait until after Katy's surgery and recovery. The timing will feel right when it's meant to happen.' Emmy nodded as if agreeing with herself.

Tom was blunt and to the point. 'You're kidding yourself.'

Emmy swore. She knew Tom was right. All her defences went up. They lined up in front of her. 'I'm not!'

'Sorry, not sorry, but you are. I'm not just going to say what you want to hear, Ems. That isn't me.'

Emmy went nuclear. Tom P Carter just got a little bit more attractive, if that was even remotely possible. 'No. I've noticed,' Emmy said with a smile breaking the tense air.

'Happy to be here for you, but if you want my opinion *and* you ask me for it, I'm not going to lie. I'm not going to just sit on your side of the fence if I don't think it's right. Simple as that.'

Emmy smiled gratefully. 'Thanks for listening. I know I can be a bit defensive about this.'

'Just a bit!'

'Sorry.' Emmy fiddled with the zip on her jacket, feeling bad for snapping.

Tom bumped her shoulder. 'No worries. I care about you and want to help, but I'm not just going to blindly say something I don't think is fair, and this isn't right in my humble opinion.'

'Actually, you know what? I'm grateful for that. I'm lucky to have you in my corner.'

'Always.'

The tension dissipated somewhat, even though Emmy was prickly. The bottom line of it was that underneath her excuses, she knew Tom was right about needing to come clean to her family. The weight of the secret was getting heavier by the day. The fallout was inevitable. The thing was that she was trying to kid herself, as Tom had said. She was not looking forward to when it all came to a head. Not at all.

22

E mmy hustled along the pavement to the pub, pushed open the door, and scanned the interior to look for Amy. She'd not seen too much of Amy, mostly because she'd been avoiding situations where she might get into deep conversation. Plus, if and when she had been with Amy one-on-one, she'd kept things well away from anything remotely connected to Katy. Weaving her way between the pub tables and chairs, she made her way towards the conservatory tucked away at the back of the pub. She, Amy, and Cherry had been to the pub many times. It was just along the road from Amy's house and housed a beautiful old heated conservatory out the back, leading to a gorgeous pub garden which they'd utilised many times in the summer months. Emmy spied Amy sitting at a table in the corner in a secluded nook overlooking the beer garden.

Amy looked up from scrolling her phone and waved Emmy over eagerly. She got up and kissed Amy on the cheek. 'Hi, stranger. It feels like I haven't seen you for weeks.'

'Oh, does it?' Emmy pretended as if she hadn't thought the same. She knew it had been ages because she knew very well she'd been avoiding Amy. The knowledge did not make her feel good.

'I was starting to think Love Emmy x and The Old Ticket Office had swallowed you whole.'

Emmy laughed. 'I know, I managed to peel myself away, ha ha!'

'I'm *so* glad you're here. I could really use a proper catch-up and vent session. It's been too long.'

'Lucky you've got me then,' Emmy joked.

'Well, that's what sisters and wine are for, right? Venting.'

Emmy felt her insides shudder at the 'sister' word. 'Spill all the happenings. Is it Dee at work again?'

Amy slid the glass of wine she'd bought Emmy over the table. Emmy accepted and took a sip, and then listened as Amy rattled on about her latest mishaps and work projects. Emmy felt her shoulders relax as she settled back in her chair. The wine did its job, and she soaked up Amy's little snippets of normalcy. It felt nice to just chat. Amy put her elbow on the table and raised her eyebrows. 'So, what's been going on with you, Ems? You've been really quiet.'

Emmy stiffened. Where to even begin considering she knew that their other sister was not well and having surgery, and it was consuming her thoughts? She tied herself in knots inside as she felt the lies begin to bubble. 'The usual. Work has died down a bit, as it does at this time of year, which has been good because Love Emmy x has been flying along since the whole Peaches thing, as you know.'

Amy narrowed her eyes. 'Sorry. You seem stressed again.'

'A lot going on with the shop and stuff.'

Amy raised her eyebrows. She was clearly unconvinced. 'Try again. I know you, remember? Something deeper is up. You have the post-Kevin look again. It's been gone for a while, but it's back with a vengeance. What's really up?'

Emmy fidgeted with the stem of her glass. She looked across

the conservatory and closed her eyes briefly for a second. Emotions, guilt, and secrecy all swirled around in her head like crazy. All of a sudden, something snapped, and all of it came crashing down around her. She was going to tell Amy. It hit her like a tonne of bricks. She couldn't continue with it anymore. No more lies. Where to even start? All the secrets swam around her head in a big fat, turbulent whirl.

'Ems?'

Emmy put her hands in front of her face for a second. 'I have something big I need to tell you.' Emmy hesitated and studied the bottom of her wineglass. She winced at what Amy was going to say about having been kept in the dark. Tom's words shot through her head about bottom line, none of it being right.

Amy frowned. 'Are you okay? You look *bad*.'

'Yes. I'm fine. I'm not sure how to say this…'

'Oh my god! Are you pregnant? Flipping heck! Oh! Blimey, Ems! I didn't see that coming! Pregnant! Wow!'

Emmy shook her head and swallowed. She half-wished she *was* pregnant. That would have been a whole lot simpler and a much, much happier piece of news. 'God no. That won't be happening anytime soon. Ditto getting married.'

'What then? You're freaking me out.'

'I promise I wanted to tell you sooner. But it was just, well, really complicated. It *is* really complicated.'

Amy's eyebrows shot up. 'What in the world is going on? You look terrible. What did you want to tell me?'

Tears sprang to Emmy's eyes. She took a breath, grimaced, and blurted. 'I've been talking to Katy again. We reconnected a while back.'

Amy's mouth fell open. Clearly, whatever she'd thought was going on with Emmy, Katy wasn't it. Emmy rushed to fill the silence. 'I saw her out of the blue. I followed her. I didn't know what to do. I spoke to her.'

Amy just stared, lips parted in shock for a moment, and then she seemed to regain her senses. She leant forward intently, eyes burning with questions. 'Katy reached out? After all these years? How? When? Why didn't you tell me?' Amy's words tumbled out in a bewildered rush, and she squinted her eyes.

'No, no, she didn't reach out!'

'What? How did you speak to her then?'

'I saw her randomly at a train station,' Emmy clarified.

Amy frowned. 'When? What do you mean?'

'Ages ago,' Emmy said and closed her eyes for a brief instant.

'I can't believe it.' Amy swore over and over again. She put her right hand to her forehead and rubbed it as if trying to make sense of what Emmy was telling her.

Emmy clutched her glass. 'I know I should have told you sooner. But Katy swore me to secrecy about reconnecting.'

'Mum is going to go ballistic! What the actual? I don't know what to think. Wow!'

Emmy felt a little bit of her die inside. What Amy had said about their mum was not what she wanted to hear. They both knew it was true.

Amy shook her head over and over again. She looked more shocked than angry. 'I just can't believe you kept this from me, Ems. Katy is my sister too.'

Emmy felt *terrible*. She felt tears on her cheeks. 'I'm so sorry, Ames. The secrecy has been agony.'

'I'm stunned. This is such a surprise. Of all the things I thought might be going on! This wasn't one of them.'

'Katy *begged* me not to tell anyone yet.'

Amy's expression clouded. 'Oh right, so she gets to dictate the terms, does she? That sounds like her,' she said tightly.

Emmy shook her head. Emmy wasn't happy, but she was surprised Amy wasn't more angry or upset. She'd braced herself for much worse. Raised voices, tears, perhaps some shouting. Mostly Amy just seemed shocked, which made Emmy feel sort of worse in a way.

Amy looked puzzled. 'I wish you'd trusted me enough to just tell me.' She swore. 'I can't believe this.'

'I didn't know what to do.' Emmy splayed her hands out in front of her helplessly. 'You know what Katy's like.'

'Well, no, actually I don't these days. I can see that it would have been hard, though.'

Emmy sagged in relief. 'It's been dreadful feeling caught in the middle. I wanted to tell you everything from the start. I *hate* keeping secrets. I'm useless at it, as you well know.'

'I don't know what to say. Sorry, so you've seen her since. How is she? Where? So many questions.'

'She has a daughter,' Emmy blurted out.

Amy swore too loudly. A man looked over from a table opposite and shook his head. 'Poor Mum.'

The relief of finally telling Amy whooshed around Emmy so quickly she felt a bit lightheaded. She dabbed at the corner of her eyes. 'I'm glad to have it off my chest now. The guilt has been killing me lying to you.'

'That's the least of your worries. Just wait until Mum finds out.' Amy added a funny sound at the end, and the tension broke a bit.

'Don't even go there.'

'So, is this what was wrong before?' Amy asked and then swigged from her glass.

'Yep.'

'So, catch me up properly. God, it's been such a long time that you've been acting weird. I knew something was wrong. I *knew* it. I know you, Ems.'

Emmy began filling Amy in about following Katy to the flat, about Elodie, about helping out with babysitting when Katy'd had a few childcare issues, and about how well Katy was doing. She felt a combination of dreadful and almost jubilant. As if she was purging something that had been stuck in her throat for a very long time. Which, in fact, she was.

Amy looked far from jubilant. 'I can't believe all of this has been going on, and you've said nothing! Mum and Dad have helped you with the shop and all that, and you've had all this going on underneath. How could you have done that? After everything they've done for you, Ems.'

Talk about making someone feel a million times worse. 'I know. I do know that, but I don't know what to say.'

'The shop opening, all of that, and you were seeing Katy all along. Ouch. We've mentioned her a few times too. Bloody hell, Ems.'

'Yep. There's nothing I can say to make it any better. I'm well aware of it. Katy was adamant, though.'

'No change there then,' Amy said sarcastically.

Emmy took a big gulp of wine. 'I know it's a lot to take in. I hate that I've kept this from you, But Katy was so insistent. She made me promise not to breathe a word until she was ready. Especially not to Mum and Dad,' Emmy explained. 'She's just not interested.'

Amy exhaled heavily. 'I can't say I blame her in a way. I remember it all from before. Mum was *incensed* by it. Remember? They're going to flip their lids.' She absentmindedly shredded a beer mat as she processed it all.

'Exactly. So I was stuck between a rock and a hard place. I hated lying but didn't feel like I could break Katy's trust either.'

'I get why you felt trapped. I probably would have done the same. Maybe. No, no, I wouldn't, ahh, I don't know.'

Emmy felt so relieved that Amy hadn't shouted or stormed off or both. 'Thanks, Ames, that means a lot. I've felt so torn and so guilty all the time.'

Amy leant back in her chair, eyebrows knitted together as she processed it all. 'I just can't believe it. After all these years, she just pops back up out of the blue? She didn't think to let her own family know she was okay all this time. That's so messed up. Just so messed up.'

'I know. Believe me, I was furious with her at first, too. But she explained how she felt as if she had to make a clean break when she left. She's happy, and I don't know, just wants to keep it that way.' Emmy didn't know whether or not to tell Amy that Katy had been pregnant when she'd left. She decided against it. Another secret.

Amy shook her head. It was as if she'd read Emmy's mind about pregnancy. 'That's still no excuse. She didn't even tell us she was having a baby! We have a niece we knew nothing about until now. Mum is going to be devastated when she finds out. God, it's horrible. Just so mean!'

Emmy nodded. She had thought the exact same thing so many times.

'I can't believe you've been babysitting and everything too,' Amy continued and shook her head. 'What's Elodie like?'

Despite everything, Emmy couldn't help but smile. 'She's really sweet. Shy at first, but once she warms up to you, she chatters away. She looks so much like Katy, it's scary. Like they look like twins. Two peas in a pod.'

'And Katy's doing okay? She's got herself together?'

'Seems to be. She's got a gorgeous flat, a really good job and Elodie goes to a little childcare school. Yeah. You'd be surprised.'

Amy processed what Emmy was telling her and took another long sip of wine. Emmy could see the questions whirring in her sister's mind. 'I can't believe it.'

'I'm just so sorry I didn't tell you sooner.'

'Has she even asked about me?' Amy's voice sounded small.

Inside, Emmy winced. She and Katy hadn't spoken too much about the family at all. She felt yet another lie slip out. 'A bit.'

'I want to see her,' Amy stated flatly.

Katy's health issue and surgery flagged in the front of Emmy's brain. 'Thing is, she's had a few health problems.'

'Like what?'

'Fibroids, and one of them needs to be removed.'

Amy's eyes widened in concern. 'Fibroids? Is it serious?'

'They're benign, so not cancerous. But there's one that's quite large that's causing a lot of pain and other issues. So she needs to have surgery to remove it. It's not all sorted out yet. She's having more scans.'

'Blimey. That's got to be scary when you have a little one.'

Emmy nodded. 'Exactly. She's putting on a brave face, but I can tell she's anxious about it all.'

'At least it's treatable. Surgery is no joke, though,' Amy replied as she twirled the stem of her wine glass, clearly churning over everything Emmy had said.

'No, it's not.'

'I guess she doesn't want to see me.' Amy shook her head.

'We haven't talked about it fully,' Emmy lied. They hadn't really talked about it at all. She felt pang upon pang of guilt. 'I should have told you sooner so you could have seen her before the surgery if she, well, you know, if she wants to. I'm sorry, Ames. I just didn't know what to do.'

Amy waved a hand dismissively. 'You need to tell Mum and Dad at some point. This is not good. We're all *supposedly* so close. What a joke that is.'

Emmy's shoulders slumped. She knew Amy was right, but she was totally and utterly apprehensive. She wasn't sure if telling Amy had been the right thing to do, but now, at least some of the guilt had eased a little bit. However, they were both now in on the secret, and, at the end of the day, Emmy wasn't sure whether that was a good thing or not.

23

Emmy's stomach churned with nerves as she made her way up the steps to Katy's house. Standing in front of the pale blue door at the front of the block for a moment, she gathered herself and then buzzed the intercom. After making her way up the interior stairs, she stood outside Katy's flat and waited for Katy to come to the door.

When Katy opened the door, she smiled. Katy looked a little bit brighter than the last time Emmy had seen her, so that was a plus. 'Hi,' Katy greeted.

Without preamble, Emmy led right into a question about the latest lot of scans. 'How did it go?'

'Well, the fibroid situation isn't good. The biggest one is massive, the size of a small baby's head, apparently. We already knew that, but it's clearer now.'

'So it definitely needs to come out as they said, does it?'

Katy nodded as Emmy put her bag by the dresser and took off her jacket. 'Yep. That's what she said.'

'What did they say about treatment?'

'The consultant said it needs to be removed, just as she initially thought. I'm being scheduled soon.'

'That's quick!'

'I know. Thank goodness for that health insurance. Apparently, it would be a different story otherwise.'

'I bet.' Emmy raised her eyebrows and followed Katy into the kitchen. 'At least it will be out of the way.'

'Yeah. I just hope Elodie is okay. Tea?'

'Yes, please. Don't worry about that. She'll be fine.'

Katy poured boiling water onto tea bags in two mugs. 'I don't have much choice in whether I worry or not. I can't fall apart. I don't have time,' Katy joked. 'I haven't put this in my planner.'

'I'm here if you need help or just need someone to lean on,' Emmy stated, not really laughing at Katy's joke. She was so tense with it all that she wasn't feeling jovial in any shape or form. She was just more than grateful that the news hadn't been worse.

'I'll remind you that you said that when I'm drugged up and loopy as a patient from hell,' Katy said with a half-laugh.

Emmy shook her head at Katy's humour. 'I'll keep the wine and dark chocolate stocked for nursing you back to health then.'

'Ha. I'll need the hard stuff for sure. I'm progressing from wine to whisky or tequila.'

Emmy took the mug of tea and sat down. 'What a turn-up, eh?'

'I know. I knew things weren't right.'

'Hmm.'

'It's funny how you are the one who knows your own body best. I just *knew*.'

'They do say that,' Emmy agreed.

Katy yanked the lid off a biscuit tin and passed it over to Emmy, who took out a Bourbon. 'I just couldn't keep putting it down to being a mum. The pain in my stomach wasn't just my period, either. That's what the GP initially said.'

'Thank goodness you went in the first place and then pushed for the right diagnosis,' Emmy noted.

'I probably would have been fine. People have fibroids for years, apparently. Not as big as this one, granted, but they do have them without problems.'

'I didn't really know much about them until this.'

Katy dunked her biscuit in her tea. 'Me neither. Apparently, they're really common. I am now, however, an expert.'

Emmy nodded, taking a sip of her tea. 'At least it seems there's a fairly straightforward fix. How long is recovery supposed to take? You said like four weeks, didn't you?'

'Could be four to six weeks,' Katy said with a grimace. 'I'll be out of action for a bit between the surgery and healing. Good luck to me trying to do that with Elodie around.'

Emmy made a funny face and nodded. 'I can help out.'

'Thanks. I'm not the best at being waited on hand and foot, though.' Katy flicked her hand dismissively. 'I'll be fine.'

'You'll just have to get used to it,' Emmy teased.

Katy's tone changed. 'I'm scared about complications or it not working. And about handling Elodie while I recover.'

'Just focus on yourself. Elodie will be fine with her dad, plus she's already sorted for the daytime. Honestly, she's the last of your concerns, really. You have to focus on *you*.'

Katy mulled it over for a second. 'Yeah, I suppose the daycare bit is not that different, and she loves being at her dad's.'

'Nope.'

'Yeah, you're right. Anyway, enough doom and gloom. Distract me – how are things with you and Tom?'

Emmy launched into an update, more than happy to discuss something to up the beat of the conversation. As they chatted, she didn't mention to Katy that Amy now knew that Katy was back on the scene. With Katy's state of mind, she didn't need to know that and have something else to worry about on her plate.

157

Emmy swallowed. Yet again, she'd lied by omission. She told herself that all of it would sort itself out in time. She crossed her fingers and hoped not sure if it would.

24

It was a week or so later, and Emmy drummed her fingers on the steering wheel as the ferry slowly made its way towards Darling Island. She smiled over at Callum in the passenger seat.

'So how was practice?'

Callum nodded. 'Yeah, you know what indoor training is like. A mixture of boring and chaos.' He held out his phone to show her a blurry video of his teammates messing around.

Emmy chuckled. 'Not serious then. I'm so glad that costs me so much money.'

'Nup, not serious out of season.'

They chatted back and forth about this and that, and when the ferry was about halfway across the water, Emmy's phone buzzed with an incoming message notification.

'It's probably your dad making sure you got picked up,' Emmy said as she looked down. But the preview notification on her locked screen wasn't from her, Kevin, and Callum's group chat. It was a message from Gemma, the assistant to mega-influencer Peaches. She frowned and tapped on it.

Gemma: *Hi, Emmy. I thought I would text you as a heads-up*

because I've sent you an email. Peaches is hosting a charity cocktail party in London and hand-selecting guests. Loads of influencers and industry people are going. You have been invited to attend. Let me know if you can come. Thanks so much. Gemma.

'Oh my!' Emmy gasped after she'd tapped on the email and read the attached invitation. The event was more than fancy. She reread the invite, just to be sure. 'Wow.'

'What's that?' Callum asked.

'I just got invited to an event with that Peaches influencer. Like a really highfalutin fancy-pants event!'

Callum looked suitably impressed. 'Cool!'

'It sounds like it'll be very posh and glamorous,' Emmy mused as the ferry got to the other side, the gate opened, and she crawled the car forward in the line of disembarking traffic. She imagined Peaches' elite social circle and grimaced. Maybe, actually, it wouldn't be that much fun. 'I'll need to dress up if I go.'

Callum made a face. 'Ugh, I hate dressing up. At least there will probably be loads of nice food, right?'

Emmy laughed. Trust Callum to cut through the glamour to the thing most important to him. She ruffled his hair. 'I bet the food will be good if she's got anything to do with it.'

'Do you get to take a guest?'

'Why? Do you want to come?'

Callum side-eyed. He paused for a second, clearly wondering if he should pretend. 'Nah, not really. Not my scene, is it?'

Emmy felt absolutely relieved. There was no way she'd want to drag Callum around something like the event she'd just read about. He'd be bored out of his brain and watching cricket videos on his phone in about five minutes flat. 'I didn't think you'd want to.'

'Not for me.'

'Nope,' Emmy agreed, nodding her head.

'What, so are you going to go with Tom?'

'I don't know. I just opened it. Have a read.'

Callum finished reading the invitation and tapped at the venue. 'Wow! It looks really fancy. He'd like it.'

'You reckon?'

'What's her name again? The influencer?'

'Peaches.'

Callum tutted. 'I know that, duh. Who doesn't? She has a trillion followers, and her whole life is out there on YouTube. I mean her real name.'

'Kim.'

'Pah! Gold.'

Emmy mulled over the invite the rest of the drive home. A fancy cocktail party surrounded by influencer elites and industry bigwigs was way outside her normal scene and her comfort zone. So far, from what she'd seen by way of the invite, the party was on a completely different planet from the one she normally inhabited altogether. But she had to admit, part of her fancied it. It would be a chance to get dressed up and do something completely different in her life. She needed a little bit of razzle-dazzle and to get away from the humdrum.

Once they'd got home and lugged in their stuff from the car, Emmy showered and dried her hair. She pulled on her softest white jogging bottoms and a big sloppy sweatshirt and cosy slouchy socks and spent an hour or so pottering around the house getting her work bag re-packed, putting a cottage pie in the oven, and ironing a few of Callum's school shirts.

She was sitting with Tom and the cottage pie later when she brought up the invitation. 'Well, some news from me today that's not about either of my sisters. I got invited to some posh cocktail thing by Peaches.'

'Sorry, do you mean Kim?' Tom joked.

'Ooh, catty Tom is out to play. Callum said the same!'

'Ha.'

Emmy pulled the invitation up on her phone and handed it to Tom. He was quiet for a second as he read it. 'You have to go.'

Emmy gave him a sceptical look. 'Do I? It seems way over the top. I can just picture it now – schmoozing and air kisses with social climbers all night.' She pretended to gag.

Tom laughed. 'It could be fun!'

'Maybe.'

'Am I the plus one?' Tom asked with raised eyebrows.

'Yup,' Emmy said as she dolloped a gigantic blob of Daddies sauce on the side of her plate.

'Right. It'll be an experience.'

Emmy grinned, picked up her phone, and navigated to the invitation again. 'It will.'

'Very fancy. I suppose I can clear my busy social calendar,' Tom joked.

'I literally have nothing to wear.'

'Can't help you there.'

'How do I fit in with the glamorous influencer set, eh?'

'Can't help there either. I think that's a job for your sister.'

Emmy giggled. 'Which one?'

Tom shook his head. 'Don't even go there.'

25

E mmy sagged back against the worktop in Tom's kitchen, phone clutched tightly in her hand. She'd had a strange lingering dread about Katy's operation, which it seemed had been totally uncalled for. Katy'd had her surgery, and it had gone well; she'd spent a few nights in recovery and was not feeling great at all, but overall, she was fine. Elodie was with her dad, that hadn't been a drama, and Katy was in a much better way than she'd hoped.

Emmy had been on tenterhooks the whole time the surgery had been taking place. On top of that, keeping the secret still ate away at her conscience whenever she thought about it. She'd been over and over again in her head when the right time would be to tell her mum and dad, plus Amy was now also weighing in her thoughts on the matter. The secret, rather than getting better, as she'd initially thought, now felt as if it had grown. The ethics of continuing the secrecy in light of Katy's surgery and Tom's take on it gnawed at Emmy. Sometimes she felt as if the problem was actually living in her head with her. She pressed her palms to her eyes until she saw starbursts, wishing she had an easy answer.

Tom smiled. 'Any other texts from her? Is everything okay? How is she doing?'

'She's alright. All that worry, and it turned out fine. I don't think it fully hit me how worried I was. Underneath, I felt as if something bad was going to happen.'

'You have a lot going on.'

'Not as much as her!'

'True. You've had a busy few months, though, plus you're holding down two jobs, Ems. Plus, there's Callum and a hundred other things.'

'Like millions of people in this country do every single day. It's nothing special.'

'Okay then,' Tom agreed as he shook his head and rolled his eyes. 'Millions of people don't have two jobs, a new house, a shop, and a teenage son.'

Emmy ignored all that. 'I'm just so impatient and wish I could fast-forward through this part to when she's back home recovering. I do worry about all this.'

'One day at a time. She's getting the care she needs. Look at it that way.'

'How are you always so logical?' Emmy asked with a laugh. 'I need to train my brain to think like that.'

'Am I?'

'Yup. Whilst I am beginning to think that I overthink every-thing in my life.'

'Like what?'

'Like everything – the whole situation with the secret.'

'Any more thoughts about telling your mum and dad?'

'I don't know. I just don't know how much longer I can keep hiding this from Mum, especially now the surgery's over and now that Amy knows.'

Tom seemed to be choosing his words carefully. The last time he'd spoken up, it had become quite tense. 'I do think you need to tell your mum sooner rather than later now that Amy knows. Amy is right.' He held up a hand when Emmy immediately opened her mouth to protest and interrupt. 'Just hear me out. Let me throw this in the ring. How would you feel if it was Callum?'

Emmy bit her lip. Tom P Carter had cut to the chase as he always did. He wasn't just logical; he was direct, blunt, and straight to the point. She went to do the knee-jerk reaction thing that it was Katy's choice but changed tack. 'It's not that simple.' She hated how defensive her voice sounded.

'You're tied up in knots about it. Enough is enough if you ask me.'

'You're right that it's been agony keeping this from Mum,' Emmy conceded. 'Katy's been through enough already, and now all this. It's not the time.'

Tom nodded slowly, but it was clear he didn't agree. 'It's an impossible situation either way. But Katy keeping your family excluded like this, even now, and forcing you to keep a secret – yeah, not good from my point of view.'

'What are you saying?'

'I'm sorry, but it just doesn't sit right with me. It's actually quite nasty. You're kind of enabling it by going along with it. I'm calling it, Ems.'

Emmy recoiled. 'Nasty?' She set down her mug with more force than necessary.

Tom held up both palms in a conciliatory gesture. 'Just saying it as it is from my perspective.'

Emmy didn't want to get in another spat with Tom, but he had some sort of knack for pushing her buttons. 'I don't think it's particularly *nasty*, though. Is it? I don't know what to think anymore.'

'You're shouldering an impossible thing here, and now Amy is in on it too. I'm trying to give you the voice of reason from the other side of the fence.'

Emmy shrugged half-heartedly. She didn't really want

reason's voice. She knew Tom wanted to help, even if he sounded judgemental, but she was prickly about the whole thing. Prickly and over it. 'The problem is that there is no good option where someone doesn't get hurt.'

'I'll support you either way.' Tom shrugged.

Emmy swooned when he said that. She loved it. So much. This was the second rough patch she had gone through since he'd been around. The first one, she'd more or less been dumped by him. She didn't want that happening again anytime soon. 'I'm still working this all out,' Emmy said, which was the truth.

Inside, she just wasn't very sure how it was going to turn out, and she didn't like how that made her feel at all. This was one situation that was not going to sort itself out in the wash.

26

Emmy was just back from an early morning cup of tea and a fry-up with Tom. They'd chatted holiday plans for the following year, discussed a jewellery conference Emmy was hoping to attend, and all manner of other things. Emmy'd had a busy few days and was gearing up to pop over to see Katy, who was now home and convalescing. She walked back to her flat to hang some washing, grab some soup she'd made for Katy the day before, and get her coat and bag. She thought about the fact that Katy now knew that Amy knew. Emmy had told Katy over the phone that Amy knew about the secret. That had been about it, and not much had happened apart from Amy and Katy, consequently, exchanging a few texts. As she sorted the washing out before she left, Emmy was mulling over the fact that Amy wanted the two of them to meet up.

As far as Emmy knew, Katy had been okay on the outside about Amy, but Emmy wasn't so sure. Katy had reiterated more than once that she was fine. Emmy was pretty sure that inside, Katy *wasn't* fine. Katy'd done the thing people do when they say they're fine – they sigh at the same time and flap a little bit, and then repeat that they are fine many times. Katy'd also said, in the same breath, that she wasn't bothered. Emmy could tell that she was most certainly bothered.

About twenty minutes or so after stepping out of Tom's flat, with the washing on the airer by the window and having dumped chicken, an onion, and curry paste in the slow cooker, Emmy was in her little car pulling onto the lane. Just as she got to the end of the lane, Russell, in his grey sports car, was heading the other way. Emmy squeezed her car into a spot on the left so he could pass. She smiled, nodded, and raised her right hand in a little waving gesture, hoping he would get the message that she didn't want to stop and chat. He didn't. She could already see him smarming through her window. Russell clearly wanted to seize the opportunity to talk, and so he positioned his car so that Emmy had little choice but to roll down her window and speak to him. Thoughts of the look on Peaches' assistant Gemma's face went through Emmy's mind as she pressed the button on her door and plastered her work smile on her face. Her work smile was pleasant enough; it said I'm professional and helpful, but you don't know me in the slightest. Russell didn't give a stuff about what sort of smile Emmy was displaying. He was too concerned with the smarm he was laying on thick.

As Emmy looked out of her car window and into Russell's car, she took him in as he revelled in the sound of his own voice. She'd seen his sort in many different guises many times before. The fast, very expensive car, the designer logo on the sunnies, the I'm-just-back-from-Marbella (or some Spanish coastal resort that was just as tacky) tan. All of it making him assume he was so much more important than anyone else. It made Emmy cringe.

'Hi,' Emmy said brightly, pointedly not using Russell's name.

'Hi, Emmy,' Russell drawled. 'How are you? I've been meaning to stop in and say hello.'

I'd really rather you didn't, Emmy thought. *Please don't bother.* She kept her voice high and happy. 'Ahh.'

'I've heard you've been importing some VIPs to Darling and bringing them to your little shop.' Russell was doing a very good job of being condescending about The Old Ticket Office. He enunciated the word 'little' with a horrid tone.

Emmy pretended she didn't know what Russell was talking about. Of course, he was referring to Peaches. 'Sorry?'

'Peaches and her entourage. One of the most famous accounts on Instagram, no less.'

Emmy wasn't surprised that Russell knew who Peaches was. He struck her as the sort that would be all over the Gram like a rash. 'Oh, yes.'

'Hitting the big time, are we?'

Emmy wanted to tell Russell to get lost or words to that effect. 'Ha!'

'I met the assistant in the lane. Nice girl. Loved chatting to her.'

Emmy stopped her face from snarling. Gemma hadn't liked chatting to him, that she was certain about. Emmy cut the conversation dead. 'Look, sorry, Russell. I must get off. I'm running a bit late for something.'

Russell nodded. 'Sure. See you around then. I'll stop by.'

Emmy made a non-committal sound and smiled as Russell inched his car past and flashed a very white megawatt smile in her direction. He made Emmy's stomach turn. She shook her head as she pulled back out and made her way in the direction of the ferry. Who even let him on Darling Island in the first place? He definitely shouldn't have been granted a resident pass, that was for sure.

E mmy balanced a tray laden with chicken soup, French bread, and lemon barley cordial in her hands as she nudged the sitting room door in Katy's flat open with her hip. 'Knock knock. Room service is here,' she joked.

Cocooned in a nest of blankets and pillows on the sofa, Katy, with a pale face, looked up from her phone and smiled. 'Thanks, Ems. Homemade soup – I must be sick.'

'Made with my fair hands. How are you feeling?'

'Not too bad. Look at you being all domestic, bringing me lunch. I knew you saw me at the train station that day for a reason – bringing me soup and looking after me when I'm not well.'

Emmy placed the tray carefully on the coffee table and then pulled the table over towards Katy. 'How's the pain?'

'Not as bad as I thought, actually. I haven't even taken anything since this time yesterday.'

Katy winced slightly as she adjusted the pillows propping her up. Emmy could tell by Katy's careful and guarded movements that she was putting on a brave face.

'Good.'

'I feel like I've been through the wringer a bit, but I'm glad to be home. The worst of it is over, by the looks of it.'

Emmy sat on the other end of the sofa. 'It makes a huge difference being home. You're on the mend now, hopefully.'

'Yeah, I'll be up and about properly soon. I'm not the best patient while stuck recuperating, but I'm forcing myself not to do anything much.'

Emmy chuckled. 'Ahh, yep, trust me though, if anyone offers to wait on you hand and foot, take it.'

Katy laughed as she shuffled up the sofa and leant forward to the soup and bread. 'I don't have a lot of offers on the table,' Katy said as her phone pinged. She read a message as she dipped a piece of French bread in her soup. 'Elodie's dad is going to have her again this evening. He's going to come around here after he picks her up and then take her back to his house.'

'It's all worked out well then.'

'Yeah, much easier than I thought it was going to be. I suppose that's because I've recovered quickly. Plus, Elodie's weekday routine hasn't really changed much. She's just staying at his more.'

'You're a trooper,' Emmy replied. She thought for a second how strange it was to be sitting with Katy in Katy's sitting room after having made her soup and chatting away. She was so happy to have Katy back in her life, and now Amy was in the know, too.

As if reading her thoughts, Katy brought Amy up. 'So, now we're all back in contact.'

'Yep.'

'How was that?'

'What?'

'Telling her.'

Emmy went to say 'fine' but changed her mind. 'She was shocked and surprised.'

'Yeah, she said in her text message.'

'How do you feel about it?' Emmy asked, not sure if she wanted to know the answer or not.

'I don't know, really. Emotional.'

'Me too.'

'Yep,' Katy agreed with a nod.

'Probs not the best time to talk about it,' Emmy noted.

Katy chuckled. 'I've felt better. No time is a good time to talk about it, though.'

'I guess not.'

'At least she knows now. I know I asked a lot initially by telling you to keep it a secret. I can see it must have been hard for you not to tell her,' Katy admitted.

'I'm a big girl.'

'Ha.' Katy rolled her eyes.

'One day at a time. I'm just glad we're together again, sort of.'

Katy smiled but looked a bit weary. 'She said she wants to meet up.'

'Yep, when you're up to it.'

'We'll arrange something when I'm back up and about, shall we? Get a date put in the diary.'

Emmy was surprised that Katy was willing to put a mark in the ground. She didn't want to make too much of it, though. She tried to keep her body language and her voice casual. 'Yeah, sounds good to me.'

Once Katy had finished the soup, Emmy tidied the kitchen, put the plates in the dishwasher, and sorted another tray so all Katy would have to do was put a bowl in the microwave later. She gazed out Katy's kitchen window and thought about Katy and Amy meeting up and the fact that there was a date being talked about for the three of them to get together. It seemed like things were on the mend. It felt strange picturing the three of them together getting on normally after so long. Maybe they could finally move forward. Hopefully, the Bardots were on their way to being back together. She could but wait and see.

27

Emmy moved through the familiar same old same old at work, smiling and making polite small talk on autopilot. Nod, smile, deal, nod, smile, deal. She dealt with a woman who was asking why she had to queue up and couldn't go right through, and a man who was not happy because he hadn't bought the drinks package because he'd thought that alcohol was included. Emmy stopped herself from saying 'boo hoo', smiled, and ploughed on through it all with her work face on. Usually, at the port, as the day unfolded, she got lost in other people's problems; today, not so much. Her thoughts were tangled up in the conversation a few days before with Tom about Katy, Amy, and Emmy being back in touch but their mum and dad not knowing. Tom's approach had been direct and to the point. What he'd said had pushed her buttons.

As she assisted with scanning tickets and answered mundane questions, she mulled over his blunt assessment of the situation with Katy. Had she really been enabling Katy by keeping her mum in the dark? Emmy flinched to herself and shook her head. Sighing as she deliberated, she plastered a cheerful smile back on her face as the next passenger approached the counter waving a large bottle of vodka in her direction. Her own problems played second fiddle at the port. *Here we go,* she thought to herself as the vodka was plonked down with a bang in front of her. She'd seen it all before. Nod, smile, and deal.

During a brief lull between customers, Emmy's thoughts inevitably spiralled back to the situation. The more she mulled it over, the more she understood Tom's logic on a basic ethical level – given the magnitude of everything that had happened, and the fact that Katy had now had surgery too, excluding her mum seemed bottom line just wrong. It was all now beyond a joke.

There were other things to consider, though, things Tom knew nothing about and didn't understand. Namely, Katy's stubbornness and how her lingering hurt ran deep. Katy was prickly even mentioning Cherry, that's how much what had happened in the past affected her. Emmy had only just managed to carefully foster trust between them again herself, and now an Amy meeting was on the cards. One wrong move and the whole tower of cards would fall in a heap, and Katy would be off.

Emmy chewed her lower lip and sighed out through her nose. The facts of the matter were that Emmy felt torn equally in both directions. She wanted to understand Katy, but she hated deceiving their mum. It was as simple and cut and dried as that. As she mulled it over and thought about what she was going to do, no path looked pleasant; all of them looked fraught with all manner of dramas.

Rubbing the crease between her eyes, which now felt as if it had become permanent, Emmy weighed both sides again and again. Was she enabling Katy? Was Katy out of order? What was the right thing to do? As Tom had pointed out – how would she feel if it was Callum? She knew she'd feel *really* upset. In fact, she didn't even want to think about something of the same ilk happening with her and Callum.

Emmy sighed, shoulders slumping. It wasn't that hard to

work out; she realised Tom's assessment was pretty much bang on if you looked at it without any emotion. But old grudges and disgruntled family blood ran oh-so deep. Had Emmy been so focused on 'keeping the peace' in the short term she'd lost sight of things? Possibly. Had she not had the gumption to get stuff out in the open? Definitely.

She sighed for about the hundredth time. As she'd thought many times before, there was a part of her that wished Katy would just put up and shut up. Couldn't headstrong Katy just chuck it behind her and get on with it? Shouldn't reconnecting their family take priority? Clearly not.

Emmy weighed it all up as she went around in circles and filed through grumbling passengers and problems. Despite her mental distraction with the Katy thing, there was one problem after another, and the rest of Emmy's shift passed in a bit of a hectic blur. As it often did, the more she got into it, the more the mindless routine of assisting travellers and answering questions settled her thoughts. She found herself naturally compartmentalising like a pro and forced herself not to think about anything else. Instead, she maintained a professional demeanour on the surface and let everything else frantically paddle in the turbulent waters underneath. Oh yes, Emmy Bardot was the epitome of calm and collected on the surface. From the outside, it looked as if she had her act together and then some. Internally, she flapped around like a headless chicken running around without a clue what was going on.

By the time she got back to her car at the end of the double shift, hung her uniform jacket on the little hook on the handle in the back, and got in the driver's seat, she was mentally wrecked and physically exhausted. She shivered at how cold it was in the car, whacked on the heater to full, pressed the heated seat, and pulled out of the car park in a hurry to get home.

Her dashboard lit up with a call from Tom, almost as if he'd known she'd been both thinking about him most of the day and that she was on her way home.

'Hey. How are you?' Tom asked.

Emmy pretended she was a lot happier than she actually was. She made her voice chirpy and bright. 'Good. Really good. How are you?'

'Great. Rough day or good day?'

'Oh yeah, fine. Just a regular old day. Can't wait to get home. It's so cold!'

'I just got home. It was freezing on the ferry.'

'Lucky. I wish someone could pod me to Darling in an instant. I cannot wait to get home and get my soft clothes on.'

'Yeah. Tell me about it.' Tom's voice changed and got more serious. 'Look, I wanted to apologise about before.'

Emmy wrinkled up her nose. She pretended she didn't know what Tom meant, as if she was all breezy and nonchalant and hadn't been thinking about his blunt assessment of her predicament all day. As if she was totally fine. 'Sorry? What do you mean? Apologise about what?'

'The Katy thing. I was out of line the other day. I've been thinking it over.'

Emmy continued to act as if she hadn't been dissecting his words to within an inch of their life the whole day. She waved off the unnecessary apology. 'Don't be silly, you were only trying to help. All good. It's good for me to talk about it, anyway.'

'Yeah, I was possibly a bit blunt. I've been thinking about it on and off.'

Not as much as me, mate, that I know for sure. 'It's fine.'

'I shouldn't have said anything,' Tom said, the regret in his voice palpable.

'Actually, it's good to get different perspectives,' Emmy stated breezily.

'Whatever you decide, I'm behind you one hundred per cent.'

'You're not going to dump me this time?' Emmy giggled, breaking the serious atmosphere.

'I don't think so,' Tom fired back. 'If you're careful.'

Emmy continued with the banter. 'Even though I'm ethically unsound?'

Tom didn't really laugh. 'Yeah, sorry about that.'

'You were right about needing to tell Mum now Amy knows. Keeping things from her feels more and more wrong the longer this goes on. Something has to give.'

'That can't have been an easy conclusion to come to, considering what Katy has said.'

'I just hope Katy will understand when I tell Mum.'

'Give her time. Once the anger fades, she'll see you were only trying to help.'

Emmy nodded, hopeful at Tom's optimism. Tom, though, did not know her mum underneath. He hadn't seen the half of what Cherry was like. She knew the conversation with her mum would be more than agonising. Cherry Bardot was not going to take the fact that Emmy had been outright lying for ages well. Plus, she'd told Amy first. Her mum would also be *furious* about that. Cherry Bardot always liked to be in charge.

Tom swiftly segwayed into a different subject. 'Anyway, change of subject. I thought you might be up for some comfort food and another brainstorming session tonight. We'll make an actual plan for the influencer stuff - you need to get a plan together and get it sorted before the cocktail thing. Fancy that, or are you too shattered?'

Emmy was glad to talk about *anything* other than the Katy problem. 'You know how to woo a girl.'

'Ha! I thought you liked me being CEO of Love Emmy x?'

'Of course. I was joking. I need to get the influencer thing lined up in time for the party or even before, yeah, you're right. The timing couldn't be better, really.'

'I'll bring a bottle of wine and a bolognese, shall I?'

'Your offerings just keep on getting better,' Emmy joked. 'That sounds perfect. You know how to wine me and dine me.'

'See you soon then.'

'Yep, can't wait to get home.'

Emmy kept her eyes fixed ahead, watching as a car in front of her made a dangerous right turn. She shifted in her seat and thought about Katy, her mum, Amy, Callum, and her dad. Time for push to come to shove and see where it all ended up. Hopefully, she wouldn't be in a heap under it all on the floor.

28

A few days or so later, nothing had changed, and Emmy picked at her salad in the canteen at work. She gazed blankly out the rain-streaked windows and thought more about her conundrum. The sky full of grey clouds and dreary drizzle matched her brooding mood perfectly. To be quite honest, she was sick and tired of the whole thing but couldn't get it to leave her head. She needed a shock of electricity to zap the whole blasted thing away and let her get back to her life.

Jessie breezed over to the table she always sat at with a tray in her hand and a beam on her face. 'Hiya! How are you?'

Emmy let a cherry tomato roll off her fork untouched, and she made a funny face. Jessie's eyes narrowed. 'That good, eh? What's occurring?'

'Ahh, nothing. I'm fine.'

'Any passengers waving bottles of vodka at you this morning? Lost passports left on trains?'

Emmy shook her head. 'Nope. Give it time.'

'Everything okay?'

'Oh, yeah, all good. I just have a lot spinning around today. More of the same I was telling you about before.'

Jessie nodded. 'The stuff with your sister?'

Emmy faltered slightly. 'Yep. It all feels impossible either way.'

'Nightmare.'

'Everything has become such a mess. I feel so trapped, keeping secrets from Mum. Now Amy knows it feels *much* worse, not better. Katy made me swear not to tell.'

'What's Amy said?'

'Just that Mum is going to be really upset and that she's not happy to be in cahoots about it.'

Emmy summarised what had been going on, including Katy's health and how firmly Katy still refused any reconciliation with Cherry and that Katy and Amy were planning on meeting up.

'Really tricky one,' Jessie sympathised.

Emmy nodded miserably. 'Exactly. I just don't know what to do.'

'What about Tom? What does he think?'

'Yeah. We had a tense talk about it. He thinks it's time Mum knew. He said it maybe felt like I was enabling Katy being in control of the situation by complying with what she wants to happen. As if I have no choice in the matter and it's all up to her.'

'He has a point,' Jessie said bluntly.

'I know, but that annoyed me too! Ahh, nightmare! And I can see his point, yep, even though I hate feeling judged for how I've handled things.'

Jessie mulled over the quandary. 'I don't think either of you is necessarily right or wrong here.'

'Maybe.'

'Thing is, you know your family best. Deep down, go with your gut.'

Emmy nodded. 'Yeah. You're absolutely right. I've got myself so tangled up trying to over-analyse every angle that I've lost sight of going with what I actually think.'

Jessie smiled. 'It'll all work out on the wash as they say.'

'Thanks, I hope so. That's what I started off telling myself at the beginning of all this.'

Glancing at the time, Emmy pushed back her chair and gathered up her tray and phone. 'Well, back to it then.'

'Good luck with it all.'

'Thanks.'

That evening, Emmy collapsed onto the sofa, emotionally exhausted. Between fretting over Katy and stewing about telling their mum, she felt completely and utterly drained.

Tom came out of the kitchen with two mugs of tea and joined her on the sofa. 'Rough day?' he asked, handing her a mug.

'My head is spinning. I talked to Jessie at work about it,' Emmy said and then proceeded to fill Tom in on Jessie's view and advice that Emmy should trust her gut.

Tom nodded. 'She made a good point. At the end of the day, only you can decide what feels right, though.'

Emmy sighed. 'I know, I just feel so torn. I hate lying and sneaking around with Mum.'

'Understandable,' Tom said. 'There's no easy answer.'

'I'm starting to think you are right, though. I need to rip the plaster off and just tell Mum. Keeping this secret is eating away at me.'

'You just need to stop dicking around and making excuses. It's getting boring.'

Emmy's eyebrows shot to the top of her head. 'Ever the voice of reason.'

'The voice of reason? That's a new one for me. I've been called much, much worse.'

29

Emmy propped open the shop's back door, letting fresh air blast through the storeroom. With her hands on her hips, she surveyed the space critically. While it was far from a mess, it was a tad on the cluttered side, and unlike its counterpart on the other side of the wall, it was hardly aesthetically pleasing for the social media queens of the world. Time for that to change. Her dad was on his way to help out with her vision to transform the space for the influencer workshop that was being planned since the brainstorming sessions. She'd not hit go on publishing the event yet, but the digital media side of it was ready. All she had to do was get the actual space spick and span. She and her dad had a lot of work on their plate. It was a daunting task, and to be quite honest, Emmy was in two minds whether or not to push on through with it, but it had been Bob who had been full of enthusiasm that had fuelled her on. He'd given her a little bit of a poke to continue stoking the fire of her small business dream. As usual in her life, Bob had been on the sidelines cheering her all the way.

Emmy stood still for a second and assessed the room. It had the bones alright; it just needed a lot of sprucing up; some of the old filing units from its insurance days still stood in situ, there were the odd few piles of paperwork here and there, and plastic tubs were stacked neatly full of Emmy's curated jewellery, and the little kitchen area wasn't that pretty. Though it was a work-space, overall it was a bit of a wasted, under-utilised space, and despite not having a whole lot of energy for the project, Emmy knew once it was finished, it would give her another string to her bow. She just needed a whole lot of energy to crack on and be done with it, which is where, as per usual, Bob came in.

Hearing the back gate open, she made her way outside to find Bob strolling down the path laden with paint tins and drop cloths. Bob's smile lifted Emmy's spirits immediately. 'Hi Dad, how are you?' She leant up on tiptoes to kiss his cheek.

'Good, darling. How was your week?'

'Long one at the port.'

'I bet.'

'Keeps me with a roof over my head, as they say. I'm grateful for a job, right.' Emmy gestured to the old building, 'It means I get to work on my dream.'

'I should say so. Never be afraid of hard work and dreams, Ems. That's what I always say, as you well know.'

'Nope. Right, well, seeing as you are looking full of beans, let's get this sad little storeroom looking shipshape,' Emmy said with a laugh.

'Aye, aye, captain,' Bob said and gave her a salute.

When they got inside the back door, Bob put his stuff down and stood for a second beside Emmy. He sucked air in through his teeth and winced a little bit. 'Well, as we said when you first moved in. It's definitely got potential.'

Emmy laughed. 'That's one diplomatic way to put it.' She tapped a neat stack of huge plastic tubs on the right. 'Watch your step back here. Don't want you crushed by an avalanche of Love Emmy x specials.'

Bob peered around. 'It reminds me of when you first moved

in. Where shall we start?'

'Umm, probably clearing those rickety old cabinets along the back wall first. Then we'll actually have space to work. I know we should have done it in the first place, but the front was a lot more important then.'

'Ahh, yep, and you wanted to get the shop open.' Bob rubbed his chin. 'It won't take long. It looks a lot worse than it is, in actual fact. Rome wasn't built in a day, Ems. One step at a time and we'll get there.'

'I blimming well hope so, Dad.'

Bob chuckled. 'Let's get to it then. The quicker we start, the quicker it'll be done.'

They started to carefully shift an old filing cabinet away from the wall, and as it rattled, Emmy remembered the furry guests she'd seen on her first night in the flat. 'You don't think there will be anything horrible behind here, do you?'

Bob shook his head. 'Hopefully, you saw the back of them but you never do know in these old buildings.'

'The pest control people said these places down this end of Darling are riddled with them, though.'

'Prepare yourself then.' Bob chuckled.

'Ugh, I do not need rodent houseguests.' Emmy shivered dramatically. 'Let's get this over with.'

Once the old cabinets had been hauled outside via a lot of pushing and shoving, Emmy and her dad stood surveying the space anew. The absence of the old insurance office furnishings made the room feel airier, but it needed a lot of love. Bob ran a hand over the wall in front of them. 'I'll just give the walls a good scrub before I prime and paint. That way, the fresh coat will really pop.'

'You sure? Or how about we just whack it on?'

Bob chuckled. 'There's a lot of old dust in these walls. The paint will go on better after a wash, or yeah, we just prime over the top of it and bodge it.'

Emmy started to slide the enormous plastic tubs full of her stock into the centre of the room. 'You're the expert.'

Bob hefted brushes and rollers out of a box. 'Ems, I was joking. I'm not a bodger. I'm going to clean them first. It won't take long. It will really freshen the old place up. Get those windows propped open, too.'

As Bob gave the walls a vigorous scouring, Emmy sorted through various boxes that had made their way into the store-room when the shop opening had been her top priority. She tucked inventory back away in the tubs and swept dust from the floor where the filing cabinets had stood.

Humming along to the radio with her dad, she was glad he'd pushed her to get stuck in. As she sorted and cleaned, her mind only wandered occasionally as to what to do about Katy. She was grateful for the distraction. By late afternoon, they'd cracked on. As was usual around her mum and dad, Emmy had wondered where Bob quite got his energy from. He was perched on the top of a ladder, reaching up to cut in along the ceiling edges with a trim brush. Emmy brought down a cup of tea from the flat and stood admiring how the primer was already changing the place.

'It's already looking so much cleaner and brighter in here. I can actually visualise it as a real workspace now.'

'Amazing what a little love can do, eh? This room was just crying out for it.'

'Yeah, thanks for this, Dad. Your pushing has made me get on with it. I was dreading it, to be quite frank.'

Bob winked. 'I'm your dad, that's my job.'

Emmy ducked her head as Bob came down so that she could hide a sudden prick of tears at the corner of her eyes. Bob was black and white about helping her, always had been. Here she was avoiding the truth left, right, and centre, and Bob was blindly helping her to follow *her* dream. The horrid tormenting guilt reared its ugly head yet again.

Oblivious to what was going on in Emmy's head, Bob took his mug of tea, and Emmy fussed around as if she was fine when she really wasn't. A few hours later, Emmy stood looking up at the freshly painted workshop wall and assessed their progress. The previously gloomy stockroom had been utterly transformed thanks to her dad's efforts. As was usual in her life, her dad had come up trumps.

Bob stepped back as well, rolling his shoulders before glancing around approvingly. 'Well, I'd say this space has officially been brought back to life.'

'It looks incredible, Dad. Seriously, thank you so much for all your help today. I really didn't fancy it, and you just got on with it.'

'Anytime, kiddo. You know I love tackling projects together, even though I'm a bit slow these days. Knee replacements do that for you.'

Emmy swatted Bob's arm. 'Oh please, you've had more energy than me all day! I should be thanking you for keeping me on my toes.'

Bob chuckled. 'Not for much longer. I need to put my feet up.'

'We need another tea.'

'Always time for tea with one of my girls.'

Emmy's eyes suddenly stung with tears. She managed a jerky nod, unable to trust her voice. She had to look away under the pretence of tidying a paint tin to hide her abrupt wave of emotion. She didn't know what was wrong with her, but things were coming to a head.

Oblivious, Bob just carried on. 'You've really made this little place your own, Ems. You should be so proud.' He gestured around. 'I always knew you'd get out of that mess you-know-who left you in. It's just taken a bit of time.'

A lump lodged in Emmy's throat. She blinked fiercely and didn't say anything.

Bob seemed to pick up that Emmy was emotional. 'Sorry, didn't mean to get all mushy on you but, well, you know.'

'No, no, it's okay. I just wasn't expecting you to say that. Just blame Kevin, eh?'

'Always,' Bob bantered. 'I really love that we're doing this together,' Bob stated. 'It's been great seeing how it's all come together.'

'Yep, me too.' All of a sudden, Emmy knew it was time. *No more lying.* She couldn't take it a second longer. She turned her head to the right and thought for a bit. 'Dad, I've got something to tell you.'

Bob frowned. 'Like what? Something happened with Tom?'

Emmy bit her lower lip. Where to even begin unravelling the whole story? 'No, not at all.' *A Tom problem would have been a whole lot easier to deal with,* she thought. 'I, err...'

Bob's eyebrows raised. 'Has he asked you to marry him? Blimey, that's a bit sudden!'

'Gosh, no! I don't want that anyway!'

'What's up then?'

Emmy blurted it out as quick as a flash. 'It's Katy.'

Bob went very still across the room. Emmy forced herself to continue. 'I've been in contact with her.' Emmy's voice cracked.

Bob stayed where he was. 'Right.' He studied Emmy for a moment and shook his head.

Emmy held her breath as she watched the play of emotions flit across her dad's face – confusion, hurt, disbelief. 'Katy? As in, your sister who up and left years ago, that Katy?'

Emmy nodded. 'I know this is a *massive* shock. And I'm so sorry I didn't tell you and Mum sooner.'

Bob just stared blankly, clearly struggling to absorb the bolt from the blue. Emmy heard herself babbling. 'I randomly spotted her at the train station months back, and we reconnected. She swore me to secrecy while she figured things out. But keeping it from you and Mum has been eating away at me.'

Bob sank heavily onto a nearby stool, shaking his head over and over again. 'Blimey, Emmy, this is the absolute last thing I expected to hear today.' He raked a hand over his head, looking shell-shocked.

'I know. I'm sorry.'

'I don't even know what to say or what to ask.'

'It's complicated. She's been through a lot.'

Bob stared at the floor, looking gutted. 'She's not the only one.'

'Yeah, I know. She's going through something now, too.'

Bob narrowed his eyes. 'What do you mean? Is she alright?'

'She's had some health issues come up recently. Fibroids that needed surgery.'

Bob exhaled heavily and leant back against the wall as if the wind had been knocked out of him. 'Ames? Does she know?'

Emmy nodded solemnly. 'She does now. They haven't met but we're planning it now.'

For a long, tense moment, Bob just sat silently processing it all. He swore under his breath. 'Your mum will be devastated you've been in contact and that Katy talks to you and not us.' He shook his head, looking *very* troubled.

Emmy's eyes welled up. 'I'm so sorry I didn't tell you and Mum sooner.'

'I don't know what to say.'

'Mum is going to be so angry.'

Bob exhaled heavily again. 'It won't be easy, that's for certain.'

'The thing is. Katy still doesn't want to know us, I mean, she doesn't want to be involved in the family,' Emmy said, stumbling over her words and not making much sense. She didn't want to say that Katy wasn't interested in talking to either Bob or Cherry. 'What is Mum going to say? She's going to be furious.'

Bob thought for a bit. 'Leave your mum to me.'

'What do you mean?' Emmy had already mentally prepared

for the inevitable blow-up with her mum. She'd played out the various scenarios in her head, bracing herself for the bomb going off. Both of them knew what Cherry was like when things didn't go her way.

Bob screwed up his lips. His voice sounded strange, like Emmy had never heard it before. 'I'll deal with your mum. She's not behaving like she usually does about stuff like this.'

Emmy was surprised, to say the least. Bob mostly toed the line where Cherry was concerned, just as they all did. Emmy was completely and utterly wrong-footed by Bob's out-of-character adamant tone. 'Okay.'

Bob squinted. 'So hang on, how did you meet up? On a train, you said?'

'No, I saw her from a train window when I had to go and get that helmet for cricket all that time ago. Remember that?'

'Wow. Right.'

'So now we all know except Mum,' Emmy stated.

Bob shook his head and rolled his eyes. 'Christ alive.'

'What happens next?'

'I don't know. I'll think about it for a week or two...' Bob said noncommittally.

'Oh, okay, right, yes, I thought you'd want to tell her straight away.'

'It's been years, Ems. You really think a week is going to make much difference now?'

Emmy nodded. 'I suppose not.'

Seeing her dad's face made Emmy feel a trillion times worse. She now wished she'd not told him. His reaction was very odd and the same as Amy's had been. It was different from how Emmy had imagined. Both of them had been more shocked and surprised than angry. Emmy knew one thing for sure – she'd opened the can of worms, and they were now relishing in wriggling all over her head.

30

Emmy was all over the show after the fallout from the day before telling Bob about Katy. She didn't really know what to think. She *did* know she felt both worse and better at the same time, so that was weird. So many conflicting feelings all at once. After dealing with it all for a long time, it felt odd that now Tom, Amy, and her dad all knew. Only the most important person left to go. Yikes.

Thinking of her mum made the guilt slam through Emmy's body at a million miles an hour again as she stood in the yard. She grimaced as she looked around at the backyard. Her mum had been there right by her side, helping and planning its makeover, whilst Emmy had lied the whole time.

It was cold and foggy in the yard, but thanks to Cherry and elbow grease, it was looking so much better it was barely even recognisable. The moss, which had more or less covered everything as far as the eye could see, was mostly gone. No doubt it would creep back in with the cold, but it no longer covered a vast majority of the area. All along the back, hanging baskets full of pansies cheered; the window boxes, which had been wonky and full of weeds, now danced with greenery and winter colour. The shed, though, was the main show-stopper. It, too, like the rest of the place, had been well overdue for some love. Now it was duck egg blue, its door was now back in place, fairy lights ran around the gutter, pots stood on either side of the door, and there was even a mat to welcome anyone who might be passing. The beds down the side of the path were weed-free and full of healthy-looking shrubs, and there was even a little seating area with its own chiminea in situ. Not that Emmy had found the time to sit by the chiminea with marshmallows, but give her time.

She smiled as she heard a car pull up in the lane, and as she made her way to the gate, Tom came through from the other side. He held up a white paper bag in one hand and had two coffees balanced in the other.

Emmy didn't feel very smiley. 'Hi.'

'Blimey. What's happened to you?' Tom joked. 'Some strange sort of mid-life crisis by the looks of it.'

'Life crisis more like,' Emmy replied with a frown.

'Now what?'

'Dad knows.'

Tom swore. 'Now we're in trouble.'

'Tell me about it.'

Tom handed Emmy her coffee and looked around at the yard. 'At least the yard looks good before the going got tough.'

Emmy chuckled. 'I know. It does look better.'

'That's an understatement. Amazing what a bit of hard work and thought does, right?'

'Yep.'

'Cinnamon buns right out of the oven, pretty much. Are you warm enough to sit out here?'

'Brr. Just.'

'I think you need what is commonly referred to as a patio heater out here.' Tom looked up at the wall above the back door to the shop. 'One of those slimline ones there should do it.'

'You've done enough for me,' Emmy said as she plonked herself down on an outdoor chair by the wall in the corner.

'So, the lovely Bob knows. How?'

'When he was helping with the storeroom. I just couldn't stand it any longer. The same as what happened with Amy pretty much. It all came to a head.'

'How was he?'

Emmy grimaced and screwed her face up. 'Yeah, strange and very surprised. Like not as I was expecting. Not at all.'

'Right. Not angry?'

'Not really.'

'I suppose it would have been both a shock *and* a surprise.'

'Yeah.'

'So, he's going to tell your mum, is he?'

'Not yet, no.'

Tom's eyebrows shot to the top of his head. 'What? When then?'

'The whole thing was out of character. He said he wanted to think it over for a bit. He said he needed some time.'

'Fair enough, I suppose. It's completely out of the blue.'

'Yeah, I guess so. I don't know. No wonder I look like I'm having a life crisis. I'd sort of imagined all kinds of different scenarios when they found out. Him being like this wasn't one of them.'

'What do you mean?'

'For a start, he wasn't angry, not really, anyway. He kept saying that he would deal with Mum. That in itself is not like him. You know what he's like.'

'That *is* strange from what I've seen of him so far. He's so easy-going...'

'I know. Precisely. So goodness knows what's going to happen next.'

'How long did he say he was going to think about it for?'

'He wasn't sure. He noted that a few more weeks after all this time wouldn't make much difference.'

'I suppose that's true to be fair. So you'll now just have to wait and see.'

'I know.'

Tom raised his eyebrows and widened his eyes. 'I'll provide the popcorn.'

31

Trying to only concentrate on her business and nothing else, and now that the storeroom was done, Emmy sat looking at the landing page she'd created for the exclusive influencer workshop she and Tom had originally brainstormed. She'd optimistically set the ticket cap at twenty-five, hoping demand would be high, but wasn't really sure what to expect. After tweaking it way too many times, changing things completely on the template, and then going back to the one she'd started with in the first place, she made another graphic for her socials. Her Love Emmy x Instagram account had really grown since the Peaches episode, and she was trying to milk it for all it was worth. She had her fingers crossed that other influencers would take up her workshop event and be just as smitten with Love Emmy x as Peaches had been. All of it was very much the unknown.

She posted, sent a message to Amy to tell her to have a look and sat and waited. Five minutes went by. Nothing. Knowing she was being completely ridiculous expecting anything right away, she sat with her chin on her hand and tapped her phone repeatedly to refresh. Not a sausage. She was learning that the small business game was a strange, sometimes exhilarating, but mostly quite scary one. She'd also learnt, more through luck than judgement, that hard work and slow and steady won the race. Tucking her phone in her pocket and closing her laptop, she went to the shop window and continued with her earmarked job for the day, a total redressing of the window display. With a podcast playing in her ears, she got lost in the world of small independent silversmiths and fussed for ages with lovely new necklaces she'd commissioned until they were just right and forgot about the influencer workshop completely.

After finishing the display and packing up a few orders, she put a load of parcels in the basket of her bike, wheeled it along through the yard, hopped on, and cycled along the lane. Weaving in and out of the back lanes of Darling, she tried not to think about anything; not that Bob now knew about Katy and that her phone would ring from her mum any second, not that the influencer event would be a dud, or that, as usual in her life, she would mess everything up.

She stopped at the post office, chatted to Xian from the bakery, who was in the queue in front of her with a gigantic parcel she was sending to Vietnam, and then made her way to Darlings. Once she'd locked her bike in the bike rack, settled in a seat in the corner window seat in Darlings, and had a lunch basket and a milky coffee in a bowl in front of her, she slipped her phone out of her pocket. Forcing herself not to look at the event page, she scrolled through the news, perusing the latest happenings in the world. As she was shaking her head in sadness at a news article whereby an ambulance had been caught up in an accident, Amy's name went across the top of her phone. Emmy shuddered and closed her eyes. She'd been waiting for the bomb to erupt with her mum. This might be it. Emmy blinked hard, trying to clear her head before answering.

'Hello?' Emmy said and waited for the fallout. It didn't come.

'Ems!' Amy squealed. 'Go you! Have you seen your Instagram? How are you breathing?'

Emmy frowned. 'What?'

'I wondered why you hadn't messaged me again, that's why I called. Instagram! Peaches has tagged your event. It's sold out!'

'What the?'

'I know!'

Emmy fumbled to open the app and navigated to Peaches' grid. As Amy had said, the workshop invite Emmy had designed was reposted to Peaches' stories and her grid and her millions of followers.

The caption read simply, *'Don't miss this exclusive workshop with my new fav @LoveEmmyx Limited tix, so grab yours quick... these won't last long, I'm sure.'*

Stunned and surprised, Emmy scrolled the likes and comments. Holding her breath, she tapped back over to the workshop ticketing page. Her jaw actually dropped; the ticket remaining counter was red. Her event was already sold out.

'Oh my gosh!' Emmy said.

'Unreal!'

Emmy shook her head. The power of social media. It had taken mere minutes after Peaches' endorsement for the event to completely sell out. It was only twenty-five tickets, but still. Emmy sank weakly back in her chair, a tad on the overwhelmed side, and sort of scared at the same time as feeling ecstatic.

A slightly hysterical laugh bubbled up. 'When I posted it early this morning, there wasn't even a single like. I put my phone away and forced myself not to look at it.'

'Well, you've well and truly sold out. No going back now.'

Emmy felt adrenaline zooming around her body. 'This is big.'

'You *so* deserve this moment, Ems.'

Emmy just kept shaking her head as she held her phone out in front of her and continued to watch the likes and comments on Peaches' post. 'Do I?' She swore. 'Just hoping I can live up to the hype now,' she joked weakly.

'Are you joking? They're going to be obsessed with every-thing, just like Peaches was.'

'I hope so.'

'This is just the beginning, trust me.'

'Well, I had better get planning then so I don't disappoint!'

'Yep, I need to go, too. Just wanted to make sure you'd seen it. See you later.'

Emmy was still floating on cloud nine later that evening as she sat at Tom's kitchen island and recounted the whole story. 'I honestly can't believe the workshop sold out just like that in minutes,' she kept repeating.

'Well, you'd better get used to it, because it looks as if Peaches is happy to give you free shoutouts left, right, and centre. What a person to have in your corner, eh?'

'I legitimately can't believe it sold out just like that.'

'You need to get the power of Peaches on speed dial from here on out,' Tom joked.

'I know, it's just unreal. That one mention from her is worth its weight in gold in terms of exposure.'

'Absolutely. You need to run with it.'

'Yeah, I need to stop second-guessing myself and just fully throw myself into planning. This has to be really good for Love Emmy x.'

'It is.'

'I've so much to sort out for the event. I'll have to make up things for them when they arrive, with a little Love Emmy x item inside,' she mused. 'Don't they call it swag or something?'

'Not a clue. The last time I went to a conference, I got a free pen. Does that count?' Tom laughed. 'I don't suppose these influencers, with the gilded life, would settle for a plastic pen, would they?'

Emmy laughed. 'I'm sure they expect more than a pen.'

'Yup.'

'I need to give them the full 'influencer experience', Emmy said as she Googled how to create an influencer event and scrolled. 'I looked at loads of these sites before when I was doing the invite and sorting out the date. Apparently, it's a good idea to do an Instagrammable backdrop for selfies…'

Tom raised an eyebrow. 'A backdrop, really?'

Emmy nodded as she squidged up her mouth, frowned, and continued to read the article on influencer events and how to make the best of them. 'Apparently, they practically breathe hashtags and filters. You need to do stuff to make their followers green with envy.'

'Just shove them in the shop and storeroom, surely? That's what you did with Peaches. The shop is the backdrop. Pop the harpist in the corner…'

Emmy put her phone down. 'Duh. Of course.'

'Just call me your marketing exec.'

'I need them to *rave* about Love Emmy x.'

'You'll pull it off. I'll be your assistant,' Tom joked. 'If I'm there, they'll stay.'

Tom might have been joking, but she loved that he was both interested and supportive. It meant the world to Emmy. She was also not stupid; there would be an influencer or two who wouldn't mind exploring the world of Tom P Carter, of that, she had no doubt. 'I'll have you working into the early hours. No breaks, sick pay or any support are offered by the employer. No flexibility either and definitely no working from home.'

'What about my workers' rights?'

'Not available at Love Emmy x. Take it or leave it.'

'I like it when you crack the whip, Ems.'

Emmy laughed and then sighed. This latest Peaches thing

was surprising and astounding. Love Emmy x was doing better than she'd ever hoped. Not only that, she and Tom were good. Plus, Callum was doing okay. Overall, most things were going well. All she had to do now was sort out the mess in her family, and all would be right in the world.

32

Emmy walked from her car across the car park and made her way to the port terminal. She'd followed her usual routine of getting dressed at home after a shower, doing her hair and make-up in the car, and going through the motions of her routine on autopilot. Unfortunately, autopilot had not reached her brain, which hadn't stopped thinking about the fact that her dad now knew about Katy but that Katy did not know that their dad knew. She presumed her mum didn't yet know either. Tom knew all of it, too, so there was that as well, and Callum didn't have a clue any of it was going on, or so she assumed. Complicated. Overall, Emmy felt like absolute crap.

A biting wind blew leaves around the car park tarmac, and thick grey clouds zoomed overhead, threatening rain and a miserable day. Emmy tightened her huge scarf around her neck and stuffed her hands in her pockets. Just as she was getting to the inner gate, she saw Jessie coming the other way. Jessie, in a gigantic black coat, scarf, and beanie, and with her coat hood up over the beanie, waved a gloved hand. 'Hi stranger. How are you? Brrr! How cold is it?'

'Good. I haven't seen you for ages. How was the holiday?'

Emmy asked. Jessie pulled her hood down, and Emmy took in her tanned face. 'Jealous! I can see by your face that you had a nice time.'

Jessie sighed. 'I so did! Take me back. It was more than brilliant. I'm counting down the days to the next one.'

'Ooh, nice,' Emmy replied with an envious but happy sigh.

'How are you? Good? How's the shop? What's the goss?'

'Great, actually. Really good. I have loads to fill you in about that.'

'Like what?'

'Like the fact that my own event sold out because of Peaches doing another post.'

'Blimey! She sure does like you. So the event sold out? Wow?'

Emmy flicked her hand. 'Yep, loads to tell you about that.'

'What about all that stuff with your sister? How's she doing with the fibroids now? All recovered? What about the family dramas you've been having? Where was I up to in the saga?' Jessie joked.

Emmy let out a huge sigh. 'Oh gosh, do you really want to know?'

Jessie laughed. 'Sounds ominous. What's the latest?'

'Well, how long have you got? My dad knows, Amy knows, Tom knows, but Mum does *not* know at the moment. Oh and Amy, Katy and I are meeting up.'

Jessie pursed her lips. 'Ooh, really? Right. Yikes.'

'I know.'

'How did all that come about then?' Jessie asked as she flipped her hood back up and shoved her hands in her pockets against the wind.

'You knew about Amy, right?'

'Yeah, but your dad? When did you tell him?'

'I just blurted it out all of a sudden, exactly the same as what happened with Amy. I didn't even mean to. It was when we were doing the storeroom makeover.'

Jessie's eyes widened as she took a packet of Polos out of her pocket and offered one to Emmy. 'How did that go down? What did he say?'

Emmy took a Polo and popped it into her mouth. 'The whole thing was quite bizarre. I thought he was going to be concerned about Mum. It was surprising.'

'Right, and he wasn't?'

'Not as much as I thought. Mostly, he was shocked. He said he'd deal with it.' Emmy shook her head as if trying to understand it herself. 'All quite strange.'

'Interesting,' Jessie said as they arrived at the terminal, and she put her bag out for a security check.

'Yup,' Emmy replied as she followed suit.

'So, now what?'

'So, now I don't know. I've been waiting for a call or something, but nothing so far.'

'Right. Does your sister know your dad knows? Katy, I mean.'

'Nooooooo!'

'Oh.'

'Yes, you are right. I do move from one secret to the next,' Emmy said at the same time as shaking her head.

'Your life is nothing but interesting,' Jessie noted with a chuckle.

'Tell me about it.'

Jessie checked her watch. 'Time for a quick coffee?'

Emmy looked at the time on her phone. 'Just.'

They made their way to the canteen and continued to chat. As they walked in, a din of conversations and clatter of cutlery enveloped them as Jessie started to peel off layers of clothing. Emmy continued to fill Jessie in on the latest developments. 'So now my dad knows I've been in touch with Katy again, but Mum and Katy herself are still completely oblivious.'

Jessie laughed. 'It's like one of those little wooden dolls.

What are they called? Yeah, matryoshka dolls. Your doll keeps opening up with layers of secrets and surprises.'

'I know, right? It's why you should never lie. Tom did say this ages ago. He's clearly one step ahead of me.'

Jessie was sympathetic. 'Blimey, no wonder you look ready to keel over. This leading a double life lark…'

Emmy sighed. 'You've no idea.' Emmy actually felt something like an over-inflated balloon. She was constantly one pinprick away from completely popping and losing the plot. The question was: who was going to be the person to stab her in the side?

Jessie took a sip of her coffee. 'Complicated, that's what families are. They always are, and it doesn't matter what walk of life you are from. I mean, look at that lot in the palace. That didn't end well.'

Emmy chuckled. 'We've got nothing on them when you say it like that.'

'Nup. It makes you feel better, actually. Everyone is in the same boat. So now what?'

'I mean, where do I even go from here? Everything is such a mess.'

Jessie stirred sugar into a latte. 'At least your dad seems to have taken it surprisingly well, all things considered.' Jessie nodded, turning her lips upside down and making a funny face. 'Could have been a lot worse if you ask me.'

'I know. I was braced for him to freak out. But telling Mum is going to be the real explosion, no question. At least, I thought that was the case, but it seems he's going to deal with it.' Emmy checked her watch with a groan. 'Anyway, enough about my melodrama for now. I need to start heading in before I'm late.'

As they began gathering their things, Jessie laughed. 'Chin up. You'll muddle through.'

'I hope so. I just have to keep reminding myself I didn't cause this problem in the first place.'

Jessie chucked. 'Nah, you just made it much worse.'

Emmy tutted as she walked to the briefing room. She'd weathered worse storms in her life, she told herself. When she'd first been on her own with Callum, little parts of her had felt desperate; that had been the pits. Nothing could be worse than that. Now, at least, she'd told people the secret that had been eating her up inside. That made a little bit of a difference. Things were moving in the right direction. She hoped.

33

It was a few days or so later and Emmy had been run off her feet all day in the shop. She loved the days she spent all day long chatting to customers and doing her jewellery thing. She was good at it; she knew her stuff, and it was obvious to all and sundry that she was in her element when surrounded by sparkly things. She hummed under her breath as she tidied up the shop for closing, looking forward to an evening at home doing absolutely zilch. Her feet needed to be well and truly up. As she put things away and closed her laptop, her phone began buzzing in her pocket. Assuming it was Callum who was at Kevin's, she pulled it out and was surprised to see a call from her dad. Her dad was not one for phone calls. Text messages, the shorter, the better, had been invented for him. She grimaced, knowing it would be about her mum, swiped, and put her phone to her ear bracing herself.

'Hey, Dad, everything okay?' She didn't even bother to sound breezy. Her voice was loaded with concern.

An ominous pause came from the other end. 'Hey, Ems. Look, I'm going to tell Mum.'

Emmy's pulse raced. She plonked herself down near the ticket counter. 'Yep.'

Bob sighed heavily. 'I've spent ages thinking about it and I've mulled it over, and I'm going to tell her.'

Emmy blinked. 'Okay, yes.'

'As I said, I'll deal with it, but we really should work out how and when and what to do about Katy.'

'Yep.' A dozen emotions swirled through Emmy – most of them dread. She cradled the phone closer to her ear. 'How do you think Mum will take it?'

There was another heavy sigh. 'She'll be very upset, of course. Hurt that it was kept from her for so long. The thing is, as I said, I've said all along that, well, actually, let's not get into that.'

Emmy wasn't sure what her dad was trying to say. He wasn't making much sense. 'Sorry?'

'I'm not letting your mum do her usual thing with this. We've *all* suffered because of it.'

Emmy shook her head. *What the?* 'Have we?'

Bob sounded weird to Emmy. She'd never heard his voice sound as it did. It surprised her. 'I knew it at the time, too. She always wanted you girls to be a certain...' Bob stopped in his tracks. 'Anyway, sorry, yeah, Katy was always a bit different. She wasn't going to follow anyone's path.'

Emmy was gobsmacked both at Bob sounding quite incoherent and that he was saying things she hadn't heard before, as if he'd never really agreed with what had happened with Katy in the first place. She was surprised, to say the least. 'Sorry, you're not making much sense, Dad.'

'Yeah, sorry Ems, I'm not sure why I'm calling...' Bob let the sentence trail.

Emmy didn't know what to say or really what Bob was saying. 'Right.'

'The time has come for me to put my foot down about all of

this. I never had my say...' Bob trailed off again as if lost in his own thoughts.

Emmy could almost hear her mum's agitated voice at Bob speaking up. 'I see.'

'I'm going to say my piece.'

'Sorry. I should have told her myself from the start,' Emmy said miserably. 'I'm so sorry.'

'Not your fault.'

Emmy bit her lip hard. Right from the start, she'd hated lying. Knowing her mum, she just didn't see how it was going to end well, and Bob's attitude had totally thrown her, too. 'Okay.'

As if reading her thoughts, her dad added, 'I've spent years toeing the line, Emmy. Time for that to change. It's been a very long time coming. Very long.'

Emmy nodded mutely, alarmed and surprised at Bob's voice. She didn't know what to think, and she certainly didn't know what to say. 'Okay. Thanks.'

After mumbling some vague reply, Emmy ended the call. She'd been prepared for her mum to be upset and furious. She'd been prepared for Bob to be cross. She'd not been prepared for Bob to say he was putting his foot down and for the whole thing to be going down a path she'd not even imagined. It was almost as if he was a completely different person from the one she knew. Stranger things happened at sea.

However confident Bob thought he was in dealing with it, though, Emmy wasn't quite so sure. There was also the fact that she had to tell Katy. But the thought of voicing the whole messy truth and dissecting what they were going to do made her shake her head. She didn't have the energy, the inclination, or the mental capacity. She'd leave it for a bit. Deal with it the next day. She'd said that too many times before.

34

Emmy hurried along the pavement with her phone to her ear. She'd just had a text from Callum to tell her he'd changed his plans and was not staying with Kevin but at a friend's. All of Emmy's mum radars went off at once, not believing him in the slightest. She called Callum, but it went straight to voicemail; she then messaged him again. After calling him and then messaging with a threat, she'd finally spoken to him, told him there was no way he was staying with a random friend she'd never even heard of, and told him Kevin was picking him up.

She'd then phoned Kevin, listened as he'd warbled on about his latest money woes, wondered if he was gambling again, decided she didn't care, told him to ensure he was on time to collect Callum, and got off the phone before Kevin could say much more at all. She hurried along the pavement towards a florist on the corner of the road with her work lanyard swinging around her neck. Her car keys jangled, her heels clipped along the pavement, and she grasped her iPad in her left arm. Emmy was busy and late because she'd had to cover for someone at work; her feet ached, her brain fizzed, and part of her wondered what she was doing with her life altogether.

She stopped for a second and gazed at the beautiful florist just up the road from Amy's house. The storefront wore oversized, galvanised planters overflowing with blooms, shelves lining the walls held hessian-wrapped potted plants, and buckets filled with fresh flowers stood in clusters, each with little handwritten tags. Emmy loved the little florist and often stopped on the way to Amy's to pick up a bunch of flowers. She stood for a bit and just stared at the bouquets for a second and tried to forget her day and the not-so-joyful joys of parenting a teenage boy. Callum was pushing his boundaries, and she wasn't particularly enjoying it. She took a deep breath, plucked a bunch of pale pink flowers from the centre of the jumble of posies, inwardly gasped at the price, and bustled through the door and into the shop.

After paying, she hurried back down the road, flowers in hand, on her way to Amy's house where Amy was home alone, and the pair of them were looking forward to a bottle of wine and a pizza delivery. Though Emmy was looking forward to unwinding with her sister, her frustration with Callum still simmered, and she was concerned about Bob. She couldn't stop replaying her terse conversation with Callum in her mind. He was pushing her buttons big time, and dopey Kevin wasn't helping matters either. As she approached Amy's front door, she took a big, deep breath in. All she wanted to do was sit, relax, and enjoy a night with Amy without *any* hassles.

She pushed her finger into the bell, and a second later, Amy appeared at the door in soft grey joggers, a matching grey sweatshirt, fluffy slippers, and her hair up. Emmy couldn't wait to get her work uniform off and do the same.

'So glad you're here. Did you get stuck in traffic?' Amy said as Emmy stepped in.

Emmy felt herself instantly begin to unwind as the smell of

Amy's house hit her. 'Not too bad. I had to stay a bit to cover for someone, and I've been dealing with Callum apparently staying over at a friend's I've never heard of.'

Amy laughed. 'Just blame Kevin.'

'Check. Already done that.'

Emmy put her huge tote bag over the bannister, slipped off her shoes by the mat at the front door, and handed Amy the flowers. 'Ahh, so happy to have finished those shifts. Where is everyone?'

'At their grandma's, as planned. We have peace and quiet.' Amy jerked her thumb up the stairs. 'Everything is ready for you up there in the spare room: clean tracksuit on the bed, etcetera. I left that new conditioner I was telling you about in the bathroom. Looks like you need a shower and a glass of wine.'

'I so do,' Emmy said and joked. 'Do I really look that bad?'

'Yep. You do. You need sister therapy and not your other sister, me. Ha ha!'

Twenty or so minutes later, Emmy's damp hair was twisted up on top of her head, she had a soft white tracksuit of her sister's on, and she was more than ready to relax. The house felt calm and quiet. Amy ushered her into the sitting room. 'Wine or tea first?'

'Wine, definitely wine,' said Emmy emphatically, collapsing onto the sofa.

Amy laughed as she poured them each a glass of white, handed Emmy one, and settled comfortably into the armchair across from Emmy, tucking her feet beneath her. 'Alright, out with it. What's Callum done now?' Amy asked, sipping her wine.

Emmy recounted the last-minute change of plans and Callum dodging her calls. 'He's testing his limits lately, seeing what he can get away with. It's like I'm constantly worried.'

'Part of the territory, I suppose. He's good overall. What more can you ask for?'

'He is. I know,' Emmy said as she sipped her wine. 'Right, enough about my drama! How's your week been?'

As Amy launched into a story about her new yoga class, Emmy settled into the sofa cushions and felt more content than she had for a while as she just listened to her sister chat. The cosy room, the soft clothes, and letting someone else be in charge soothed her work week edges. Amy's house was beautifully decorated, tidy, clean, and somehow like slipping on a favourite old jumper. It was warm, familiar, comforting, and had seen her through a crisis or sixty-five.

By their second glass of wine and the arrival of the pizza, Amy had launched onto the topic of their dad knowing about Katy. Amy put her wineglass down and picked up a piece of pizza. 'So, a bit of a turn-up for the books. You suddenly just blurted it out to him?'

Emmy sighed. 'Exactly.'

'How did that happen?'

'I don't know is the honest answer. It was the same as with you. I couldn't stand it anymore.'

'How was he?'

'Odd. Very odd. Surprising.'

'You said that on the phone. What do you mean?'

'Like not what I would have thought. As I told you, he said he would *deal* with Mum.'

Amy's eyes went wide. 'That just doesn't sound like Dad. *Deal* with her?'

Emmy took a long sip of wine before responding. 'I know. That's what totally threw me. I was gearing up for a lecture, but instead, he was oddly calm about her. It was so out of character.'

Emmy recounted her phone conversation with Bob in full detail. She'd already told Amy the conversation over the phone, but face-to-face, she went into a lot more detail. 'I was sure he was going to blow up at me, but he just seemed sort of calmly weird.'

Amy shook her head in disbelief. 'That's *so* unlike him. He's normally very defensive over family. Remember how he reacted when all that stuff was happening?'

Emmy grimaced at the memory. 'Don't remind me. So that's why this calm reaction threw me. Maybe he's mellowing with age?'

'Or feeling guilty,' Amy suggested. 'Didn't Katy say about how it's always Mum's way, blah, blah, blah. Maybe Dad's had enough of that. I'm not siding with anyone, but Katy does have a point.'

Emmy nodded. 'She definitely said that. Who knows what Dad really thinks?'

Amy took a bite of pizza. 'I wonder if Dad feels bad about how things went down with Katy? Maybe he regrets not doing more to keep her around? She needed help. Who knows?'

'Possibly,' Emmy mused. 'When I said we'd been talking, he looked sad, almost. He kept muttering about how families should stick together. I've never heard his voice sound like that.'

Amy nodded. 'Makes sense. Still, weird he didn't say much about you going behind Mum's back.'

Emmy felt a prickle of unease at Amy saying she'd gone behind her mum's back. It felt horrible for it to be spelt out in black and white. 'That's what worries me. Whatever he says, she's going to lose it when she finds out about me and Katy. I'm just waiting for the phone to ring.'

'Nothing new there then,' said Amy ruefully.

'I should have just told everyone in the first place,' Emmy said, putting her wine glass down and rubbing her temples. 'I don't know what I was thinking.'

'Don't beat yourself up about it. Too late now. It will all work itself out.'

'I know, but I hate feeling like I've created more family drama.'

'We're the Bardots. We thrive on drama.' Amy laughed.

'Don't say that.'

'Just blame Kevin.' Amy giggled.

'This is one thing I actually *can't* blame him for.'

'There's no point dwelling on it now. What's done is done. We'll deal with Mum's reaction if and when it happens. You're going to have to give Katy a heads-up. Then there's the whole you, me and Katy meeting up.'

'Let's not talk about it,' Emmy said. 'I just want to chill.' She'd deal with the fallout when it happened.

By the time the pizza was finished, Emmy was feeling the wine – she'd not eaten much all day, and it had gone straight to her head. She tried and failed to stifle a hiccup, which made Amy burst out laughing.

'We need water.'

'And bed. I need to go to bed and sleep.'

'Yeah, same. I'll make a cup of tea, and then we'll hit the sack.'

Half an hour or so later, Emmy was sitting up in bed in Amy's spare room waiting for a text from Kevin. Once he'd replied that Callum was safe and sound and she'd also had a goodnight text from Tom, she sat for a while just staring out the window down into Amy's garden. She watched as an egg chair hanging from a tree swung back and forth in the wind, and the leaves on the trees lining the back fence fluttered. Loads of things ran through her mind as she stared – Callum, her dad, her day at work, the Love Emmy x influencer event, a dress for the cocktail party or lack thereof. She then thought about Katy and the conversation with Amy about their dad and how the situation was going to resolve itself.

The thing Amy didn't quite yet grasp was that from what Emmy'd seen so far from Katy, nothing was going to change, despite what anyone thought. Emmy had a suspicious feeling that Katy wouldn't be changing how she felt about their parents anytime soon. Katy was just as headstrong as she'd always been, but now she was also different: more grown up, more educated, more independent, more articulate, and *definitely* happier. She'd made her own way in the world, was doing well, and carried with her a strange sort of confidence that she didn't want her mum involved in her life. Emmy winced at the thought that she and Amy were going to be the ones to deal with the fallout from that.

35

A couple of days later, Emmy smiled at someone she recognised from the ferry who cycled away from Darlings café on their bike and waved to her. She'd picked up her iPad at home, put it in her bag, dropped off a couple of parcels at the post office, and was on her way to Darlings for a morning basket and a coffee. It couldn't have come soon enough after a busy few days. From the road, Emmy hustled along with her chin tucked in her scarf – on the freezing cold day, Darlings was looking very inviting. With a nippy wind biting at her cheeks, a warm orange glow came from the little bow window at the front of the café. The tables outside were empty, wind blew leaves around underneath, and even though it was the middle of the morning, the coach light by the front door was lit. Emmy had really come to love Darlings. It felt like a little bit of escapism away from the humdrum and bustle of her real life. She'd go in, make herself comfortable, wait to see what arrived in a basket and feel herself almost slip on down into another world. She'd got to know Lucie, who worked in Darlings part-time, and the owner, Evie, who seemed to know everyone and was always whizzing here, there, and everywhere and doing six things at once.

Emmy pushed the door open and stood for a second on the mat and just looked around. The decor was so good, and now Emmy, with her new shopkeeper eyes, knew why. It was because the whole place simply said, come on in, sit down, spend a bit of time with us, take the weight off your feet, and chill out. The little tables and smiles from the staff felt a bit like the feeling at the end of the day when you got home – all of it a bit of a jumble, the light soft and glowing, the chatter low, a clink here and there of cutlery and china.

Emmy appreciated how hard that whole little scenario was to pull off. She knew only too well how much hard work would have been put in behind the scenes to make Darlings lovely. Because of her experience in dressing up The Old Ticket Office and making it work, she knew that Darlings, its decor and how it was run, had been thought through to within an inch of its life. Every single thing was just nice and just right.

Evie smiled and waved from behind the counter at the far end and pointed to a table right in the corner by the window. Emmy gave her a quick thumbs up and shimmied her way in and out of tables until she got to the table Evie had gestured to. Emmy took out her iPad, hung her jacket and her bag on the back of the chair, and kept her scarf around her neck. A couple of minutes later, Evie zoomed over and said hello.

Evie beamed. 'How are you?'

'Good, good. What about you?'

'Great, actually, thanks. Tom said your sister wasn't well?' Evie frowned.

'Ahh, yep, she's fine now. She went in for surgery for fibroids.'

'Oh right.'

'Nothing too serious, though the operation was actually

quite a big one. She's done well, though. Yeah, she's on the mend.'

'Good to hear. Yep, Tom came in and said you were making chicken soup to take around there.'

'Yep, that's right. It went down well,' Emmy joked. 'I've done something right.'

'How's the shop?'

'Really good, actually.' Emmy held her iPad up. 'I brought this with me to check a few figures and such.'

Evie shook her head. 'Goodness, I forgot to say! Peaches came in here and gave the place a shout-out. Did you see?'

Emmy looked surprised. 'What? No! I didn't see that!'

'Yeah, on her stories. I've had loads of DMs about baskets. She showcased one of them saying they were recyclable and such a good idea. You have to laugh.'

'Blimey, her reach is far and wide. Oh, great, I'm pleased to hear you got some of the Peaches' love. Darling is getting it left, right, and centre from her.'

'I know. We should be very honoured. Right, what can I get you? Basket? Coffee?'

Emmy basked a little bit and loved that she was now treated like a true Darling-ite. No questions, just that she'd be delivered a basket and a bowl. Worked for her. A few minutes later, a small white basket with a blue and white napkin was in front of her. She picked up the pretty coffee bowl and examined the navy blue and white Paisley pattern on the side, took a little sip, and felt herself instantly relax. She dipped into the gingham napkin and smiled at the regular fare she'd come to expect in a Darlings morning basket; on the left, a stack of what looked like homemade biscuits sat next to a mini croissant. A little ceramic dish held a thick pat of yellow butter, and there was a small made-for-one pot of jam. Emmy, now used to the odd combinations sometimes found in the baskets, picked up one of the biscuits, decided that the butter was meant to be spread on top of it, did so, and popped a bit into her mouth. Oh yes. Evie, as usual, was a pro and the biscuit and butter combo was a dream. Emmy had never in her life had what was, by the taste of it, a homemade digestive, but she'd be finding it hard to go back to one bought from Sainsbury's ever again.

A few minutes later, Evie zipped past. As she did so, she raised her eyebrows. Emmy picked up one of the biscuits and nodded enthusiastically. Evie laughed. 'You like?'

'Where in the world did you get these? What even are they?'

Evie tapped the side of her nose and chuckled. 'Classified information. I cannot possibly divulge.'

'Ha.'

Evie stopped at Emmy's table. 'You went to Lovely Bay, didn't you? Tom said Holly recommended it to you as well.'

'Yeah, we went for a day out not long ago.'

'Yep, I did too. These are from that shop in the main street there,' Evie explained.

Emmy turned her mouth upside down. 'I don't think we came across that shop. I thought it was all about the secret chowder in Lovely Bay.'

'Yeah, it sells all sorts of baked goods and stuff. We had a cup of tea in there, and once I tasted one of the biscuits, I got a job lot of them for here. There were loads of different ones. I got chatting to the owner. Really nice woman.'

'Right. Well, I need to buy a load of them too. They're outstanding.'

'I know. How nice are they?'

Emmy shook her head. 'The butter too, though, right?'

'Yeah, totally makes it. If I had a pound for everyone who has said the same thing as you...'

'You'd be rich.'

'I would indeed.'

About twenty minutes later, Emmy had thoroughly enjoyed nearly all the biscuits and had received a top up of coffee. She had an organisation document open on her phone for the influencer session at Love Emmy x.

Since the tickets had sold out quickly because of Peaches' shout-out, she'd had to get her act together without too much mucking around. She'd sourced pretty earrings as a gift for each attendee. Lucie, who she knew from Darlings, had handmade individual fabric bags, and she'd ordered a whole ream of new foliage and greenery to go in the flower installation around the front for an exclusive winter theme for the influencers to use as a backdrop. From a standing start, the influencer event was not only sold out but ready to go. It was all lined up to take place the weekend after the cocktail party, and Emmy had made up enough goodie bags and bits and bobs to add in a few extra social media queens she might meet at the cocktail party.

As she sat lost in a world of her own with her hands cupped around the little coffee bowl and gazed out the window of Darlings, she felt quite pleased with herself at a few things in her life. Yes, there was the whole family drama sizzling away on the sidelines, and goodness only knew what was going to happen when her mum found out, but at the end of the day, she could cope with that. Overall, things were not bad; she was doing okay, thank you very much. She'd gone and moved herself and Callum to Darling Island, and it had turned out to be one of the better choices she'd ever made in her life.

36

Later that day, Emmy was in a clothes shop and not in a good mood. She rifled through yet another rack of dresses, her frustration mounting by the millisecond. She'd already been to four different boutiques searching for the perfect dress, or really any dress, to wear to the influencer cocktail event. In fact, she'd graduated from searching for a perfect dress to any item of clothing whatsoever that didn't make her feel either four hundred years old or resembling a pudding or perhaps a deflated vanilla soufflé or any combination of all three. Attractive was not a feeling that could be attached to the way she felt.

Shoving aside a glittery sequinned number that resembled a disco ball, she huffed out an irritated breath. Dress shopping and outfits for special occasions had never really been her forte. Why was it so difficult? Why were the mirrors so bad? Why were the floors always covered in dust bunnies? Why in the name of goodness did the curtains never ever close properly? She was beginning to feel like the dowdy, ugly stepsister trying to pull together a look glamorous enough for a ball she wasn't even that sure she wanted to go to.

'How are you getting on?' a perky sales assistant called out from her pew behind the sales desk for the second time. 'Seen anything you like?'

Emmy resisted the urge to snap. Since when had clothes shops started employing people younger than her son? The poor girl was only doing her job when she wasn't head glued to her phone. Emmy swallowed her irritation. 'Thanks. Not yet, unfortunately.'

'Feel free to take your time browsing.' The girl flashed a smile showing impossibly white teeth, ignored a pile of jumpers and a shelf full of jumbled mess right in front of her, and dipped her head back to her phone.

Emmy idly shuffled through a few more options half-heartedly. Deciding that she'd have a go at anything, she selected several dresses to try, none of which had jumped out at her. She lugged the hangers to the fitting room past the salesgirl, who was now draping herself over the counter, beside another girl doing the same thing. Both had their phones in their hands and heads down, completely oblivious to anyone in the shop. Emmy was glad they didn't notice her as she struggled to shimmy around three open cardboard boxes blocking the corridor and had to tug at a curtain to pull it open. The dresses draped on the less-than-clean floor, and Emmy took a deep breath to steady herself.

She wrestled her way into the first dress, a black halter style that she hoped somehow might slice off a few pounds. That was a joke and a half. As she struggled with the zip and then turned to the mirror, she nearly cried. It had not sliced off anything. The dress, whose label told her it was very expensive, didn't live up to the price tag hanging from its neck. It looked cheap, nasty, and clung to everything. Every little lump, bump, and curve showed. The Darlings baskets she'd indulged in that morning said hello from somewhere in her middle region.

Emmy's heart sank down to the floor and made acquaintance with the dust bunnies. The Emmy staring back at her from the mirror wasn't quite the person she'd imagined in her mind going to the cocktail party. She sucked air in with a gigantic inhale, turned sideways, and winced. Dreadful. Hopeless even. Sighing, she shimmied her way out of the dress and forced herself to move on to the next option.

With the next dress finally over her shoulders, she hesitated again, sucked everything in before fully facing the mirror and braced herself. Her shoulders may have slumped at what looked back at her in the mirror. A V-neck gaped awkwardly, and the calf-length skirt with a side slit brought stumpy legs to mind. Emmy pressed both her palms to her flushed cheeks and let out a dramatic sigh. She'd picked out dresses she normally wouldn't have touched with a barge pole, hoping she might be surprised. She was surprised, alright, and not in a good way.

'Everything good in there?' the salesgirl called out.

Emmy tutted quietly to herself. The young salesgirl was the last thing she needed at this point in the manoeuvre. She turned her back on the dreadful mirror. 'Yes, fine, thanks.' It wasn't, and *she* wasn't anywhere near fine. 'I'll try on one more, but I'm not having much luck.'

Emmy was relieved to hear the salesgirl's footsteps retreat back out into the shop. The last thing she wanted was any help. She scrunched her eyes shut, told herself to get it together, and struggled out of the dress. As she put it back on the hanger, she reminded herself that it was just a dress and what she looked like was a first-world problem. But she kept thinking about all the polished, airbrushed industry influencers who would be strutting around at the party. She would not only be mingling with them, but hoping they would buy into her and Love Emmy x. She *needed* to look the part.

She swallowed down her spiralling self-doubt and wrestled her way into the final option – a shimmery champagne-coloured gown with duchess vibes. She held her breath, turned to the mirror, and looked so bad it was comical. Rather than weep, she burst out laughing at the image in the mirror. Clearly, the dress had been designed by someone who didn't know a real body. Possibly if it was being worn by someone tall and willowy, it *might* have worked. But for someone short-ish and with a few extra pounds normally very cleverly concealed around the middle, it did not even remotely work.

She took the dress off and decided there was no point and that she was in the wrong shop. Forcing the issue was only going to make her feel a million times worse. She took the defeat on the chin, pulled her clothes back on, and redid her hair. She picked up the rejected dresses, fought with the dreadful too narrow curtain for a second and stepped out of the fitting room.

The salesgirl looked up from her phone with a half-interested look on her face. 'No luck?'

I need a lot more than luck after what just happened in there. 'Thanks, but no.' Emmy went to hand the girl the dresses, but the girl went straight back to her phone. Emmy was left holding the dresses up in the air. She looked around the shop and decided that there was no way she was going to put them back on their racks and do the girl's job for her. She laid all three of the dresses on the counter. The girl dragged herself from her phone screen, lazily pushed herself up, and tutted that Emmy had given her something to do. Emmy turned on her heel and made her way out of the shop.

Well, she'd learnt one thing, and that was that the whole episode had been a horrid, deflating experience. As she walked along, she shook her head. No wonder there were influencers all over the internet gushing and whatnot about how wonderful Love Emmy x was. The whole customer experience Emmy had just received compared to what she had created at The Old Ticket Office was like chalk and cheese. She may not have a dress to wear to the cocktail event, but she'd had a very important lesson in shopkeeping and how *not* to do it. She tucked the information into her head, glad to see the back of the shop, and vowed never to enter it again.

E mmy fished her phone out of her handbag as she stomped towards the car park, the image of herself squeezed into the hideous dresses made for willowy mannequins still fresh in her mind. She jabbed at Amy's name on the screen. Amy picked up, and Emmy launched straight into it. 'You will not believe the disaster I've just had trying to find a blimming dress for this influencer thing. God, it was soul-destroying. Awful!'

'Oh no, what happened?'

'Where do I even start? I've been to four shops now and it's been a nightmare from start to finish. Nothing has fit right, the selection has been rubbish, and the sales staff look like I could have given birth to them. Honestly, I don't know how some of these places stay in business.' Emmy moaned and word-vomited the whole horrible trip and details of her frustrating time as she walked to her car. She described how she'd thought she would be clever and try something different. She whinged about how expensive everything was and how the disco ball number had made her look like a glittery sausage, and the cheap feeling but very expensive black halter dress had clung to every lump and bump and anything else that it could find.

'It couldn't have been that bad. Surely?' Amy ventured.

'*Worse* than bad. I'm not sure I can go.' Emmy totally dramatised. 'The last one was the worst. It was some champagne-coloured monstrosity that must have been designed for a super-model because it just hung off me like a sack but a badly fitting sack. I'm telling you, Ames, it was *bad*. I burst out laughing, looking at myself in the mirror because it was so comical how terrible I looked.'

Amy made sympathetic noises on the other end of the line. 'Sounds like a disaster.'

'At this point, I'm ready to give up and just wear a bin bag,' Emmy said glumly. 'I don't even know why I'm bothering with this cocktail party thing anyway. It's not really my scene, is it? I might not go.'

'Too right, it's your scene!' Amy said firmly. 'You've worked your bottom off with Love Emmy x, and you deserve this. You're going, the end.'

Emmy smiled. 'My confidence has taken a knocking. When did I turn into someone lumpy, old and haggard?'

Amy laughed out loud. 'You're not haggard! I get it, I really do. What are your plans for the rest of the day?'

'I'm just getting in the car now. I'm working on the online store and then I'll have a look at a few dresses, I suppose. At least I'll be able to cry into my own mirror if I do it at home.'

'You know how much I love me a bit of online shopping. I'll put together a little list for you. I'll WhatsApp them over so you can have a proper browse from the comfort of your sofa.'

'You're a star. That might help. Thanks.' The thought of tackling dress shopping from her sofa made Emmy feel slightly better. 'Lucky I've got you.'

'Go home, make a cup of tea, and put your feet up. Ames to the rescue. By the way, anything on Dad?'

'No, nothing, you?'

'Nup. Okay, touch base later.'

'Will do.'

Emmy tutted as she got to her car. What an absolute debacle and complete and utter waste of time the dress-shopping expedition had been. She should have asked Amy in the first place. Amy was good at dress shopping and dressing up to the nines.

Once home, Emmy left her shoes in the storeroom, so glad to be home it was untrue. She called out hello to Callum and flicked the button on the kettle before she'd even taken her coat off. She then headed upstairs to her room, had a shower, and changed into comfy joggers and an oversized jumper. Catching a glimpse of herself in the mirror, Emmy paused. The oversized jumper and joggers looked a whole lot better than any of the dresses, that she knew for free.

'So much more me,' she muttered to herself. Perhaps that was the root of it all – trying to squeeze herself into things that just weren't her cup of tea in the first place. She should have stuck to her guns: little black dress and Love Emmy x jewellery.

Feeling much better, she wandered back downstairs to the kitchen, made herself and Callum a cup of tea, toasted two slices of bread, slathered on a load of butter, topped it with Marmite, and delivered it to Callum in his room. With her cup of tea in hand, she curled up in the corner of the sofa and scrolled through her phone, skimming work emails and confirming an upcoming online meeting.

As she sat and decompressed, the familiar sounds of the flat, the trams outside, and the little comforts of home worked their magic. Emmy ever-so-slowly felt her stress over dress-gate ebbing away. Curled on the sofa in her comfies, she sat drinking her tea and spent a productive hour tidying up her inbox and reviewing the latest sales figures. She shook her head at her numbers – she might have a long way to go, might not have a dress for the influencer event, and she certainly had a few lumps and bumps, but since the Peaches thing, business was doing very well. The numbers were telling her in black and white that for the sake of Love Emmy x, she definitely needed to go to the cocktail event.

Just as she was finalising an email, her phone dinged with a WhatsApp message from Amy. She smiled as she scrolled down; there were about half a dozen dress options, along with a few notes. Amy had even colour-coded her recommendations into 'top tier,' 'possibles,' and 'maybes.' Emmy nodded and smiled. If there was one thing she knew, it was that she might be very good at jewellery, but Amy was a *master* at dressing up. She read Amy's bullet point notes – good cut, nothing too slim fitting on the tummy, fabrics that draped rather than clung, and highlighted Emmy's good bits, which according to Amy, were her shoulders, back, and clavicle.

Amy had sent a voice note telling Emmy to call as soon as she'd looked through them all so they could narrow it down together. Dress-gate wasn't going to win. Emmy Bardot was going to the ball.

37

Emmy had been in the shop all day. It had been long, productive, and full of sales. She wasn't going to argue with that. However, her feet ached, her temples seemed to thump of their own accord, and her neck was so tight it felt as if someone had actually pulled the muscles taut from above. She pottered around in the kitchen, clearing up after Callum had made himself a toasted sandwich, wiped down the surfaces, and sprayed the sink as she waited for Tom to arrive. Her mind raced about the conversation she'd had with her dad about her mum. Bob had finally told Cherry what had been going on. It had not gone down well. A Bardot earthquake had occurred.

Emmy kept glancing impatiently at her watch, desperate for Tom to arrive. Right on cue, she heard the gate to the lane clang open, the back door open, and heard his footsteps thudding up the stairs. Emmy rushed to the top of the stairs to see Tom with a beam on his face. In one hand, he had a bottle of wine, and in the other, a massive family-size bar of Dairy Milk. Emmy giggled in relief; bless him, he'd come prepared and had known exactly what she needed.

'You have supplies.' Emmy laughed, grabbing the chocolate

from him and ushering him in.

Tom kissed her on the cheek. 'How are you? You sounded really stressed on the phone. So your dad's told your mum. Wow. It's all out in the open now.'

Emmy put the wine in the fridge, filled the kettle, and swished out the teapot. 'I don't even know where to start.'

Tom sat down at the kitchen table. 'What happened? Is everyone okay?'

'Physically, yes. Emotionally... that's another story,' Emmy replied as she poured the water into the pot, stirred it, and put the lid on.

'So your mum knows now. It's been a long time coming. Thank goodness for that is all I can say.'

Emmy ripped open the Dairy Milk, broke off a huge piece, and continued, 'Yep. Apparently, she completely lost it. So much for Dad dealing with it.'

Tom's eyes widened. Emmy knew he'd only seen the lovely get-her-own-way side of her mum. Tom sounded surprised. 'Really?'

'Dad said it was okay at first, but then as she learnt more, she started shouting and slamming things.'

Tom frowned. 'That's not the Cherry I've seen. She's always so supportive and lovely to you.'

Emmy raised her eyebrows. 'Precisely. *To me*. Katy would say that's because I toe the line.'

'And Katy doesn't, I mean, *didn't?*'

'Nope. Anyway, Mum said to Dad that she'd tell Katy exactly what she thought of her for making me keep the secret. That's the way the conversation went.'

'So, what did your dad do?'

Emmy shook her head and frowned. 'That's the surprising part. He said he wasn't going to let Mum ruin this for me or Amy. That he would handle her and for me not to worry.'

Tom looked as shocked as Emmy had felt hearing her dad

sound so strangely firm. 'Wow. That's not like the Bob I've seen.'

'I know! My first thought was, who is this man, and what has he done with my dad?'

'Too funny.'

'The man I know does what he's told,' Emmy corrected herself. 'I don't mean that in a bad way, but, well, as you know, it's always really Mum who calls the shots.'

Tom shook his head. 'There must be more to this than you know.'

'He was *so* calm when he spoke to me. He kept repeating this wasn't good for any of us. That he wished he'd intervened sooner. He said Amy and I deserved to have our sister back, and he wouldn't let Mum ruin it.'

'Blimey, bit of a turn-up for the books.'

'Those were practically his exact words. I nearly dropped the phone.'

Tom let out a low whistle. 'What changed, do you think?'

'Guilt? Maybe he blames himself for how things went down with Katy back then.' Emmy shrugged. Emmy was confused by the whole thing. She'd wasted hours of her life feeling guilty and spending too long wondering what would happen. With her dad dealing with it, it had gone a completely different way to any of the scenarios she'd foreseen in her head.

'Could be guilt, yeah.'

'It's a bit late now. But still, better than nothing, I suppose.'

'So, has your mum called?'

'She texted. Amy and I have been summoned.'

'When? I'll make sure I'm out of the country.'

'Just waiting to see when Amy can do it.'

Tom swore and then joked, 'Will you need chaperoning?'

Emmy stuffed a huge piece of chocolate into her mouth. 'I'm not looking forward to the conversation with my mum.'

Tom joked, 'Nah. Don't blame you. I wouldn't even want to be a fly on the wall.'

38

Emmy and Tom had been on a bike ride around Darling, their destination being the old beach huts on the far side of the island. Lucie from Darlings had recommended them as a good spot to sit with a cup of tea on a windy day to blow away the cobwebs. It was certainly a windy day, and they had collected a couple of Darlings baskets on their way through to accompany the flask wedged in the front of Emmy's bike basket.

As they cycled along, Emmy could see the beach huts in the distance. She could make out their Darling Island blue and white colours and the requisite bunting flapping like crazy in the brisk, cold wind. After locking their bikes in the bike rack, they did exactly as Lucie had recommended and made for a bench slap bang in the middle of a long line of beach huts sheltered from the vast breeze coming in off the sea.

Emmy's cheeks were flushed from the wind, her nose felt cold, and her earlobes were chilly. She sighed as she walked along with the bike basket tucked into the crook of her arm 'Wow. She was right. What a lovely spot.'

Tom followed her gaze out to sea. 'No fog but a lot of wind.'

'Lucie said it would be sheltered and a good place for these,' Emmy replied, holding up the Darling Baskets.

'Yep. Good. I'm ravenous. I'm the one with the bike without the assistance of a battery.'

The wind whistled around them, and the sea crashed and banged on the shore as they made their way to the huts. Emmy stopped by a Municipality of Darling Community Noticeboard and perused the many notices neatly displayed behind glass doors. Darling was a hive of activity according to the community events – the Darling Variety Club (founded in 1982) was looking for new members for its Shakespearean performance, the Darling Horticultural Society was organising a coach trip to Lovely Bay, and a man named Ron had a 'Wanted' sign fixed right in the centre. Ron was on the lookout for a bandsaw, whatever that was. The Tuesday Art Group met on the second and fourth Tuesdays of the month from 2 to 4 pm in members' homes. The sign told Emmy that usually, there were three or four of them who could all paint a little and to bring your own ideas and paint in acrylics, pencils, and watercolours.

'Fancy joining the art group?' Tom asked with a chuckle.

Emmy shook her head. 'I'm just about able to draw a circle, so that's a no from me.' She paused for a second and pointed to the largest poster. 'But I *do* fancy that.'

Darling Twilight Markets are back. Come and join us for a drink and DJ's sausages (limited batch). Also on offer – Darling Bay Preserves (special marmalade on sale), Darlings will be providing food baskets (first come, first served), and Josie's eggs will be available (first in best dressed). All the usual stalls and raffles you know and love, including handmade cards, gifts, tombola, beer tent, Fleur and Follie homewares. Please drop donations in the hall foyer. From 5 pm at the Coronation Pier Village Hall. (Braziers on the beach, weather permitting.)

Emmy turned and looked up at Tom. 'Yes, I do very much fancy that. Have you been to it before?'

'Many a time with Leo and co. Not for a while, though.'

'Good?'

'Err, let's just say I may have rolled home once or twice.'

'That good, eh?'

'If it's not too cold.'

Emmy screwed her face up in question. 'Sorry, it's on the beach, is it? Surely it's not warm enough?'

'You'd be surprised, but it moves to inside the hall if the weather is terrible.'

'So what, there are braziers on the beach?'

'Yeah, and chairs and blankets. It's a funny old Darling thing.'

'I like the sound of it. How come I don't know about it?'

'Goodness knows. The posters are all over the ferry and the tram, and every other post on the community's Facebook page is about the market. It's like a Darling institution.'

'Right. Well, we're going,' Emmy said as she turned away from the board and headed to the bench.

'The brazier bit is sort of invite-only.'

'What?' Emmy frowned. 'It doesn't say that on there.'

'No, I know. It doesn't *say* that in black and white, but yeah, you don't go to that bit unless you're a resident and someone has to sort of ask you.'

Emmy didn't really understand. Tom wasn't making much sense. 'I wouldn't be invited?'

'No, no. *We* would. That bit is just for Darling-ites mostly. There's the market, and then it moves to the beach weather permitting afterwards, and basically everyone drinks the Darling ale or hot toddies at this time of year and gets a bit sozzled.'

'I see.'

'Have you met Vanessa?'

'No, don't think so. Who's Vanessa?'

'She's in charge of the markets and Coronation Hall. She and her husband run the kiosk by the pier when it's open,' Tom said.

'Oh yeah, I know the one you mean.'

'She's always in Darlings, too, when she's not in the kiosk. I thought you might have met her in there.'

Emmy shook her head. 'Nope.'

'Anyway. She runs the event, so we'll just message her and tell her we're in for the beach bit.'

'Right. So we don't actually get invited, or we do?'

'Well, initially, you do in the early days. But now, no, because obviously, I've done that bit already.'

'Clear as mud.'

'It's one of those funny little Darling things,' Tom said and waved his hand dismissively.

Emmy smiled as she sat down on the bench. Chilly, salty air whipped around her head, a plethora of clouds moved swiftly across the sky, and Darling Island was giving her all the feels. 'I like the funny little Darling things.'

'Yeah.'

'Better than family drama things,' Emmy noted with a funny smile.

'Absolutely. We've had enough of those for a while.'

Emmy put two cups on the bench and poured in hot water from the flask. 'We need more Darling, less drama in our lives.'

'So you won't be inviting either of your sisters, Mum or Dad to the market?'

Emmy giggled as she handed Tom one of the cups. **** *no,* she said in her head. 'Absolutely blimming well not.'

'Can't say I'm disappointed.'

'I'm not sure I'm even going to be alive once I've attended the showdown with Mum.'

Tom fake-shuddered. 'Don't even joke.'

39

The doorbell on the front of the shop door went. Emmy rushed down the stairs, expecting a delivery. As she crossed the shop, she could see the postman standing in the recess. She slid two bolts across and pulled the door towards her. Paul looked up from his satchel.

'Morning.' He craned his neck back, taking in the flower installation around the top of the shop. 'Looking lovely. I meant to knock before and say.'

'Thanks.'

'How's it going?'

'Yeah, really good.'

'Rumour has it you had a visitor.'

'I did.'

Paul squinted. 'Some big person on Facebook or something, was it?'

'Instagram. Yep, it's been amazing.'

'Well done you. Glad you had a bit of luck come your way.'

'Thanks.'

'Rightio, what have we here then? A few parcels for you.'

Paul pulled out his satchel and started handing them over. 'Been busy shopping? Anything nice?'

'Not really. They're dresses. I had a disastrous shopping trip, so I went online to see what I could come up with. This is the result. The influencer who came here invited me to a charity cocktail party.'

'Looks like you've got a few options here, at least.'

Emmy balanced the parcels in her arms as she chatted with Paul. 'Hopefully, one of these dresses works out. My sister helped me whittle it down to this lot. I couldn't find a single thing I liked in the shops.'

'Ah, the old charity cocktail party.' Paul nodded knowingly. 'I get dragged along to those every year. I spend the whole night trying not to spill wine down my one and only suit.'

Emmy laughed. 'Hopefully, there will be some good prizes up for grabs. I need to win a weekend spa break.'

'Now that sounds more like it.' Paul chuckled and patted the parcels. 'Well, I'll keep my fingers crossed that the perfect dress is in this little lot then.'

'Thanks, Paul. I appreciate you lugging them all over here. I won't be ordering any more, though.' Emmy laughed. 'If none of these are any good, I'm wearing a ten-year-old little black dress, which is probably what I should have done in the first place.'

'No worries. See you later.'

Emmy clicked the door shut behind her and carried the parcels through the shop, up the stairs to the flat, and then up the next set of stairs to her bedroom. She dropped them on the bed, opened her dresser drawer, rummaged around for some scissors, and started to slit open the satchels. She pulled out a silky emerald green dress with a low cowl neckline. It was one of the ones Amy had recommended that Emmy was in two minds about. It looked nice but wasn't quite her thing. She'd decided to order it anyway and see what happened.

The second parcel revealed a pink dress that was pretty, but Emmy instantly realised that in the flesh, it was far too casual. Emmy wrinkled her nose and moved on to the next parcel.

The third dress was a safer bet – a black flowing midi dress with thick lace sleeves and a high neck. More classic and understated. By the time Emmy got to the last satchel, she wasn't in love with any of the dresses, and she had yet to even try them on. *Here we go again,* she thought.

She unzipped the last garment bag hopefully. Things were looking up. Better, much better. A simple black velvet fitted dress with long sleeves and a completely open back. A thick band of diamanté ran from the neck down the open scooped back. The band caught the light as Emmy held it up.

'Bingo,' Emmy said to herself as she held the dress up against herself. The dress was classy and very simple but, at the same time, fancy by way of the sparkle going down the back. It wowed right away. It razzle-dazzled. It was definitely the one. If she could get in it, she was wearing it. She nearly cried in relief.

A few seconds later, she was down to her underwear and slipping herself into the dress. She stood in front of the mirror and felt as if she'd been transformed. Her mind flitted to the hideous changing room with the dust bunnies where she'd felt short, squat, lumpy, and anything and everything in between. What looked back at her was far from lumpy or squat. Emmy Bardot had grown two feet. She turned and looked over her left shoulder at what was looking back at her in the mirror. The whole thing was cut like a dream. Her muffin top, which had remained a constant stubborn companion in her life since the moment she'd had Callum, had somehow disappeared. The fat deposits she hated, that had taken up residence on the top of her arms, were nowhere to be seen. The handles that lived on the top of her thighs had been scooped, skimmed, and sculpted. As she looked in the mirror and squinted, life for Emmy Bardot was very, very good indeed.

Emmy snatched up the invoice note from the bed. The dress was not cheap. She didn't care. It was staying. She went back to the mirror and giggled. 'Team Diamanté for the win.'

40

E mmy sat in the front passenger seat of Amy's car with her stomach churning. Rain poured down the windscreen, the sky was full of thick grey-black clouds, and as they pulled onto the driveway of their mum and dad's house, the car sloshed through water in the gutter. They both hustled out of the car, ran through the heavy rain, and then stood on the front porch for a second.

Amy looked at Emmy. 'Ready for this?'

'No. Not at all.'

Amy rolled her eyes. 'Dad says she's fine now.'

'She's *not* fine. How can she be fine? No way in the world is she fine. Would *you* be fine?'

Amy gave a funny little smile. 'Dad said she's been warned. That in itself is odd. What does that mean? Dad has warned Mum, what? He's never behaved like that.'

'Who even is he?'

'Don't know. I'll believe it when I see it.'

Amy pressed the doorbell. They heard it ring in the depths of the house, and a couple of minutes later, their mum opened the door. Cherry beamed; her hair was done, her face was on, and she was breezy, so *very* breezy. Plus, she had heels on indoors. Cherry never ever wore shoes in the house. Emmy shuddered. 'Hi, Mum.'

'Hi, darling! How are you?' Cherry asked, her smile unnaturally bright.

Emmy stopped herself from frowning. Was her mum going to shove it under the carpet? Surely not? 'Good.'

Cherry started to bustle. 'We're having our boozy lunch in the comfort of the conservatory today. It's nice and toasty in there. I've had the heating on full blast, and the wood burner is on.' Cherry clapped her hands together. 'Excellent!'

Amy side-eyed behind their mum. Ominous. Cherry sounded *very* bright and *very* breezy. 'Good, it's freezing, and where has this rain come from?'

Emmy bundled in on the talk about the weather. The longer they kept the conversation off the secret, the better she'd feel. 'It wasn't even forecast.'

Amy followed suit. 'It just came down out of nowhere as we were driving along.'

Emmy added, 'It's pelting down.'

Amy deposited a Waitrose finger sandwich platter on the kitchen island next to an oversized dish with Cherry's favourite pesto pasta. Cherry opened the fridge and pulled out a bottle of bubbles. 'What say we start with a few bubbles?'

Emmy was now extremely worried about Cherry's strange act. Cherry's voice sounded very odd. She was putting on some sort of peculiar, breezy, slightly upper-class, and definitely not normal accent. Hyacinth Bouquet sprang to mind. She was purposely avoiding the Katy topic. It almost felt worse than confronting it head-on. Emmy thought she'd been more or less prepared for what was going to happen. It was not this. Her mum's behaviour had completely thrown her. A surprise if ever she'd had one. 'I'd love a glass.'

'How nice is it to have the house quiet and just be us girls?' Cherry singsonged.

Emmy shuddered. This was not going to end well. Over the years, their boozy lunches had been held in all manner of venues and had dealt with all sorts, but not the re-emergence of a family member who didn't want to see Cherry. It was not good. A few minutes later, as the rain pummelled on the conservatory roof, Emmy clung to her glass for dear life. She scooped up a handful of nuts from the dish on the coffee table and watched her mum continue the strange show she was putting on from the other side of the room. It went on for ages, with neither Emmy nor Amy saying much at all. They couldn't get a word in edgeways. Emmy took a large gulp of champagne as Cherry breezed around the conservatory, topping up her glass with forced cheeriness. Emmy and Amy exchanged tense looks, both unsure how to broach the subject of Katy.

'Oh, I almost forgot the olives and cheese!' Cherry suddenly exclaimed. 'Let me just pop back to the kitchen.'

Cherry hurried out, her heels clacking on the floor. The second she was gone, Amy immediately turned to Emmy. 'This is *so* weird,' she whispered. 'Why is she acting like everything's normal?'

'Normal! This is far from normal! She has heels on inside!' Emmy shook her head helplessly. 'It's like she's in some sort of denial or something. I thought she'd be upset and angry and wanting to interrogate me.'

'I'm not sure what to think. What in the name of goodness has Dad said?'

'I don't know,' Emmy said with a shake of her head. 'I'll say it again: she's wearing shoes *indoors*.'

'Unbelievable. We are so in trouble.'

'I thought…' Emmy started and then stopped. 'I don't know what I thought, but this wasn't it.'

'Should we just come right out and bring up Katy?' Amy

whispered uncertainly. 'Maybe we need to be direct, or she'll just avoid it all afternoon.'

'I guess we should. But go gently, the last thing we want is her storming off or something. I don't know. This whole thing is so baffling. She's had her hair done!'

Amy grimaced. 'There is the biggest surprising elephant ever known to man sitting in the corner of this room.'

'I know. You'd better give him a bucket of champagne.' Emmy giggled. 'This is not going to end well.'

Amy nodded as they heard Cherry returning, still chattering brightly about nothing in particular. She set down a cheeseboard and bowl of olives with a flourish. 'There, now we've got all the nibbles we need! Isn't this just lovely? Lovely. So nice to have you two here. Lovely.'

'Mum. I know you probably don't want to discuss this, but we can't pretend like nothing happened,' Amy said.

Cherry's fixed smile faltered slightly, but she kept it pinned in place. 'Oh, goodness, what do you mean, darling?'

Emmy took a deep breath. 'Katy. You know we've been in touch with her again. Emmy's been seeing her, and I'm going to meet up with her, too.'

Cherry's smile vanished instantly, her bubbly facade gone in an instant. Her face clouded with loads of things, but mostly what looked like anger, hurt, bitterness, and indignation all rolled into one. It wasn't a pretty look on her face. 'Ah. Yes, well.'

Emmy heard herself speaking too quickly. 'I'm so sorry I didn't tell you sooner, Mum, but Katy was very clear she didn't want me to say anything yet.'

Emmy instantly knew she'd made a wrong move. Cherry whirled around in a flash. 'Oh, so we still have to bow down to Katy's wishes, do we? She swans off without a word for years, but she still gets to decide when we're allowed to know she's alive? Typical.'

'I know it's unfair, Mum, believe me. I was upset with her too.'

'Upset doesn't even begin to cover it!'

Amy shifted in her seat. 'I felt the same.'

'Now she thinks she can just waltz back into your life as if nothing happened? And leave me out,' Cherry hissed.

Emmy shook her head. 'It didn't happen like that. It was so out of the blue, running into her. But she seems different now. She's really turned her life around.'

'Isn't that wonderful for her!' Cherry said, grabbed the bottle of champagne, and refilled her glass. A tiny splash of champagne landed on the coffee table. Cherry didn't bother to clean it up.

Emmy and Amy exchanged worried looks.

'Mum, please try and stay calm. Getting worked up won't help anything.'

Cherry bared her teeth. 'I tried to put on a brave face. Your dad has warned me not to overreact because of *you two*. How am I supposed to react when my daughter is suddenly back in touch with you all behind my back?'

'It's a shock.'

Cherry's face crumpled. 'I just don't understand. How could she do this? Why didn't she want me to know?'

Emmy perched on the arm of the chair and put her hand on her mum's back. 'She was in a bad place back then with the drugs and partying. She doesn't want any drama.'

Amy passed Cherry a tissue, and she dabbed at her eyes, smearing her mascara. Amy raised her eyebrows. 'Bit late for that.'

'It still doesn't excuse what she did. We're her *family*.'

Emmy hesitated, unsure whether to drop the next bombshell. 'She doesn't really want to be part of it, though.'

Cherry calmed down. 'I heard.'

'How are you with that?'

Tears pooled in Cherry's eyes. She seemed a bit lost for words. 'I'm used to it.'

Amy squeezed her eyes together and then wiped the corner of her right eyelid. 'We're just going to have to play it by ear. It all needs time to settle.'

Cherry just kept shaking her head. 'Your dad has said just to let it lie and that I'm not to react. He told me not to cause a scene and behave normally.'

Amy chuckled. 'So you got your hair done and are wearing heels in the house.'

Cherry looked glumly at her feet. 'Dad said to leave it to you two and see what happens. He said I'm not to do my normal meddling. He said Katy and you two can take as long as you want.'

Emmy nodded and then shook her head. 'I don't really think there's much else we *can* do.'

'So, what, we just do nothing? We continue and see what happens, do we?' Amy asked. 'You're happy with that, Mum?'

'No,' Cherry said resignedly, 'but your dad has warned me that it is what it is, and I have to…'

'Since when did you start listening to Dad?' Amy said with raised eyebrows and a half-smile, attempting and failing to lighten the tension in the air. 'You've always called the shots.'

Cherry didn't smile. Not even a sniff of one. 'Since he threatened to leave.'

41

Emmy and Amy were back from their afternoon with Cherry, and the pair of them sat huddled on the plush sofa in Amy's sitting room, the rain still tapping against the windows. Amy passed Emmy a biscuit tin, and Emmy rummaged around at the bottom and then dipped a Garibaldi in her tea.

Amy shook her head, 'Well, that was a turn-up for the books. Blimey, this is going from bad to worse.'

Emmy fiddled with the rim of her mug. 'I can't believe it. It was as if Mum was someone else.'

Amy put her mug on the coffee table, leaned back, and crossed her arms. 'I know. It was like she was putting on a show, but for whom? For us? For herself? It was all so...' she trailed off, searching for the right word.

'Surreal?' Emmy offered, a look of confusion on her face. 'Nuts?'

'Exactly. Surreal.' Amy sighed deeply. 'I mean, we knew she'd be upset about Katy, but that. What even was that?'

Emmy thought about the initial staged cheeriness of the lunch and how the conversation had rapidly gone downhill.

Emmy shook her head, her mind racing. 'Do you think we should have handled it differently? If I had told her sooner, right at the beginning of all this, would that have helped?'

'You said Katy was adamant about keeping it quiet. You were just respecting her wishes and caught between a rock and a hard place, so no, that wasn't an option.'

'But at what cost?' Emmy's voice cracked. 'Ames, this is a nightmare. Mum was so weird. I'm concerned for her mental health.'

'She was.' Amy shook her head repeatedly.

'Pretending everything was fine, wearing heels indoors, for heaven's sake. Her hair, too!'

Amy exhaled. 'Maybe we underestimated how much this would affect her. We were so focused on Katy and ourselves.'

They sat in silence for a moment, the only sound the rain and the distant hum of the house. Emmy's thoughts turned to Bob and to the warning he'd apparently given their mum. 'What do you think Dad said to her? To make her act like this?'

'Well, she said that he'd said he'd leave. Imagine Dad speaking to her like that! They've always been the perfect Mr and Mrs. There must be things we don't know,' Amy said as she shook her head in disbelief.

'It must have been serious. I've never seen Mum like this. It's like she's walking on eggshells, and that's just not her, is it? She's normally the one who calls all the shots.'

'Exactly,' Amy agreed. 'She's always been one to bowl on in and take charge, and there she was at first being all strange and avoiding the biggest elephant in the room.'

'We'll have to talk to Katy.' Emmy shuddered, her voice tinged with doubt. 'She won't listen. She's always been so stubborn anyway.'

'Mum said Dad said to just leave it for a while anyway.'

'What, so we just do nothing?'

'He said to let things work themselves out.'

'What about Mum, though?'

Amy picked at the fringe of the throw on the back of the sofa, her brow furrowed in thought. 'Not sure.'

'You're right. We should do what Dad said. Give it time. See if Katy warms up to the idea of seeing Mum.'

'I guess there's not a lot else we can do,' Amy said as she traced the patterns on her mug with her finger.

'But it feels like we're just waiting for something to happen. It's so passive after all this drama.'

'I know, but what else can we do? If we push Katy too hard, she might back off completely. And that won't help Mum at all. Dad clearly doesn't want that which is why he's told Mum to wind her neck in.'

Emmy sighed, a long, drawn-out sound. 'I just hate this. Mum has always been our rock, and now she's crumbled because of *me*. After everything she's done for me.'

'No! There's a lot to this. Dad does have a point that it's always her way. That's why we need to be careful. It's like untangling a massive knot. You can't just pull at it; you have to work it loose bit by bit.'

Emmy nodded slowly, the analogy making sense, and then she joked. 'You're being very counsellor-like, Ames. What's happened? So, you're saying we should keep talking to Katy, keep building that bridge, and just see what happens?'

'Yep, one day at a time.'

Emmy turned her mouth upside down. 'What if Katy never wants to see Mum?'

'We can't control that. We can be there for Mum, I guess, if that happens. What a mess.'

'We'll try to show Katy that Mum's changed. That she's not the same person she was back then.'

'Pah! Has she, though? One little episode today, and that's just because Dad has basically threatened her. It's all quite mind-boggling.'

248

'True.'

'What an emotional few days. Next I get to see Katy again after all this time – more drama. I half-wish that wasn't booked in. I'm not sure I can take much more family stuff,' Amy joked.

'Too late. You're not backing out now,' Emmy replied.

Amy nodded. 'We just have to get on with it I suppose.'

'It'll be fine.'

Emmy didn't feel as if the meeting between Amy and Katy would be fine. 'So, I guess there is some sort of conclusion to all this,' Emmy mused. 'You and me continue with Katy and Mum and Dad just have to wait and see what happens. That's basically what Dad is insisting happens, isn't it?'

'Yup.'

'We tell, or *I* tell, Katy that Mum knows, and we just go from there.'

'Yeah, and we plod along and let it all sort itself out in the wash.'

Emmy nodded. If that's what Bob Bardot was mandating was going to happen, it would have to be a good enough conclusion for her.

42

E mmy sat in the service station car park she'd arranged to meet Amy in and watched one lorry after another pull into various spots on the far left. She then let her eyes follow their drivers as they jumped out of various cabs and walked over towards the coffee shop. After she mindlessly watched a long line of drivers do precisely the same thing, she picked up her phone, answered a couple of emails, sent a text to Callum instructing him that Kevin was collecting him, and then sent a message to Katy.

Emmy: *Hey. I'm just waiting to meet Amy now. Are you sure you're happy with this?*

Katy: *Yes.*

Emmy smiled. As usual, Katy was short, sweet, and to the point.

Emmy: *See you soon, then.*

Katy: *Will do. You okay?*

Emmy was pleased to be asked if she was okay. Throughout the whole thing, she'd felt stuck in the middle of everything, and as if her opinion didn't really matter. It didn't really, but that was a whole other conversation for another time.

Emmy: *I'm fine.*

She decided to tell the truth. She wasn't really fine.

Emmy: *Bit nervous about all of this, to be honest.*

Katy: *Same.*

Emmy: *At least we're moving forward.*

Katy: *Yes.*

Emmy watched as Amy drove into the car park in her fancy black German car. She reversed into the spot next to Emmy, smiled and waved, grabbed her bag, walked around the front of Emmy's car, and made a funny face. Emmy leant over the front seat, yanked the handle and pushed the door. Amy got in, put her bag in the footwell, and settled into the passenger seat. Emmy could tell just by looking at Amy that she was tense, even though Amy was pretending she wasn't. Amy fiddled with the strap on her bag. 'So, here we are. This is really happening. We're going to see Katy.'

'Yep.'

'I'm quite nervous.'

'No way, really?' Emmy said in a jokey, sarcastic way.

'Is it that obvious?'

'Very. You're fiddling. You never fiddle.'

Amy immediately dropped her bag handle. 'It's been so long. What do we even talk about?' Amy fretted.

'I have no idea. It all feels huge. Can't be worse than Mum and the heels.'

Amy laughed. 'Good point. What if it's too weird? Or she hates me?'

'There's a lot of baggage floating around. But she said yes, so that has to be a good sign. It'll be fine once we break the ice. Too late now.'

Easier said than done, Emmy thought. An awkward silence descended as they both worried.

The heavy family stuff that had gone on felt as if it was sitting in the car between them. Emmy's mind spun with questions about how it was all going to go down. Her stomach churned as she pictured the arguments Katy'd had with their mum, mostly centring on the fact that Katy had been taking drugs and wasn't going down a path Cherry had wanted her to go down. It had not been pleasant for anyone involved.

Amy punctuated Emmy's thoughts. 'Do you think she's changed a lot?'

Emmy paused, considering. From what she'd seen, Katy was *very* different but still quite strong-willed and passionate about what she thought was right and wrong. Her opinion of Cherry was not the same as Emmy's or Amy's. She didn't want to give Amy any preconceived ideas. 'I think she's the same Katy with a different side.'

'I feel weird.'

Emmy tried and failed to sound confident. She mostly sounded wobbly. 'I'm sure we'll just click right back into place. We're still sisters at the end of the day. Honestly, it'll be fine.'

'So, what's the plan when we get there?'

'Just play it by ear.'

'Okay, that's not really a plan, but a good plan. What about all the stuff that went on? The arguments and everything.'

'Don't even go there. She's touchy. I've nearly messed this up several times.'

'Right. That hasn't changed then. So, what, Katy just gets her own way? What Katy wants, Katy gets?'

Emmy shook her head. 'You see, that's not going to work.'

'No. I suppose not.'

The majority of the rest of the car journey went by in silence. Amy was clearly not in any mood to chat. Emmy was the same. When she pulled the car into the kerb outside Katy's flat, Amy peered out the window. On the bright, chilly day, the house looked as lovely as it had the first time Emmy had been to visit; the pale blue front door was flanked by pots overflowing with white and purple pansies, and matching hanging baskets swayed beside the door. Amy squinted and craned her neck to see to the top of the house. 'Oh, right, okay, right, yes.'

'Not what you expected?'

Amy shook her head. 'Not at all. It's really nice.'

'I know.'

'Like, much better than I expected. Much.'

'Yep. For goodness sake, don't say that.'

'Nope. I won't. I was expecting something a little bit more...' Amy trailed off.

'Rough?'

'Ha. I was going to say tatty.'

'I was the same. Wait until you get inside.'

Emmy turned off the ignition, checked her phone to see if there were any messages from Callum, answered one from Tom about their plans that evening, and grabbed her bag from the back. 'Time to face the music,' she joked. 'Ready?'

'As I'll ever be.'

They got out of the car and stepped along the pavement in brisk, chilly air. Emmy buzzed the intercom, the door clicked, and as Amy stepped in, she stopped for a second on the doormat and peered up with her chin raised. Her eyebrows shot to the top of her head. 'Wow, this is lovely.'

'It is.'

Amy whispered and joked, 'I need a flat. A little private place to go on my own.'

'You and me both.' Emmy chuckled as they walked up the first flight of stairs to Katy's flat. Katy was waiting at the door with a pensive look on her face.

Katy gave Emmy a brief, tight hug before turning to Amy. They stood awkwardly for a moment before Amy stepped forward and lightly put her arms around Katy.

'Hey,' Amy mumbled.

'Hi, Ames. It's really good to see you.'

An uncomfortable beat passed before Katy gestured them

inside. 'Come on in. It's quiet. Elodie's dad took her to childcare today.'

Emmy and Amy followed Katy down the hall to the kitchen. Emmy could feel Amy looking around at the beautifully decorated flat. This clearly wasn't the dreary flat Amy had envisioned. The air was tight, tense and uncomfortable. Emmy wasn't really sure what to do or say.

'Wow, the flat is gorgeous,' Amy enthused as Katy made tea.

'Thanks. It's taken a while to get it to feel homey, but I'm happy with it now.'

'Really lovely.' Amy emphasised the word 'really'; it came out as if she hadn't been expecting the flat to be nice.

'Surprised?' Katy said, breaking the air with a funny smile.

Amy quickly recovered. 'No, no. Not at all.'

An awkward silence descended as Katy made the tea. Emmy wracked her brains for an icebreaker, but her mind kept tumbling, and she felt as if her tongue had been glued to the roof of her mouth. 'How are you feeling? You look so much more comfortable than you did after the surgery.'

'I'm doing well. Recovering slowly but surely. My energy levels are finally back to normal,' Katy noted. 'Yeah, I'm fine, actually.'

'I'm glad. You seem to be healing well.'

'I know, it was a rough few weeks. But I'm getting stronger every day. Just taking it slowly, well, I'm trying to. You know how it is.'

Emmy nodded. 'You're sounding very zen about it all. I'd be going mad being housebound for so long.'

'It forced me to slow down a bit, which was probably a good thing.'

Amy spoke up hesitantly, 'One of my friends had the operation, too. She said it was painful.'

Emmy was grateful Amy was speaking.

'It was at first,' Katy acknowledged. 'It feels a bit like you've been sliced open, which I guess you have.'

Emmy winced in sympathy. 'Yep.'

'I was on strong pain relief those first few days, as Emmy knows. Could barely hobble to the bathroom. And, of course, having Elodie...'

A flicker of emotion passed over Amy's face at the mention of Elodie. She stayed silent and fiddled with her mug handle.

'The worst part was not being able to flit here, there, and everywhere. Being housebound for weeks is not my idea of fun. You don't realise how much you do in a day when you have a little one, etcetera, etcetera.'

'The main thing is you're healing, and the worst is behind you now,' Emmy said, noting that Amy still looked tense and uncomfortable. An awkward lull followed again, and Emmy racked her brain for a change of topic, but Katy spoke again first.

'Actually, there was one strange silver lining,' she said slowly. 'Being stuck at home all this time forced me to really reflect on stuff. It made me do a bit of soul-searching.'

Emmy leaned forward. 'Like what?'

'How differently things might have turned out if I'd made other choices.' Katy flicked her hand between the three of them. 'About us...'

Emmy didn't know what to say. Amy remained silent. 'It is what it is.'

Katy looked up with an intense expression. 'If I could go back and do things differently, I would have tried harder. Leaving you two was horrible.'

Emmy blinked against a sting of tears. Amy shifted in her seat, avoiding Katy's gaze. Emmy wasn't sure what to say for the best. 'We understand why you left because of the arguments with Mum. You don't have to feel guilty.' She felt Amy bristle.

Katy shook her head firmly. 'I still abandoned you both,'

Katy said, looking sad but resigned. Emmy's heart broke a little bit. Emmy glanced over at Amy, who was staring fixedly at the table, face blank. Amy was clearly feeling very uncomfortable. Emmy wished she could erase the past, wave a magic wand and make everything instantly better. 'The past is the past.'

'You always were the wise one,' Katy joked in an attempt to ease the tension. 'Not sure if you get that from Mum or Dad.'

At the mention of their parents, Amy pushed back her chair abruptly. 'Sorry, I need to pop to the loo.' She turned and strode stiffly from the room.

Katy looked taken aback by Amy's sudden departure. She lowered her voice. 'This was a mistake. She seems so uncomfortable. Why did I even think this was a good idea, and why did I bring things up? Where did that come from? Ahh!'

Emmy dropped her head back for a second and closed her eyes. Clearly, there was still a lot of hurt zipping around, especially for Amy. 'This all touches a nerve. Amy really missed you, Kates, like a lot. Really a lot.'

Katy's face fell. 'I shouldn't have said anything. Maybe we shouldn't have done this. I did say that when you first mentioned it.'

'Just give her time. This is emotional for all of us.'

'Yep.'

'We just have to give everything time.'

The toilet flushed down the hall, and a minute later, Amy reappeared. Emmy turned the conversation to the shop and the influencer event. But it was all very tense. Emmy heard herself speaking and felt as if she was in a scene where she was looking on. Here she was with *both* her sisters having a cup of tea. The three of them back together again. Long may it last.

43

It was the day of the charity cocktail party. Emmy was neck deep in the fanciest bubbles in the fanciest hotel room she'd ever been in in her life, which wasn't hard because she hadn't been in many. She certainly hadn't been in any like the one she was currently making the most of. The water was piping hot, there was a cup of steaming peppermint tea beside her, and her hair, courtesy of a hairdresser just along the road, was in a very elaborate updo on the top of her head. It had to be said that Emmy Bardot was having the time of her life.

Apart from a few one-offs with Tom, it had been a very long time since Emmy had been to a hotel. Being in a rental trap, looking after a son, holding down a job, keeping a car on the road, and trying to make ends meet did that for a girl. The hotel had been booked courtesy of both Tom's organising skills and Amy's insistence for weeks, and Emmy was very much revelling in it as much as she could. Bring it right on.

Just as the hairdresser in the fancy salon not far from the hotel had instructed, she had a hairnet over her hair and a clear hotel shower cap on top of that. A couple of the super white, super fluffy, super posh hotel towels were wedged behind her neck to keep her head out of the water, and she had a fancy complimentary sheet mask attached to the front of her face. The sheet mask was infused with diamond particles and apparently was going to make her face both plump and glowing. Don't mind if I do.

Emmy had got herself quite worked up about the charity cocktail party. She'd thought she was too old, too frumpy, and way, way, way too out of touch to be there and had secretly told herself that she was going to come down with a mystery virus the day before. Even after having the dress sorted and with the knowledge that Tom P Carter would be in a dinner suit, it had been her plan to swiftly remove herself from attending at the last minute. She'd kept her plan close to her chest, intending on getting sick just before. Charity cocktail parties, posh frocks, fancy food, and five-star hotels were not the places for the Emmy Bardots of the world. Or so she thought. It had been Katy who had shaken her out of the negative self-talk that Emmy now realised had been following her around in life for years. She'd given Katy a tiny little insight into the fact that she wasn't quite sure if she was going to go, and Katy had both come down on her like a tonne of bricks and filled her with confidence all in one fell swoop.

Katy had somehow just known what to say when the little nagging self-doubt Emmy often resided with made itself known. Katy had buoyed Emmy's confidence and then some. She'd told her how amazing the Love Emmy x website was. She'd forced Emmy to listen when she'd told Emmy how pretty darn good her job at the port was, and she'd hammered home the fact that from what Emmy had shown her of Darling Island and The Old Ticket Office, Emmy should be more than proud of herself. Katy had been adamant and strong and feisty and just pretty lovely all around, really. She'd insisted life for Emmy could have gone another way if she'd let it. Emmy had opened up the centre of her chest, pulled apart her ribs, taken Katy's words, and placed them right next to her heart. She'd then listened to them for days and days on repeat. It seemed they'd worked very well indeed.

Now here Emmy was on the day, getting ready for a big do with influencers and famous faces. They weren't just any old faces either. According to the list that had arrived in her inbox a few days before, A-list celebs were at the fore. We're talking a footballer who'd splurged the inner workings of his famous life all over the TV, a princess who it was rumoured liked a drink, and a celebrity chef with messy hair, to name but a few. It seemed that Emmy had climbed up a strange imaginary ladder and, by accident, had deposited herself in a whole other A-list world. Emmy was still unsure whether she would be able to converse in the world, let alone whether she liked it or not. But she kept the words Katy had told her tucked just under her ribs and let them lead the way. Katy's words would take her to the ball.

As she soaked in the water and stared up at the ceiling, her mind went over what had happened with her mum and dad. Of all the scenarios she'd put herself through, all the scenes she'd played out in her head, all the things she'd imagined would happen once the Katy secret had come out in the open, none of them had happened. Not even close. What had actually taken place had never been on her radar at all. Bob had surprised everyone. Bob Bardot, it seemed, had played the trump card of his life.

Amy and Emmy had spent hours discussing, dissecting, and digesting it. They'd gone out for dinner with the sole purpose of chatting about its occurrence and ended up going home a bit worse for the wear. They'd also had a grown-up sleepover where Emmy had gone to Amy's, stayed over, and they'd talked about it until they were both blue in the face late into the night. Never had either of them heard their parents behave in the way that they had. Cherry had been well and truly told, Bob had been and continued to be adamant, and Emmy and Amy had been nothing short of gobsmacked.

Bob had spoken to both Amy and Emmy separately and told them that, as far as he was concerned, they were to do precisely what they wanted to do concerning Katy. He'd also told them Katy could take as long as she wanted. It was all very peculiar. Cherry, too, had made a dramatic and swift U-turn on her normal controlling behaviour where her girls were concerned, which had conversely meant that Amy and Emmy felt as if they were spinning on their heads.

Emmy let the whole thing drift in and out of her head as she carefully sipped the tea through the hole in the sheet mask and turned the hot water on with her toe. What a strange and odd turn-up for the books. She'd spent *so* much emotional energy, *so* much brain power, and *so* much inner turmoil when she'd been keeping the secret for Bob to well and truly have the last word.

Emmy heard the hotel room door open, and Tom called out her name.

'In the bath!' she shouted over the sound of the tap.

Tom appeared in the doorway. 'Wow, look at you, living the high life!' He perched on the edge of the tub and frowned. 'Err, what is that on your face?'

'It will plump me.'

'Do you need to be plumped?'

'In my face, yes. Thighs, no. Ditto upper arms.'

'Too funny. That was in that little contraption of complementary goodies on the side over there, was it?'

'Yep.'

'Nice.'

'I know, it feels very fancy-schmancy. I could get used to this hotel malarkey.'

'Me too. Maybe we should order some nibbles and champagne? Really go all out.'

Emmy wasn't sure. Another thing that wasn't really in her

world. She was lucky she was in the hotel room at all. Bubbles hadn't even crossed her mind. She decided to throw caution to the wind. 'I like your thinking. We don't want to turn up sloshed, though.' Emmy giggled and joked, 'I have a job to do and an image to upkeep.' She made a serious face. 'This is a work event for me.'

Tom went out to the bedroom and flicked through the room service menu options. 'They do fancy olives and cheeses, that could be nice.'

'Perfect.' She winced. 'How much is it?'

'You don't need to know that.'

Emmy shook her head and squinted. 'If it's extortionate, I don't want it.'

'It's extortionate. You're having it.'

Tom called down to room service and ordered the cheese and olives, plus a bottle of bubbles. 'Did you speak to your mum and dad again today? Any more drama?'

Emmy rolled her eyes. 'Oh, don't even get me started on that saga again. I've just been mulling it over. What a turn-up for the books, eh?'

'Have you spoken to them?'

Emmy sat up a bit, careful not to dislodge the shower cap. 'A quick conversation this morning. Basically, Dad told me that he's told Mum she needs to accept that we are seeing Katy again with no fuss. She's not even to mention it.'

Tom raised his eyebrows in surprise. 'Wow, really? He's on fire.'

'I know! Amy and I are so shocked.'

'Well, at least it's all out in the open now.'

'It's not gone the way I thought. I thought Mum would be unbearable, crying, and guilt-tripping me, and ranting, but there's been none of it.'

'Hopefully, she'll stick to her word now and let you handle things with Katy your way.'

'Fingers crossed. I won't hold my breath, though.'

Tom shook his head as there was a knock at the door, and he jumped up to answer it, returning with a large plate.

Emmy sat forward. 'Ooh yes, please!'

'Look at you. You're all wrapped up like a posh little parcel in there. Bubbles right up to the top.' Tom popped open the champagne and poured them both a glass. 'To a drama-free night and my lovely Ems,' he said, clinking his flute against Emmy's glass.

'I'll toast to that.' Emmy laughed. She leaned back against the tub and sipped her bubbly. She sighed as the chilled liquid hit the back of her throat. It was so good to get away. She was more than determined to put all the family issues aside and just enjoy their fancy hotel for the night. Do what she wanted to do. Stuff everyone else. She'd waited for it for a long time. She was going to rock it to the hilt.

44

Emmy looked over her shoulder in the mirror as she walked up the steps to the entrance of the building where the cocktail party was taking place. The line of diamanté dropping from the back of her neck to the base of her spine glittered in the light. She caught sight of Tom in his suit beside her and felt every single muscle inside her clench. Tom P Carter was not bad at doing fancy suits. As if sensing her thoughts, Tom squeezed her hand and smiled. Emmy beamed back.

About twenty minutes later, she had a champagne flute in her hand and found herself in the most bizarre and unreal situation of her life. Emmy Bardot – mum, port worker, and very small business owner – was standing chatting with a global football star. The same global football star who, the week before, she'd watched on the news. All very odd. She felt a bit spacey as she watched his lips move and heard his words go in her ears. He sounded so different in real life. Way too normal, but at the same time not. Her brain couldn't quite compute what he was saying. He was telling her he liked football podcasts and cooking. Something like that. She liked jewellery and Darling Island. So many, many worlds far, far apart.

Emmy smiled politely as the footballer rambled on. He did quite like the sound of his own voice. She nodded along and made 'mmm' noises whilst thinking she needed to get away from him when she got the first chance. Superstar footballers would not be interested in her shop on Darling Island or her Insta stories, and she had a job to do. She was not at the event to stroke the ego of anyone, least of all a global football player she'd never ever see again. She was dressed up with her hair done and her Love Emmy x face on to make things happen. She'd probably never get the chance again to be in the room with so many big social media stars. Plus, the footballer small talk was sort of dull and definitely one-sided. Footballers were so last year.

Just then, as if reading her mind, Tom appeared at her elbow holding two fresh glasses of bubbles.

'I got you a top up,' he said smoothly, handing her a champagne flute.

'Thanks.'

Tom turned to the footballer with an outstretched hand. 'Lovely to meet you, I'm Tom, Emmy's other half.' Tom's usual confident, slightly aloof, exponentially attractive, and definitely hot tone took over. The footballer shook his hand slightly bemusedly at Tom. Clearly, he wasn't used to people not fawning all over him. Tom chatted for a couple of minutes, right away picked up the vibes that Emmy was desperate to get away, excused them both, and steered a relieved Emmy gently away as the footballer stared after them, not used to being dismissed so promptly.

Emmy whispered to Tom, 'Honestly, he just droned on and on about himself. Thank goodness you saved me.'

'All part of my job as CEO.'

'How do you even do that confident, aloof thing?'

'Much practised.'

'I need some lessons.'

'Also fulfilling my role as your knight in shining armour,' Tom bantered.

Emmy hid a gulp. He didn't know how right he was. She loved him for it. She swooned inside.

'Some night, eh?' Tom remarked as he looked around.

'It feels so surreal. Me, little Emmy Bardot from Darling Island, hobnobbing with the rich and famous.'

Tom turned up one side of his nose. 'You're ten times more interesting than that boring footballer. Which isn't actually hard.'

'Yawn.' Emmy giggled.

'Tell me about it.'

'I can't help feeling out of my depth, though, you know? Actually, no, you probably don't know.'

Just as they were standing looking around them at the room, Peaches, followed by her assistant Gemma, and the videographer who had been at Emmy's shop, swept across the room, making a beeline for them. Peaches looked so done, she didn't quite look human. It was as if someone had airbrushed her skin and sprayed on her hair. Everything about her, including her hair, her dress, her skin and her jewellery, was the colour of a peach. Her dress was like a ripe ombre peach, her skin glowing. She looked *so* good and *so* knew it. Emmy chuckled to herself, imagining from what she'd seen as an insider how long it must have taken for the vision that was in front of her to come to life. Emmy had thought she'd made an effort by getting her hair put up and shoving on a sheet mask. Peaches clearly beat to a different drum.

'Hi!' Peaches breathed. She stood back and looked at Emmy's beautiful, simple, classic dress. 'Wow! You look amazing! Love Emmy x jewellery too.'

Emmy felt herself flush. Peaches was either being very genuine or simply shocked at how well Emmy had scrubbed up that she was very exuberant. 'Thanks.'

Peaches turned to Tom. She raised her eyebrows. Tom P Carter in a fancy suit didn't fail to impress. Peaches beamed, and Emmy introduced Tom. 'My partner, Tom.'

Peaches held out her hand and sort of preened at the same time. 'Lovely to meet you.'

Tom used the same confident, aloof tone he had with the footballer. 'Likewise.'

Emmy felt herself go nuclear as she bathed in the fact that Tom wasn't bothered by the fact that he was standing next to the vision in peach. He stepped just a touch closer to Emmy and away from Peaches. It was tiny, probably unnoticeable to anyone else but man, did that one little shift in where Tom was standing feel good.

As she stood chatting to Peaches and Gemma, Emmy couldn't get the smile off her face as she almost floated above the room. Peaches raved about one of Emmy's latest earring commissions as the videographer held up a camera not too far away from Peaches' head. A tall woman with dark hair and a bright red dress approached them, air-kissed Peaches, ignored Gemma, and turned to Emmy eagerly. She laughed and flicked her head towards Peaches. 'Sorry to interrupt your conversation. I didn't really want to talk to you, Peaches, ha.' She looked at Emmy. 'Are you Emmy? From Love Emmy x? I saw your name on the email list that came around.'

Emmy's eyes widened in surprise. She had no clue who the woman in the dress was. 'I am, yes.'

The woman started to gush. 'I knew it! I love your socials so much. Your shop! Darling Island, isn't it? I watch your stories on repeat.'

Emmy had no idea who she was talking to, but by the way Peaches was behaving, the woman was obviously a big deal. 'Yes, it is.'

'I love it! Love!'

'Thank you so much,' Emmy said, amazed anyone at the

fancy event knew her face from the few times she'd been on her stories.

'I wanted to make sure I spoke to you, and then if you wouldn't mind, I was going to ask my PA to get in touch so we can do a visit to the store,' the woman gushed. 'Could we get a quick photo? Do you do selfies for free?'

Emmy felt *way* out of her depth and totally out of her comfort zone. The gushing, the dresses, the over-the-top nice-ness, but she'd take it for the sake of Love Emmy x any day of the week. Ten or so minutes later, the whole entourage had made their way away from them. Emmy watched them in a bit of a daze. She whispered to Tom, 'I can't believe someone wanted my photo!'

'I'm standing with a celebrity.' Tom laughed and clinked his champagne flute against Emmy's glass.

Emmy shook her head. She really owed a lot to her first encounter with Peaches. It had led to lots. 'Who even was that?'

Tom frowned. 'I don't have the foggiest.'

Emmy giggled. 'Me either.'

Tom took Emmy's hand and put his champagne flute down. 'Right, follow me. We need to replicate what just happened there ten times over.'

'Do I *really* have to?'

'Yep, you *really* do. Work the room, Ems, work the room.'

45

Emmy slowly blinked her eyes open, wondering where she was. For a second, she felt confused by the unfamiliar ceiling overhead. Then, the events of the previous night came flooding back. The dress, the charity cocktail party, Tom, chatting with celebrities...

She rolled over with a groan. Her whole body felt as if something had run over it with a bulldozer or something of a similar ilk. She looked over at the chair at the foot of the bed. Tom's tie was draped over the back of it, his shirt rumpled on the seat. Emmy smiled at the sight of it. Who even was she going to a cocktail event with a handsome man in a suit? She stayed where she was for a moment, feeling the pins from the elaborate, now half-collapsed updo sticking in her head. Slowly she sat up, wincing at how much she ached and silently thanked Ms Sensible, who had popped into her head, limited her alcoholic intake to a couple of glasses, and plied her with copious glasses of water. She'd told herself that for her first ever cocktail event she wanted it to be a night to remember, but that she was not going to be paying a price for it the next day. She was so ach and tired because of the full-on social schmoozing she'd done all in the cause of Love Emmy x.

She slid out from under the thick hotel sheets and tiptoed to the en-suite, catching a glimpse of herself in the mirror. 'Good lord,' she muttered. The updo was now more of an up mess, mascara was smudged on her cheeks, and her eyes were red. For a second, she stood without moving, weighing up whether to try and make a cup of tea or not. Deciding she'd wait for a bit, she stood for a while, peering in the mirror, then turned on the shower. She stood under it for ages, thinking about the night before and letting the hot water soothe her aching muscles and fuzzy head. As she scrubbed at her face with a flannel, she remembered talking to the footballer or rather listening to the footballer. Now, none of it felt real. The glitz and glamour of it and her in the middle of it felt like some sort of weird, surreal dream. After drying and wrapped in the lush hotel robe, she sat for a bit, desperate for a cup of tea but not wanting to wake up Tom.

She sat scrolling through photos from the event on her phone. She smiled, seeing shots of her and Tom all dressed up, nodded at the fancy food and watched the video of the awards ceremony. As her mind went over the evening, she shook her head as she remembered the woman who had recognised her. Fancy someone actually knowing who she was. She had to laugh. Pottering around in the room, she finally made a cup of tea, and Tom stirred. He sat up blearily.

'Morning.'

'What time is it?' Tom said, fumbling for his phone on the table.

'Nearly eleven. I thought I'd leave you, you were out cold.'

Tom scrubbed a hand down his face. 'I'm too old for late nights like that anymore.'

Emmy made him a tea and passed it over. 'All I can offer you is a hotel biscuit.'

Tom sipped the tea. 'I could eat a horse. That was some event. Those influencers know how to party,' he said with a shake of his head.

'I was just looking at the photos. It doesn't feel real.'

'You were schmoozing with celebrities, Ems.'

'I know. We're a long way from Darling Island.'

'Yep. Take me back.'

Emmy laughed. 'Most of them just seemed full of themselves. Did you see that footballer's face when you stole me away from his dull cooking stories?'

'I wish I'd got a photo! His jaw nearly hit the floor,' Tom chuckled.

'What a night.'

Tom stretched his arms over his head and yawned. 'Well, I, for one, had an amazing night.'

'Yep. I'm glad it's over, though, too. I'm drained.'

'It was a lot of small talk. Are you worn out?'

Emmy nodded. 'I am, but in a good way. I'm still letting it all sink in.' She gestured around at the beautiful room. 'I could definitely get used to this princess treatment too.'

'Yeah. You and me both.'

'No washing up, comfy beds, room service. No Callum to clear up after.'

'Maybe we'll have to make this a new tradition then.'

'You're paying.' Emmy laughed. 'I don't want to leave, but at the same time, I can't wait to get home.'

'Tends to happen when you live where we do.'

'Yep, take me home, James, home to Darling Island. Best place in the world.' Emmy nodded. It was so true. Fancy evenings were pleasant enough, but going home to Darling Island to her own little flat and her own little business was even better. In actual fact, it was priceless.

46

The afternoon light outside the shop window was touched with the Darling fog, and inside, Emmy started to make moves to close up for the day. There was a soft, cosy glow from the little lamps and candles dotted around The Old Ticket Office and Emmy was feeling it after a long day. She was behind the counter, meticulously lining up a new batch of earrings, when the shop bell jingled. She looked up to see Russell, the creepy neighbour who hadn't been around for a while, stepping through the door. She inwardly groaned – his presence was not welcome. Emmy's heart sank; she hadn't expected, or wanted, to see him again, and especially not in the shop.

'Hello again, Emmy,' Russell greeted, his voice dripping with confidence and sass. He leaned casually against the counter, a little too close to Emmy for comfort.

Emmy didn't let him see her shudder or that she felt vulnerable. She forced a polite smile, taking a subtle step back. 'Hi, Russell. Looking for something in particular? A gift for someone?'

'Just thought I'd pop in, see your little enterprise here,' he said, his eyes sweeping over the shop. 'As I said before. Quite the cosy setup. I'm not sure why everyone is raving about it on Insta, but I guess I'm not your target customer. I see you were at that influencer event. Very interesting.'

Emmy knew she would have to be cautious about how she responded to Russell. Since she'd first met him, he'd set off alarm bells in her mind. She resolved not to let him intimidate her and nodded, her hands fidgeting with a piece of jewellery on the counter. She put one of her work voices on. 'Thank you. I pride myself on being unique.'

Russell ran his hand along the counter. 'So, this is what keeps you busy, huh? Must be nice, playing with beads all day.'

Emmy bristled at the condescension but kept her tone even. 'It's a bit more than that, but yes, I love what I do.'

Russell inched a bit closer. Emmy felt sick. 'You know, a woman with your talents should aim higher. Ever thought of expanding? I know a thing or two about business.'

Emmy bristled, feeling cornered. She moved to rearrange some items on a shelf, putting more space between them. 'I'm quite happy with how things are, thanks.'

Unperturbed, Russell continued, 'You know, Emmy, or it's Ems some people refer to you as, isn't it? You're a beautiful woman – someone like you shouldn't be hidden away in a place like this. You should be out there, being seen.'

Emmy's discomfort grew by the second, as did Russell's smarm. She didn't like the way Russell was looking at her, his gaze lingered a little too long in all the wrong places. 'I'm exactly where I want to be. Now, if you don't mind, I was just about to close up for the day.'

Russell leaned in, his tone shifting to something softer, more insinuating. 'Come on, Emmy. How about dinner with me? I can show you a world beyond this little shop.'

Emmy felt a wave of unease wash over her. She straightened up, meeting his gaze firmly. 'I appreciate the offer, Russell, but no thank you. I have plans, and as you know, I'm with Tom.'

'Too bad,' Russell said, ignoring the mention of Tom. His body language was weird, and didn't seem particularly disappointed at Emmy's rebuttal. Instead, there was a glint in his eye. As if he was thoroughly enjoying himself. 'You're sure?'

'I am more than sure.'

Russell's demeanour subtly shifted. What he thought was the charm he'd exuded when he'd first walked in morphed into something more invasive. He inched closer, his presence now looming over Emmy. 'Come on, Emmy, Ems, don't be like that,' Russell coaxed, his voice low. He reached out, his hand lightly brushing against her arm. 'I'm leaving again next week for a few months. It'd be great to get together before I go.'

Emmy recoiled at his touch, and she took a step back, trying to put more distance between them. 'I think you should leave,' she said, her voice firm yet tinged with unease. 'I'm not interested, and you're making me uncomfortable.'

Russell seemed unfazed, a smug smile on his lips. He leaned in closer, his voice a whisper. 'There's no need to be shy, Emmy. I know you're just playing hard to get, Ems.'

Before Emmy could respond, the door to the storeroom flew open, and Tom stepped into the shop. His face looked like thunder, and his expression was dark and mean. 'Mate, I think you've overstayed your welcome,' Tom said sternly. There was an edge to his voice bordering on menacing. Emmy had not heard it before. Her whole body went nuclear. He moved to stand protectively next to Emmy, his body language exuding a warning.

Russell straightened up as quick as a flash, a flicker of surprise crossing his face as he regarded Tom. He attempted to maintain his composure. 'Tom.'

Tom leant across the counter, his gaze fixed intently on Russell. 'I suggest you leave now, or I might forget my manners.'

Russell's smugness faltered, replaced by a hint of wariness. He glanced between Emmy and Tom, assessing the situation.

After a moment, he straightened his jacket and scoffed. 'I was just chatting to Ems.'

'Get out before I make you.'

'Are you threatening me?' Russell's voice was odd and goading.

Tom was on it and shot back quickly. 'I don't make threats.'

'Because it's illegal to threaten someone in this country.'

'Why would I threaten you? What have you done wrong?'

Russell didn't back down. He narrowed his eyes. 'It sounded like you were trying to be intimidating.'

'Not at all. Anyway, right, off you trot, Russell. I really hope you sleep well tonight. Make sure you put your alarm on. You do have one, don't you?'

With a glare, Russell turned and strode out of the shop. Tom turned to Emmy. 'Are you okay?'

Emmy nodded, still shaken. 'Yes, thanks to you. I didn't know what to do.'

'Don't worry, I won't let him bother you again.'

'Hopefully, you won't have to. He said he's going off again for a few months.'

'Good. Let's hope he gets the message and doesn't come back. Ever.'

Emmy let out a sigh of relief. Her hands were shaking slightly, and she felt a knot in her stomach. She locked the door and turned the sign. If she never saw Russell again in her life, it would be too soon for her.

47

Emmy stood in the hallway to the flat, wrapped her thick Aran scarf around her neck, and called out to Callum. 'There are leftovers in the fridge. Are you sure you don't want to come with us?'

'No, thanks,' Callum called back.

Emmy pulled a pompom hat that matched her scarf onto her head. She'd have been worried if Callum had said yes. He'd just finished a huge assignment and was well ensconced in a FIFA competition with his mates. Going to an evening market with his mum probably wasn't top of his list. 'See you later, then.'

'Yeah, have a nice time.'

'Will do,' Emmy called back as she shrugged on her huge coat with the faux-fur collar and cuffs and made her way down the stairs. A few minutes later, she was hand-in-hand with Tom on Darling Street at the tram shelter, waiting for a tram. Emmy stood and watched as the blue and white tram livery caught the light from the streetlight above. Above that, bunting fluttered in a quickly descending fog. Just as she was thinking that the foghorn hadn't gone off, it sounded. She laughed. 'I was just thinking I hadn't heard that.'

'We're in for a lot of fog, apparently,' Tom noted.

'Oh, I hope that doesn't mean the beach bit will be cancelled.'

'It shouldn't affect it at all.'

'Good. I've been looking forward to this all week.'

'Really? What, even now that you hobnob with fancy influencers and celebrities, you still like to go to little events on Darling Island?'

Emmy giggled. 'Thank goodness we don't have to do that every weekend. Boring.'

'Nope. This is much more my cup of tea.'

About fifteen minutes later, the descending fog had enveloped Darling, and thick swirls of it clung to everything around them. As they got off the tram, the sound of the waves crashing on the shore came up from the beach, and as they strolled along, Darling Island Coronation Hall came into view. The path up to the front porch was swathed in garlands of little gold lights, a canvas domed marquee covered in the same lights stood on the left, and a throng of people bundled up in hats and scarves made their way to the hall.

Emmy nodded to herself at how lovely it was as they stood in a short queue at the entrance adjacent to the dome tent. Behind a little table topped with a blue and white gingham tablecloth, a man in a butcher's apron stood with an iPad. He looked up and immediately recognised Tom. 'Evening.'

'Evening,' Tom and Emmy said together.

The man lowered his voice and looked at Tom. 'Slot for you on the beach. You know the score.'

Tom nodded, and Emmy had to stop herself from laughing at the seriousness of it all as Tom tapped his phone on the payment gadget. 'Thanks.'

'Bit foggy out there tonight, but we're all set. Glad to see you're dressed for the occasion. Blankets are out and the fires are going. It should be okay.'

'Too easy,' Tom replied. 'Cheers.'

The man smiled. 'Head for the sausages first before they're gone.'

Tom nodded. 'Yep, I know the drill.'

Emmy smiled. 'Thank you.'

As they headed toward the hall and made their way through a side door, Emmy was gobsmacked at what greeted her. She'd been expecting a village fete-type affair: ugly trestle tables, random plastic orange chairs, and a dusty old stage with discarded bits and bobs from various community events. There was none of that whatsoever. Instead, the whole place was lit by Moroccan lanterns hanging from a vaulted ceiling, strings of lights by the dozen, tables were draped with hessian and beauti- fully accessorised with little chalkboard signs. Each volunteer standing behind their stations was dressed in the same apron as the man at the front. All of them seemed happy.

'Oh my! And there I was, thinking we were going to be in a school hall with dodgy disco lights.' Emmy remarked in a hush.

Tom rolled his eyes. 'Darling does everything up a gear.'

'For sure.'

'Let's head to the beer tent.'

Emmy followed Tom out another door, and they stood in a queue chatting. A woman was taking orders, there was a huge stack of bread rolls in gingham napkins, and a man stood behind a triple-width barbecue turning lines of sausages. When they got to the top, a man she was sure she recognised seemed to know Tom and chatted to him about the special sausage recipe. The next thing Emmy knew, one of said sausages was in one of the rolls and in her hand, and she was standing in a little group of people, including Tom's friend Leo the Australian, Lucie from Darlings café, and Xian, one of the owners from the bakery. Emmy basked in it all: people chat- ting and enjoying themselves, the smell of the sausages, a glass of ale in her hand, and the fog in the distance hanging over the sea. The Darling community was wrapping her up and doing its thing. It was chilly and foggy, but Emmy Bardot liked it very much indeed.

~

An hour or so later, Emmy followed Tom out of the village hall towards the beach. The silhouette of the old pier could just about be seen nestled in the thick fog. The temperature had dropped, and brisk, salty sea air whipped around Emmy's head. She shook her head at what was happening on the beach; basket-shaped braziers were surrounded by a circle of director chairs, spiked candle lanterns were stuck into the sand, and people stood around chatting, bundled up in hats, scarves, and coats. The beach area was lit in a soft glow of light coming off the pier, and huge old tea chests overflowing with drinks were staggered between the seats.

The woman Emmy recognised from the tram, Shelly, bustled over to Tom. 'Evening. It's a bit chilly down here, even with the fog. You'll need to tuck yourselves up.'

Tom nodded to Emmy. 'We have blankets and more scarves.'

'Good, good. It's warmer by the fires. Anyway, the cocktails will warm you up,' Shelly said and pointed to the tea chests. 'Help yourselves.'

Tom didn't miss a beat. 'Rhubarb?'

Shelly tapped his hand and winked. 'Is there any other?'

'Thanks,' Emmy said as she tucked her scarf in the neck of her coat, not sure how long she was going to last on the beach. Darling-ites were clearly more used to being out and about by the sea in all weathers than she was. She was very glad about her decision to wear a thermal vest. Once they'd sat down, Emmy relaxed as she held out her hands to the fire, and flickers of light danced around in front of her face. She leant over to Tom's chair. 'Question: what is a rhubarb cocktail?'

'All you need to know is that they are concocted by Shelly with Darling-grown rhubarb, and they are lethal.'

'Ooh, sounds nice.'

Tom grabbed a bottle of the rhubarb concoction from one of the tea chests and poured its contents into two plastic glasses. 'Cheers, Ems. To you and me, and to Darling.'

Emmy swooned inside as she looked at Tom, and shadows and dancing orange light from the fire flickered on his face. She felt just as she had from the word go with him: safe, happy, and content. She smiled and tapped his glass. 'Cheers.'

Tom rummaged in his pocket and then put a small velvet Love Emmy x ring box on the arm of Emmy's chair. Emmy frowned and chuckled. 'What the?' She opened the box. Inside, diamonds in the shape of a flower glinted back at her. She wasn't sure what to think or what the ring meant.

Tom smiled and joked, 'I know you'll never get married again. You've told me that enough times. We already covered that.'

Emmy went more nuclear than she ever had. 'No, no, it's not that…' She trailed off, leaving her sentence in the air as she pulled the ring out of the velvet slot. 'Oh, my goodness. This is beautiful.'

'I thought you'd like it.'

'Wait, where did you get the box? A Love Emmy x box?'

Tom laughed. 'I stole it from the storeroom.'

Emmy wasn't sure what to do with the ring. She pushed it onto the third finger of her right hand. Tom nodded. 'I thought, why not? It's a Love Emmy ring.'

'A what ring?'

'A Love Emmy ring,' Tom said, as if it was self-explanatory.

Emmy Bardot had never felt anything like the feeling that rushed around her body at that moment. She repeated what Tom had said as she stared at the ring with pricks of tears in the corner of her eyes. 'A Love Emmy x ring?'

Tom shook his head. 'No, not a Love Emmy x ring, a Love Emmy ring. Just you, Ems. I love you, and this is a love ring to show it. It's just that. Love Emmy.'

Emmy pressed her lips together as a nuclear fizz went around her body and ended up bubbling up in her eyes and nose. She nodded over and over again as she held up her hand towards the fire, and the ring caught in the light. 'A Love Emmy ring. Wow.'

Emmy beamed as a tear dropped out of her right eye and slid down her cheek. Tom P Carter had played a very good card. She *was* Emmy, and she *was* loved. She took his hand and as the fire flickered, the sounds of everything going on around her seemed to somehow fade away. The crackling of the fires, the sound of the waves, the distant chatter. All of it was on the periphery of sitting rugged up in a huge coat, with a blanket on her lap, a scarf around her neck, and a hat on her head. Emmy Bardot had never felt better. She looked right into Tom's eyes. 'A Love Emmy ring. It looks like you need one too.'

Want a little bit more from Emmy and Tom? Find the epilogue here https://BookHip.com/VMPKTPF.

THE SUMMER HOTEL LOVELY BAY

MY NEW SERIES IS HERE!

An old hotel.
A beach town.
A romance by the sea.

The Summer Hotel Lovely Bay

Nina Lavendar is ready for something to happen in her life; she just isn't quite sure what. So when something a bit different lands in her lap and she sends a spontaneous, off-the-cuff email, she wonders what, if anything, will happen at all. When she gets an opportunity in a little town she has no clue about she certainly doesn't think that it's going to completely and utterly change her life.

As she arrives in Lovely Bay, Nina realises within a very short time that her silly spontaneous jaunt wasn't quite what she thought it was going to be. But with fate playing its hand she runs with it anyway and things start to happen in every area of her life. None of which she'd seen coming, especially the man that makes her tingle.

A swoon-worthy and utterly gorgeous romantic comedy that will make you laugh, maybe cry and definitely fall completely in love… and not just with the romcom but with Nina and with life in a small town tucked down on the coast.

READ MORE BY POLLY BABBINGTON

(Reading Order available at PollyBabbington.com)

The Summer Hotel Lovely Bay

The Old Ticket Office Darling Island
    Secrets at The Old Ticket Office Darling Island
    Surprises at The Old Ticket Office Darling Island

Spring in the Pretty Beach Hills
    Summer in the Pretty Beach Hills

The Pretty Beach Thing
    The Pretty Beach Way
    The Pretty Beach Life

Something About Darling Island
    Just About Darling Island
    All About Christmas on Darling Island

The Coastguard's House Darling Island

Summer on Darling Island
Bliss on Darling Island

The Boat House Pretty Beach
Summer Weddings at Pretty Beach
Winter at Pretty Beach

A Pretty Beach Christmas
A Pretty Beach Dream
A Pretty Beach Wish

Secret Evenings in Pretty Beach
Secret Places in Pretty Beach
Secret Days in Pretty Beach

Lovely Little Things in Pretty Beach
Beautiful Little Things in Pretty Beach
Darling Little Things

The Old Sugar Wharf Pretty Beach
Love at the Old Sugar Wharf Pretty Beach
Snow Days at the Old Sugar Wharf Pretty Beach

Pretty Beach Posies
Pretty Beach Blooms
Pretty Beach Petals

OH SO POLLY

Words, quilts, tea and old houses…

My words began many moons ago in a corner of England, in a tiny bedroom in an even tinier little house. There was a very distinct lack of scribbling, but rather beautifully formed writing and many, many lists recorded in pretty fabric-covered note-books stacked up under a bed.

A few years went by, babies were born, university joined, white dresses worn, a lovely fluffy little dog, tears rolled down cheeks, house moves were made, big fat smiles up to ears, a tril-lion cups of tea, a decanter or six full of pink gin, many a long walk. All those little things called life neatly logged in those beautiful little books tucked up neatly under the bed.

And then, as the babies toddled off to school, as if by magic, along came an opportunity and the little stories flew out of the books, found themselves a home online, where they've been growing sweetly ever since.

I write all my books from start to finish tucked up in our lovely old Edwardian house by the sea. Surrounded by pretty bits and bobs, whimsical fabrics, umpteen stacks of books, a plethora of lovely old things, gingham linen, great big fat white sofas, and a big old helping of nostalgia. There I spend my days spinning stories and drinking rather a lot of tea.

From the days of the floral notebooks, and an old cottage locked away from my small children in a minuscule study logging onto the world wide web, I've now moved house and those stories have evolved and also found a new home.

There is now an itty-bitty team of gorgeous gals who help me with my graphics and editing. They scheme and plan from their laptops, in far-flung corners of the land, to get those words from those notebooks onto the page, creating the magic of a Polly Bee book.

I really hope you enjoy getting lost in my world.

Love

Polly x

AUTHOR

Polly Babbington

In a little white Summer House at the back of the garden, under the shade of a huge old tree, Polly Babbington creates romantic feel-good stories, including The PRETTY BEACH series.

Polly went to college in the Garden of England and her writing career began by creating articles for magazines and publishing books online.

Polly loves to read in the cool of lazing in a hammock under an old fruit tree on a summertime morning or cosying up in the winter under a quilt by the fire.

She lives in delightful countryside near the sea, in a sweet little village complete with a gorgeous old cricket pitch, village green with a few lovely old pubs and writes cosy romance books about women whose life you sometimes wished was yours.

Follow Polly on Instagram, Facebook and TikTok
@PollyBabbingtonWrites

PollyBabbington.com

Want more on Polly's world? Subscribe to Babbington Letters

Printed in Great Britain
by Amazon